IVY'S venom

FOR ALL CONTENT INQUIRIES, PLEASE VISIT
MY WEBSITE

Dedication

Judge your strengths by your weaknesses

Prologue

"Ivy…" Her voice floats to me above the music. "Hold my hand."

"Keep both hands on the wheel," I chastise, but lean over to kiss her cheek. "Besides, you know the rules."

Her face falls at my words, but I need to make sure she understands what this is. I can't have her thinking I belong to her.

Ivy Greene belongs to no one.

Not even to pretty Charlotte Jones from Toronto.

Chapter One

Ivy

My legs gradually ease open, showing him I'm bare beneath my kilt, as I slowly run my fingers up my thigh. He's leaning against the chalkboard with his arms crossed and watching my face intently. I know he wants to peek at my pussy, but between the hours of eight and three, he needs to be professional.

"Ivy," he snarls, his black hair falling over his forehead. "Knock it off."

"I'm horny." I shrug as my fingers meet the apex of my thighs. "And wet."

"Mrs. Greene could walk in here at any moment—"

"Mrs. Greene can watch for all I fucking care," I cut him off.

He steps forward, wedging himself between my legs, and grabbing my hand just as it lands on my pussy. His rough knuckles scrape along my clit as his blue eyes flare with frustration, and I lift my hips to feel more. He yanks my hand and his out from under my kilt though and I whimper at the loss of contact.

"I said to knock it off," he growls and chucks my hand away.

"Fuck!" I hop off the desk and right my kilt. "You are a boring old man."

Grabbing my backpack off the floor, I saunter to the classroom door, flipping my long, mahogany hair over my shoulder.

"Ivy." His voice is low as he calls out to my back. "Tomorrow you have detention here for an hour after the last bell."

I grin without turning to look at him and suck my bottom lip into my mouth, then let it slowly pop back out. "Okay, Mr. O'Connor."

My instinct for fucked-up men who like girls in school uniforms still works like a charm. I had him pegged the moment I walked into his classroom at the beginning of this week and it's taken two days to break him.

Closing the classroom door behind me, I stand and watch as students make their way to their lockers, getting ready to leave for the day. I cross the hall and stand in front of my locker, grabbing the lock.

Precious Blood Academy is a catholic institute that houses immoral teenagers but prays for our souls in the process. It's not a strict school by any means. I've spent the last few years in a strict school and Precious Blood is a kitten compared to that. The only thing this school is strict about is the uniform.

"So, what is my fucked-up little cousin doing tonight?" Carmelo's deep voice rasps as he leans against the locker next to mine. His dark brown hair is getting a little too long and curling wildly around his face as his deep brown eyes twinkle with mischief.

"We were born literally three months apart. Shut up." I open my locker and hide his face from view, pulling out the textbooks I won't actually be studying tonight. It's just in case Dad does a surprise check-in.

"It's Thursday." He chuckles. "Isn't that race night down at the strip?"

The strip is an old, abandoned highway that's rarely used anymore. It was long ago replaced by a larger one and now the unruly rich kids of Whitsborough use it to drag race until my Uncle Emmett gets wind of it and shuts it down. I used to go there with Dad's newest vehicles and race them for fun, all without him ever finding out. At least, he's never spoken to me directly about it.

"Tell me you're taking the Shelby?" Cameron, who might as well be my cousin, leans on my other side. His short, dirty blond hair is highlighted by the fluorescent lamps as he grins, his dimples appearing in each cheek.

"I don't know what I'm doing yet."

I slam my locker shut, then stride out of the school and into the parking lot. Cameron and Carmelo are the only two I speak to here because I haven't really bothered to get reacquainted with the girls I used to call friends a few years ago. I've changed in the time I was away, and honestly, I'm just not interested. Who knows when I'll be shipped off to reform school again?

"Call me if you're going!" Carmelo calls out from behind me. "I don't want you to go alone."

He's always been so protective of me, and a lot of my family says he's like his father—my Uncle Carm. Uncle Carm died before me and Carmelo were born, and the circumstances around his death are pretty hush-hush. I did some digging around when I was in New York and found out my mother's side of the family ran a large mob organization back in the day. Uncle Carm was their leader for a while, and whenever I got to see Trent—my mother's business partner in New York—I tried to bleed him for information. It never worked; they're all so tight-lipped about everything.

Saying my family are tight-lipped is a fucking understatement. I grew up knowing there were secrets, secrets pertaining to our relatives who have long since passed away, and secrets that would eradicate us if anyone found out.

"Ivy!" a voice calls just as I reach my car, and I refrain from groaning out loud.

Turning around, I come face-to-face with a girl I grew up with and at one time called my best friend. Molly is sweet and innocent, but a complete loser now. I don't know what happened to her in the few years I've been away at Johnstone Reformatory, but now she's a loner who eats her lunch in the bathrooms.

I don't answer her and instead watch as she huffs her way to me. She's always been asthmatic and now that she's added braces to the mix, she's a bona fide weirdo.

"When did you get back?" she asks when she finally stops in front of me.

"A few nights ago." I unlock my M5 and throw my bag into the backseat.

"We should totally catch up." She grins wide, and I cringe as the sun reflects off all the metal in her fucking mouth.

"Listen, Molly." I cross my arms over my chest. "You're just not my type."

"What?" She looks horrified and her face turns the

color of a beetroot, making her orange hair look neon. "Not like that."

"Like what? You aren't down to eat my pussy?"

"Ivy!" she shrieks and backs away, her blue eyes shining with unshed tears. "I m–meant like the o–old days, like f–friends."

"I'm not looking for any friends." I shrug. "How's your brother?"

"What?" Her expression morphs into confusion, and I become increasingly annoyed at her stupidity.

"Never mind." I roll my eyes and get into my car. "Get lost, Molly."

I close the car door, her mouth agape, and flip down the visor. I have a date. No matter how tough I act or appear, my bright, blue-green eyes reflect my inner turmoil. I check my makeup, making sure my liner hasn't run, before slapping the visor closed again. Eyes truly are the windows to your soul, and mine are filled with inky darkness.

That's about as deep as I'll get on that shit.

After starting the car, I open the center console and pull out the already rolled joint waiting there. Time to drive and forget where the fuck I am.

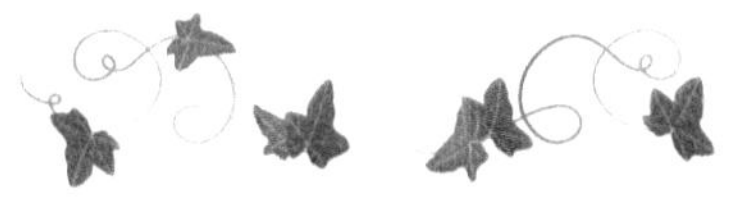

I roll into the hotel lot and throw my keys to the valet. This better be worth the drive here. Toronto is a forty-five-minute trek, and if this man's dick is subpar, I'm going to snap. Walking into the lobby, I head straight for the elevators across the room, already knowing his room number.

He has two hours to make me come, and then I need to head back to Whitsborough, because regardless of what I said to Carmelo, I will be racing tonight.

The elevator doors slide open, revealing a bellhop standing inside. He has his hat pulled down low on his face, but he fucking fills out the uniform perfectly. His face is stuck in his phone, so he doesn't pay me any mind as I get in.

"Eleven, please."

I keep my eyes on the door as his head snaps up in my peripheral vision. He reaches his finger out and presses the button for the floor, but his eyes are on the side of my face the entire time. I fucking hope he hit the right floor.

"Ivy Greene." His voice is deep and slightly familiar.

Turning my head slowly, I look into a set of light brown eyes, framed by thick black lashes, and skin the color of terra-cotta, warm and golden. His lips are turned down into a frown, but they are the sexiest set of lips I have ever seen, moist and full.

"You don't remember me." His tongue comes out to run along the plump bottom lip.

"I don't," I admit.

I can't control this immense attraction I'm feeling, like he's pulling me in, and I can't stop myself from falling.

"Why would you?" His voice becomes mean and snarky. "Why would you remember the family of the girl you killed?"

Everything stops at that moment. My lungs stall, my heart falters, and my mouth drops. What the fuck did he just say?

"Good thing Mommy and Daddy were there to make sure it was swept away." He shoots his hand out and presses the stop button. "I wanted to kill you, you know."

He steps toward me, and I wish I could get my body to work so I could move or scream, but I'm stuck, just staring at him with my mouth agape.

It takes a few moments, but it finally hits me exactly who this guy is. Now I'm the one fearing for my life, because if the tables were turned, I would've already killed him.

"Neil." My voice is hoarse and dry.

"So, you do remember me." Something close to curiosity flashes through his eyes.

Of course, I would remember him. His sister and I were best friends, and he was my first fucking crush. Neil Jones and Charlotte Jones were my first real friends outside of my family. Neil, being a few years older than us, stopped coming around as often when he hit thirteen, but Charlotte and I remained close.

Until I killed her.

"Yes." My voice cracks and I want to punch myself in the face for sounding so weak. "Your family and mine are close."

"No." He steps in closer, our chests bumping. "My father and your family are close. He's a fucking traitor for not having you charged with murder and your family as accessories."

He's not wrong.

Shaking my head, I tip my head back to look up at the ceiling of the elevator. *Did you do this to punish me, Char?*

"You're not going to fight me on any of this?" he asks as his voice pitches with disappointment.

I take a deep breath and steel my spine. I'm a fucking Greene.

"No, I'm not fighting you, Neil." I reach around him and release the stop button. "I'm late for a date, and I get grumpy when I'm late."

His brows rise toward the peak of his hat, and he steps back to the elevator wall. He's put as much space as he can between us in this confined place.

"You a prostitute or something?" He sounds disgusted.

"Or something." I shrug as the elevator dings, announcing my floor.

"Don't fucking come back here again, Greene," he snarls as I step out of the elevator.

Even in anger, even with his features saturated in hate, he's so fucking gorgeous it hurts, and I know it's karma kicking me in the ass.

"See you around, Jones." I wink and walk down the corridor.

As soon as I hear the metallic drag of the doors shutting, I let myself crash against the wall and suck in a lungful of air, then place my hand over my chest, feeling my heart beat rapidly as I breathe to slow it down. What were the fucking odds of this happening? I've been back for a few days and already shit has hit the fan.

I won't be surprised when I get shipped off again, and this time it'll be some place farther away. Mother is too busy to see what's going on with me and Dad likes to believe I can do no wrong. Then, when I fuck up, Mother can't handle it, and Dad sides with her, no matter what. I know it makes them sound like awful parents but really, they're not. My brother, Saxon, is the weird child, and most of their attention and focus is on him. My baby sister, Dahlia, has a charm that captures everyone's heart and she's honestly the easiest child to handle. And then there's me, temperamental with issues for days. So I get why they are the way they are when it comes to their oldest, problem child.

Doesn't make it hurt any less.

Pushing myself off the wall, I look toward the hotel room I'm supposed to be in. It doesn't hold the same appeal after all that, but I need it nonetheless. One of my many issues is craving my legs open and screaming with orgasms. It clears the constant fog in my head, and I'd rather it be this than hardcore drugs. Besides, it's all I've known for three years, thanks to *him.*

I shake the tall, dark figure from my mind and head to room eleven-ten, then knock brusquely, and the door opens wide to another tall, dark figure, only this one slightly more handsome.

"You're late." His voice is deep and it resonates between my legs.

"You're grumpy." I push past him and saunter into the room before hiking my kilt up a bit more on the way over, knowing it showcases my long legs, and hoping it drives him crazy. Most men liked a naughty girl in a school uniform, at least most of the men I knew, and I was hoping this one would be no different.

I stand in front of the large window as the muted sounds of busy downtown Toronto seeps through. The blinds are down but the slats are open, and I see the Toronto Harbourfront skyline next to the CN Tower. He comes up behind me, his gold badge twinkling in the late afternoon sun filtering in, and his large hands land on my shoulders.

Last night, I took Shelby out for a spin while sucking back on a bottle of whiskey and caught the attention of Officer Van Dyke. He pulled me over and could smell the alcohol pouring out of my very pores. I was resigned to the fact that I was caught, even fucking expected it, and was about to give him my wrists to seal in cuffs.

But then he recognized me.

Easy to do when you look a lot like the woman who is acclaimed for cleaning our hometown up and donating millions to charities. Or when you're part of a family that literally holds the town pillars on their backs, a real social monarchy, and watched through a magnifying glass.

Hence why I'm here. Officer Van Dyke recognized me immediately and told me about the repercussions of my actions. My chief of police uncle would be scrutinized and thrown under the bus, they would criticize my mother and father for raising such a deadbeat daughter, and finally, I would shine a negative light on the family that works so fucking hard to be perfect.

Then he put forth an offer. I meet him here today and let him fuck me. Then he would let everything go. I agreed because for one, it's an easy lay, and two, I really don't want to fuck up my family any more than I already have.

I watch the reflection in the window as his hands rub my shoulders, his wedding band shining against his pale skin. Adam Van Dyke is married with children and a prominent man in Whitsborough. I know him very well too. His daughter, Molly, and I used to be best friends.

I undo my kilt, letting it drop to the floor, my bare pussy on display, and undo the buttons of my uniform top. Then I pull the white dress shirt off and toss it to the couch as I hear him undoing the belt looped in his slacks.

The familiar, initial rush of panic seizes my chest and makes it hard to breathe. It lasts for about a minute, and then I relish in the high of being wanted, being revered. My body is my fucking temple, and as chaotic as my life is, I take care of it. I'm toned, lean, and tall for a girl, standing a few inches below six feet. I understand all too well the cravings my curves and features elicit from men, and I work it to my fucking advantage.

I pull apart the clasp on my bra, watching as my tits bounce against my chest and my nipples hardening in anticipation, and I toss it to the growing pile.

"You've really filled out these last few years, Ivy."

"Shut the fuck up, Adam." I turn around to face him and roll my eyes when I see his cock. Nothing amazing about it, less than average, and I'm regretting my decision not to bring my vibrator. "That's not going to do much for me." I point at his dick in his hand. "I hope you eat like a madman."

"Get on the bed." He grins. "Sometimes it isn't about the size but how a man works it."

He sheds the rest of his clothes in a matter of seconds, and I give his body a once-over as I scoot up the bed. He's fit for an old guy, his abs are still visible, and he at least shaves his hair. Not too bad.

I open my legs wide on the stark white bed set, my deep olive skin a contrast to the pristine sheets, and stick two fingers in my mouth. Looks like I just might have to get myself started. Pulling my saliva-coated fingers out of my mouth, I run them through my folds, hoping to get myself off.

He crawls up the bed, his face stopping above my pussy, giving it his rapt attention.

"I saw Molly today," I tell him and hope for a reaction.

His head pops up and his eyes narrow. "What did you say to her?"

"She asked me to hang out, you know, like old times." I sink the two fingers into my pussy and moan at the feeling.

"And?" he rasps, his sight back on my fingers as I try to pleasure myself.

"What the fuck did you do to your daughter?"

Again, his head snaps up. "What do you mean?"

"She looks like a fucking pariah. All that huffing and puffing, and the amount of metal in her mouth must set off the department's metal detectors yards away."

"She's developing slowly." His eyes look back up at mine. "Nothing wrong with that."

I lie back on the bed and stare at the ceiling as he licks and sucks at my pussy. No matter how hard I try to keep myself here in the present, I keep going back to when another would have his face between my legs, his fingers moving inside me, and even though I cried and begged him to stop, he would continue.

Forcing myself to look down, I watch Adam's dark hair and focus on that. No graying temples, no small bald spot in the center, and his shoulders are wider. Adam unfortunately doesn't do it for me though, and I want to slap his head out of the way to finish my own-damn-self off.

Then I see him, Neil Jones. His beautiful skin bathed in sepia, those light brown eyes framed by lush black lashes, his perfect nose dusted with freckles and a single hoop in the right nostril, and his perfect cupid's bow lips surrounded by a light shadow of growth.

I tip my head back as Adam's tongue hits my clit and moan as I imagine it being Neil.

Neil sucks my clit into his mouth, lashing his tongue over the pebbled surface, and I can feel the heat pool in my core. His long fingers slowly push inside me and I clench around him, wanting it deeper, then wanting his cock instead.

"Turn over." Adam's voice breaks through my reverie and I growl in frustration.

"Stop talking or I'll never be able to come," I snap at him and turn onto my hands and knees.

I hear the condom wrapper rip and close my eyes again, imagining it's Neil with the wrapper between his perfectly straight teeth, the sound of him sliding it down his length, and then the head being pressed to my entrance.

He pushes inside and I try really hard to imagine it wider, longer, and when the pace picks up, I try to imagine it pummeling my cervix. When none of the trying works, I bring my fingers to my clit and begin to furiously rub, giving it the friction it needs, and all before this shithead proves to be a few pumps chump.

I'm almost there, I feel it building, and I hit the precipice, only to have the old fucker groan his release. I want to scream but I continue to rub furiously, and as I crest—finally—I feel his small, limp dick slip out of me before he collapses on the bed beside me.

Fucking waste of time. I should've called his bluff and taken the charges, family be damned. I just really thought I would get at least one orgasm out of this shitty ass deal. I jump off the bed and quickly grab my shirt, pulling my phone out of my breast pocket.

Adam is still strewn across the bed, his little limp dick resting against his balls, and the condom still hanging off the end, filled with semen. I snap a photo without him knowing and quickly get dressed.

"You're leaving?" He pulls up and leans on his elbows. "I have this room for the night."

"The sex was shit, Adam." I pull on my skirt. "Why the fuck would I stay for more? Besides, I am a minor and can be seen on every camera coming into this place. You may want to fucking check yourself."

I fluff out my hair while he stares at me slack-jawed and popping his lips like a fucking goldfish.

"You better not say a fucking word." He finally regains his composure and straightens. "Because I will take your family down."

"Oh, fuck off." I wave my hand over my head as I start for the door. "Do it then, limp dick."

Chapter Two

I rush back through the lobby of the hotel and nod at the valet. He gives me a once-over then saunters outside and over to my parked matte black M5, sliding into the driver's seat. I keep glancing around me, worried I'll see Neil again and he'll make me feel things—remember things—I've worked hard to suppress.

The car pulls up in front of me and I slap a fifty in the guy's hand as soon as he opens the door.

"Wow! Thanks, hotness," he husks as he moves aside to let me behind the wheel.

I stop in my tracks and look him in the eyes. Not bad looking. I mean, his face isn't great but he has a banging body, and right now I need dick like my next fix.

"Get in." I nod toward the passenger side and his eyebrows shoot up. "You got two seconds before I'm out of here."

He scrambles around the car, yelling to his co-worker

that he's taking a break, then I slam the door and peel out of the lot before his door is even shut.

"Whoa, take it easy, hotness." He smiles at me, the expression on his face a little too eager.

"Stop calling me that." I just need him to keep his mouth shut and pull his dick out.

"Give me a name then."

I take a sharp turn into a parking garage and drive to the top.

"No," I answer brusquely and park across three spots. "Get a condom." I point to the glove box.

His smile is huge as he grabs a foil packet, and I notice his front tooth is chipped. It bothers me. I motion for him to hurry and he quickly has his pants to his thighs, rolling the condom down his length. And what a length it is. *Thank God.*

Reaching over him, I press the button to move his seat back, and then I'm straddling his waist, guiding him to my entrance.

"I can't believe we're doing this," he breathes out.

Covering his mouth with my hand, I grind out through my teeth, "Don't speak."

I slowly lower myself onto him and moan at the intrusion. It feels good to fuck something I can feel when I'm wet. Picking up my pace, I alternate between thrusts and grinding, chasing the orgasm that's been teasing me for a good hour. Then I release his mouth to reach my hand between our bodies and he watches as I rub my clit.

"Do not come," I snarl as I watch his eyes roll back. "I will fucking gut you, cut your dick off, and shove it down your throat."

His eyes widen like he realizes I could actually mean

what I say, which I do, and that maybe he should've thought this through more, which he should have.

"Okay." His whisper is hoarse and suddenly sounds a lot like *his*, the man with the graying hair.

I squeeze my eyes shut, but when I feel hands under my skirt and fingers digging into my ass, I lose it. I open my eyes to my hand around this guy's throat, and come almost instantly at the potent fear in his.

As I continue to come, clenching around him, I squeeze his throat and then watch as he comes, his face turning a deep red. I close my eyes blissfully as that figure in my mind disappears with my release, receding back into the darkest folds of my subconscious. Peace washes over me, even though I know it'll be short-lived.

I release him, and he sucks in some air while I plop back in my seat to drop the visor and check my makeup in the mirror. He pulls off his condom, ties it up, and opens the door to chuck it out.

Before he can close it, I lean over. "No, you can get out now too."

"What?" He looks at me bewildered as he pulls his pants back up.

"Get. Out." I shove his shoulder hard.

"You're a crazy bitch!" he exclaims as he jumps out of the seat.

"So I've been told." He slams my car door as I nod.

Then I circle around him once, my tires burning on the bends, and laugh when he tosses me the finger. There's a slight smile on his face though as I speed out of the garage.

After driving aimlessly for a while, my emotions begin to level out and my mind is serene, despite the chaos. I rely on certain highs to replace my life's lows, and sex is one of those highs. It drives out the shadows that always seem to creep their way back to the front of my mind.

I have no one to help me. Nobody knows what's been happening to me for the two years I was shipped off to a prestigious reform school for the unruly kids of the wealthy elite.

Why was I shipped off to a reformatory school?

Because I killed my best friend,—Neil's younger sister—Charlotte Jones, and no matter how many times I'm told it was an accident, I know the difference. My parents even know the difference since they tossed me away to some boarding school in New York and left me in the hands of the devil himself.

The cemetery comes into view and I sigh with relief. It's like my brain is on autopilot and knows exactly what I need at this moment. I pull in and drive to our family's mausoleum. It stands tall and proud, made of white brick and lined with angel statues. Our family is in there, and one in particular who means the world to me, even in death.

I enter and go straight to her plaque, immediately resting my hand against the cool metal. I try to remember her voice, her scent, but it's been so long and so many tragic things happened after she left.

Laurann Jennifer Talia (Craven), beloved grandmother and great-grandmother.

She was the one person who saw what was really inside of me, my struggle with connections, and my need to be alone. She saw my inner turmoil and showed me how much she loved me despite it. I was an angry child, and I can't really explain why, but she saw me through it. She told me I had evil that ran in my veins, but unlike others in my family, I could use it for good. She died before she could show me how, and two nights later, that evil poured out of my body, stealing my best friend in its grasp.

"Hi, Jenna." She hated being called Grandma. "I miss you. I'm back home now. I'm sorry I didn't come see you right away."

My forehead drops against the plaque, hoping to feel her and wishing she would give me a sign that she hears me.

"I'm happy to be home, but it doesn't feel like a home." The pressure is building behind my eyes. "You took my home with you when you left, and now, I can't seem to find it." Tears slip down my cheeks as I try to gather my emotions.

"We all miss you, and not one of us has been the same since you left. How do I do what you told me? How do I take hold of the evil inside of me and make it good?"

I stay for a while longer, waiting for answers, and when I get none, I leave with a heavier heart.

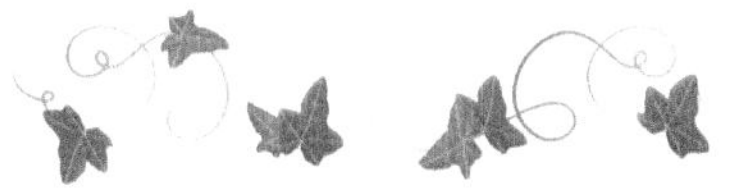

"Ember!"

I groan and turn into my pillow.

It's always the same when my dad walks through the door. He screams out for my mother and she answers with a laugh. Even after all these years, those two love each other like crazy, and it's fucking disgusting. They were high school sweethearts, even went to Precious Blood Academy together, and then married young when they found out they were having me.

I bet that's when the regret set in. Having a kid right out of high school really puts a dent in the college party scene, or when you want to hang out with your friends, and even worse when you're trying to have a date night with a screaming kid on your hip. So I get why they mostly ignore me.

On top of all that, I was apparently a tough kid. I didn't listen, I was a bully, and overall, I had a bad fucking attitude. My mother likes to remind me not much has changed, and then my dad tries to soften the blow by saying I resemble her in more than just looks.

I don't care.

"Ivy!" he yells from the bottom of the stairs. "Come down and tell us about your day!"

I can't ignore him for long. He won't allow it, and then it would get Mother started, which is something I don't want. She may be quiet and stay out of the way, but once she's set off, there's no going back.

Grumbling to myself, I roll out of bed and stand in the center of my room. This room used to belong to my Uncle Emmett when he lived here, and I still have a few posters of his on the wall. Hip-hop artists from his time, a couple of mounted skateboards, and then there's a picture of him with my Uncle Travis and Aunt Adri. When Dad offered to take them down, I refused. I chose this bedroom because he and I have the same interests.

Leaving the room, I head down the stairs as the sound of my little sister's laughter filters through my thoughts. I fight hard to keep the smile off my face at the sound but lose miserably. Dahlia will always be my weakness because she's still so innocent. She's a typical seven-year-old, full of questions and unaware of dangers. And she loves me more than anyone ever has.

"Ivy!" she squeals and wiggles herself out of Dad's lap.

"How's my pretty flower?" I bend down and let her crash into me.

"I'm so happy you get to stay home this time," she mumbles into my neck, her breath hot.

"I'm happy to stay with you too, flower." It was always the hardest to say goodbye to Dahlia after my visits because she would cry until she lost her breath, and my blackened heart would break.

"How was school, Ivy?" Dad asks as I disentangle myself from Dahlia's arms.

"Good." I shrug.

"As long as she stays away from the teachers, it will continue to be good." Saxon snickers as he comes into the room.

He's twelve going on thirty and a fucking snob on a good day. Saxon's extremely smart—fucking gifted—and looks a lot like Dad with his bright green eyes and build. He's going to be a lady-killer and he fucking knows it.

"Speaking of." I grin at him as his eyes narrow on me. "How's your teacher doing?" I waggle my eyebrows suggestively as he shakes his head.

"She's a girl." He chuckles like he got one over on me.

"And?"

"All right," Dad cuts in. "That's enough."

Saxon is looking at me, wide-eyed and confused. Good. The little shit thinks he knows everything.

"Who wants pizza for dinner?" Dad asks, and I turn, heading for the front door.

"I'll grab something while I'm out. I made plans!" I call back.

"With who?" he presses as he follows behind me.

"Molly," I answer. Might as well make her and her family useful.

"That's great, Ivy. I'm glad you're talking to Molly again," Dad says as I slip on my shoes. I don't know if he fully believes me or if he's preferring to be blissfully ignorant.

"Make sure you drive carefully." Her voice makes me halt what I'm doing. It's quiet but assertive, and I turn my head to look at her.

I really am a near duplicate of Emberlise Greene. We both have thick mahogany hair, big blue-green eyes, and stand at the same height. I'm curvier than my mother, but besides that, we are basically the same person, and she's stunning to look at.

"Okay." I nod.

"If you're taking Shelby to the strip, make sure you wash her down after, and don't scuff her," she advises just before she disappears back into her office and shuts the door behind her.

I stand there staring at the door in shock. She knows I go to the strip?

Shaking off the shock, I quickly leave the house before she changes her mind about caring. I don't know why that shocks me as much as it does because the woman knows everything.

She just doesn't give a shit.

CHAPTER THREE

Me: I'm here.

Carmelo: Pulling up in 5.

I lean back on the red hood of the Shelby and watch the gathering cars around me. The strip has become more popular since I left, and I grin as I take in the crowd. Guys and girls of all ages gathering together and panting over sexy cars.

The familiar deep rumble of an Audi R8 pulls me from my thoughts, and I look over my shoulder as it pulls up beside me. The doors open and Carmelo and Cameron slide out, immediately catching everyone's attention.

They are both devastatingly handsome and have so many girls here in Whitsborough chasing them. Where Carmelo is dark and mysterious, Cameron is fair and approachable.

Tonight, they look their part. Carmelo is dressed in

dark wash baggy jeans, a white V-neck, and his leather jacket. His black, curly hair is covered with a black bandana and his dark eyes hold a hint of trouble. He's towering over most at six and a half feet.

Cameron has on a pair of black fitted jeans, a white hoodie, and a black bandana tied around his neck. His blond hair is combed back, slick over his head, and his bright blue eyes twinkle with mischief. Cameron sucks people in and Carmelo spits them out.

They make their way over to me, and I chuckle when everyone stops to watch our exchange. This is me announcing my return, and I have two of the most popular guys ready to take up my flanks.

Carmelo and I are in the same grade, but Cameron is a year younger. I actually feel bad for him next year when we've moved on to college and he has his senior year here without us. You better believe my ass is not sticking around here for college. I have no choice but to be here now because I'm still a minor without a job and a means to take care of myself, but college gives me the option to leave.

"Cuz." Carmelo leans in and kisses my cheek. "What's up?"

"Nothing." I shrug.

"Fuck," Cam cusses as he leans in to give me a hug. Then he holds up his phone to an opened message. "Amelia is coming."

Those three words almost have me catapulting off the hood of my car… almost. I hold myself still and concentrate on my breathing. Amelia Jones is my dad's good friend, Rodney Jones' daughter, and yes, you guessed it, Neil Jones' younger half sister.

My mother apparently helped get Rodney Jones out of the street gang life, and my dad offered him a job to work for him. At the time, Rodney, who already had a son, Neil, and another baby on the way, Charlotte, took him up on the offer to provide a better life for his kids. He moved to Whitsborough and things didn't work out with Neil and Charlotte's mother, but they came to see him and us every other weekend. That's how we became so close.

Rodney ended up marrying Shay, another family friend, and they had Amelia a few years later. I haven't seen her since her sister's funeral, and I don't know how the fuck she's going to react to me.

"Tell me you're not fucking her," Carmelo groans as he looks out toward the cars lining up.

"Nah." Cam shakes his head. "Not that she isn't trying to tap though."

"Gross," I mutter. "We're all practically family."

Not that I have a fucking leg to stand on because… Charlotte.

"Lots of sexy girls here tonight," Carmelo hums, and I nod in agreement.

"Yeah, there are."

"You still swinging both ways?" Cam hits my shoulder.

"I swing all over." I shrug. "It's the soul I like, not the flesh it's encased in."

Even though most of those souls turn out to be too bright and too pure standing next to mine.

We stand in silence, watching the buzz around us as more people roll up in their souped-up cars, and I feel the flutter of excitement in my belly. I can't wait to feel Shelby's motor vibrate and roar as I leave these fuckers in her dust.

"Who's Amelia with?" Carmelo asks, and I immediately

tense as the hairs on the back of my neck stand; the surrounding air is suddenly heavy and charged with an intense energy.

He's here.

"That's her half brother, Neil. He hasn't been around since…" Cam shoots me a look.

"Since Charlotte died," I finish for him.

"Is he gonna be a problem?" Carmelo cracks his neck to the side and fists his hands. "I kind of want a problem tonight."

I don't say anything because I don't fucking know the answer. Carmelo is a fighter. It's what he's known for. Fighting is what he does, and according to our family, it's in his blood.

My gaze slips back to Neil and his youngest sister. Amelia is stunning. She has her dark mane of curls out and surrounding her face, the streetlight highlighting the blonde streaks. Her eyes, much like Neil's and Charlotte's, shine golden, enhancing her deep golden skin. She looks like her dead half sister, but she also looks a lot like her mother, and Shay is a stunner.

Walking right beside her, his stride lazy and his face half covered by another hat, is Neil Jones. They are coming right for us, and I have to tense every fucking muscle to stop myself from fleeing. I knew one day I would have to face the music of what happened, especially after seeing him in the elevator before my tryst with Adam, which shocked me to my core. I just thought I had more time.

"Ivy." Amelia's voice is smooth and thick like honey. "It's good to have you home." She leans forward and brushes her lips to my cheek. "We should talk," she whispers in my ear.

I give her a brusque nod, but my eyes haven't left her brother's form. He's standing off to the side, his arms crossed, and his attitude permeating the air.

"'Sup man?" Cam calls out to him, our ever-welcoming golden boy.

Neil gives him a nod and turns his head toward me. I can't tell if he's looking at me, but I can fucking feel it.

"Ivy, are you racing?" Amelia asks as she makes her way to Cam.

"Yeah." I nod and clench my teeth when I hear Neil snort.

"You got something to say?" Carmelo's voice is deep with restrained anger.

I reach out and place my hand on his vibrating arm. He's barely holding himself together.

"Carmelo, *relax.*"

Neil flicks the beak of his cap, and it pops up further onto his forehead, showing us his face. He is fucking heart-stopping gorgeous. His eyes narrow and his top lip curls upward. "Bro…"

"Stop, Neil!" Amelia yells. "These are my friends."

We are?

Neil growls at being cut off and snaps the cap back down his face, then storms off through the crowd. I watch his retreating back and exhale the breath I didn't know I was holding.

"Nice car." I look up at the voice and stare into a face I've never seen before.

"Fuck off, Pat," Carmelo growls.

"Hold on." This Pat holds up his hands. "I haven't seen you or this car around here before. Are you racing?" he asks me.

"I used to come here," I answer softly. "Haven't been in a few years. I may race." I shrug.

"That car is meant to be driven," he continues.

"What exactly are you getting at, Pat?" I sit up on the hood and look him in the eyes.

Both Carmelo and Cam chuckle and Pat's eyes flash with trouble. I wait patiently for him to toss out terms.

"Race me." He pops his hands on either side of me on the hood and leans in.

"Back up, man." Carmelo steps forward.

Pat is definitely older because I haven't seen him at school, and he looks more college-aged. He has tattoos covering his arms and neck, and a few teardrops decorate his face under his right eye. This one is either a legit gangbanger or a fake thug. I don't fucking care either way.

"I don't do friendly races," I tell him. "What are the terms?"

"I can see you don't need money." He looks from my attire to the car I'm sitting on. "What does a princess like you want?"

I give him a slow, raking once-over and deem him worthy of the terms I want to lay out.

"The winner gets head." I smirk.

NEIL

The anger is still all-consuming, but now it holds something else. I hate to admit it, but Ivy Greene is fucking hot, and I can't seem to get those eyes and her voice out of my head. I can still fucking smell her, that lingering citrus fragrance and something close to vanilla.

After she left the elevator earlier today, the scent wafted around me, and instead of getting the fuck out, I stayed in there for another ten minutes until it slowly faded away. She always smelled like vanilla when we were kids, and the second I smelled her in the elevator, I knew who it was.

My insides ripped apart when the first thing my heart remembered was the feelings I had attached to that scent, and then my brain kicked in to remind us we fucking hated her. She killed Charlotte.

Now she has Amelia wrapped around her finger, and all I want to do is wrap my hand around her throat and strangle her, or kiss her, maybe both. It's hard to separate shit in my head when I see her, because on one hand, she's my first veritable crush from when we were kids, and on the other, she took someone so important away from me.

"Ivy is back," I hear a few chicks murmuring.

"I heard she went to a reform school for wayward teens."

"What the fuck is a wayward?" a dumb fucking chick asks.

"Like bad kids."

"Oh, because she was the reason that girl died a few years ago, right?" another chimes in.

"Yeah, my dad thinks she should've gone to juvie for

that, but her parents paid off the judge." Fucking right, she should have.

Her parents didn't pay off anyone. My traitor father didn't press charges, and I don't think I will ever see him the same again.

"Is she racing tonight?"

"Should she even be driving?" Great fucking question.

"I saw her race last year and she's good. She came in first." Huh.

"I think your boyfriend is over there talking to her, Riley."

"What?" A tall blonde whips her head around to look. She's wearing a small tube dress in a loud pink color and tottering on heels tall enough to be called stilts.

"You should go over there," a girl pipes up. "I've heard about her venom."

Venom.

If that isn't the fucking truth. Ivy's venom is potent, and the smallest amount draws you in… then kills you.

The girl on stilts stumbles her way over toward Ivy with her band of girls behind her for backup, and I follow far enough behind not to be seen, but close enough I can hear what's going down.

"Pat!" stilt girl shouts. "What's going on?"

"Just some friendly wagering," the boyfriend answers.

"Is this your girlfriend, Pat?" Ivy's voice is like smoke and ice.

"Yes, I am!" Stilts exclaims.

"Nice," Ivy replies, and I look around the girl to see Ivy

hop off the hood of her car.

She rounds the front of her car and motions to the two guys with her to back up, then she gets in and rolls the window down as her car rumbles loudly to life.

"Pat," she calls out as the guy heads for his car. "We'll discuss details when you catch up to me at the finish line."

Cocky little bitch. I hope this fucking guy smokes her.

She drives up to the starting line and revs her engine as she waits for Pat to pull up beside her. I stand transfixed, watching her car, and waiting with bated breath for her to move.

"She's misunderstood," Amelia's voice sounds from behind me.

"She killed our sister," I growl, without taking my eyes off the snake in her car.

"Dad believes otherwise, Neil. He says Charlotte wasn't acting right for a while." Amelia's words only anger me further.

"Are you kidding me?" I turn on her. "What could you possibly know? You were a fucking kid!"

"I remember her!" she screams at me. "Charlotte wasn't perfect!"

I close my eyes and exhale, trying to breathe out the anger and inhale calm energy. I don't want people to witness any more shit from the Jones family. We've given them enough to talk about over the years.

"This isn't the place, Amelia." With a tug, I pull her over and under my arm. "I love you." I kiss her temple and hug her.

I refuse to lose another sister to the Greenes. The roar of engines and the burning of tires sounds around us, and I look up in time to see the back end of both vehicles disappear into the night, only the red taillights visible.

"You need to forgive her," she whispers to me. "You need to let go of that anger inside of you."

I don't argue with her, and I'm saved by the sound of squealing tires as the two cars come veering back. Ivy is in the lead, and in the last hundred feet, she pulls it home. I guess the bitch taught herself how to fucking drive in the last two years because she's proven herself to be a danger behind the wheel. My sister could attest to that… if she were still alive.

Her cousin, Carmelo—the one who tried to step up to me earlier—rushes to her car, screaming excitedly and pulling open her door to haul her out. Ivy's face is thrown back and pure pleasure radiates from her features. She's so beautiful that it hits me like a ton of bricks. If only her insides matched the outside.

Amelia screams and runs over, only to be scooped up by Ivy's other boy, Cameron, and my teeth clench when I realize my last living sister is chilling in the jaws of a croc. My protective instincts are telling me I need to pull her out and fast.

"You won, Ivy." The guy Ivy raced steps out of his car. "Now for your prize."

What the fuck did they wager?

Ivy grins and licks her plush lips, like a fucking croc going in for the kill.

"How do you want it?" he calls out.

Ivy backs up and scoots up on the hood of her car, spreading her legs and making her leather skirt slide up her thighs. A thin scrap of black material is nestled between her legs, and I groan when she reaches her hand under her skirt to touch herself. I'm instantly hard and completely confused.

What the fuck is going on?

Her cousin steps forward, growling her name and reaching for her, but she shrugs him off and waves him away. Then Pat steps forward and rests his hands on either side of her waist, watching her hand closely. His girlfriend is being held back by her friends as she screams at the duo, but Pat just looks over his shoulder at her and shrugs.

"A bet's a bet, Riles." He grins like the cat that got the cream. Fuck, I guess he did.

Then he reaches inside Ivy's skirt and pulls her panties down as I look around for anyone who may be recording. Why isn't anyone recording?

A guy steps up to my left, practically salivating, and the sudden urge to knock his teeth down his throat overwhelms me.

"If you want it so bad, why don't you take a fucking picture?" I snarl at him.

"Are you crazy?" He looks at me with pure shock. "Do you know who she is? Her family would make you disappear if something like that showed up on the net."

I fucking believe it. I always thought the Greene family were like the fucking mob and this guy just proved I'm not the only one.

I look back in time to see Pat's head disappear between Ivy's legs, and my body jerks forward of its own accord. I want to rip him out of there and smash his face into the asphalt. Before I can make my way to them though, Ivy's fingers twist into his hair and she yanks him away from her roughly.

"Riles," she calls out to Pat's girlfriend, keeping her eyes on Pat while grinning from ear to ear. "Your man doesn't know how to eat pussy."

The crowd bursts out laughing and Riley stops struggling, standing still.

"I know," she replies, and the crowd gasps in shock.

Pat is trying to disentangle his hair from Ivy's clutches, but she's not relinquishing her hold.

"Why don't you come over here and show him how it's done?" Ivy suggests, and the noise of the crowd dies in a hush.

Riley and her stilts step forward, and Pat is finally released, whipping around with a growl.

"I lost." He points a finger at his girl. "Not her."

"So?" Ivy taunts.

"Those were the terms!" he yells. "The winner gets head." It's looking like he lost on purpose.

"I didn't specify from whom," Ivy snarks, and the crowd comes alive with laughter again.

Riley steps up to the hood of the car and Pat grabs her arm. "Let's just go."

"I won't force you." Ivy shrugs. "I can leave here without my prize, but I will ban Pat from this night forward."

Another gasp from the crowd and Pat surges forward. Ivy doesn't even flinch as he nears her face, and it's Carmelo who steps in, his neck bulging. That fucker is huge. I wouldn't fight him unless I had no fucking choice. Even then, I'd expect to fucking lose.

Riley shakes Pat's hand off her arm and spits at his feet. "A bet's a bet, motherfucker. We're fucking over."

Carmelo and this Cam dude part a path through the crowd and drag away a struggling Pat.

The crowd erupts in a chorus of *oohs* and *aahs* just as

Riley places her hands on Ivy's knees and slowly pulls them apart. The same rush of anger comes over me, and I am jarred to the spot as I realize I don't want anyone between her legs, male or female.

With her legs spread, leaning up on her elbows, Ivy watches as Riley slowly bends down toward her displayed pussy. It's possibly the prettiest pussy I have ever seen, and I am overcome with jealousy at the girl on stilts.

Just as Riley's mouth descends onto Ivy's pussy, Ivy's head tips back and she lets out a breathless moan, causing my dick to twitch in my pants. The crowd falls to a hush again as everyone watches these girls' foreplay on the hood of the fucking car.

Ivy's hand grabs Riley's ponytail and she wraps the hair around her wrist and fist, pulling her head in closer. Riley's hands slide along the inside of Ivy's upper thighs and pushes them open wider, her tongue sinking into Ivy's core.

Riley is thorough, I'll give her that. She sucks each bit of flesh into her mouth and then latches onto Ivy's clit, sinking two fingers inside of her at the same time. Ivy is gyrating her hips against Riley's mouth as she lies back against the hood, moaning loudly.

The guy beside me curses, and when I look over at him, he's rubbing himself through his jeans. I move away from him, but I see a lot of the same and I can't blame them. This shit is hot as fuck.

"Fuck," Ivy groans loudly, my attention snapping back to her and Riley.

Watching as Ivy comes apart into the mouth of another female has me both aroused and pissed off, because I want her in my mouth and my hands around her throat.

Chapter Four

"To find the value of x, you would have to divide sixteen—" Mr. O'Connor's voice is cut off by the shrill sound of the end-of-day bell.

Students hastily get out of their seats in a rush to get the hell out of this school, and I can't fucking blame them. I have detention, so I stay seated.

"I want this page finished tonight for homework!" Mr. O'Connor yells at the students' retreating backs.

Then his bright blue eyes land on mine. Desire is apparent, and so is frustration by the crinkle between his brows. He saunters to the door and closes it behind one lagging student.

"Ivy." His voice is rough and strained as his head presses against the wood. "How's life at home?"

"What?"

"I'm always worried about my students, but after yesterday…" He pushes himself away from the door and comes to perch on the edge of my desk. "After yesterday, I was left with a strong feeling you are not okay being back here."

Is this fucker for real? Is he really going to waste my time? Mr. O'Connor is easily the hottest guy in this school and young for a teacher—just getting out of the teacher's college. His black hair is faded at the sides and long on top, styled into a flipped front. Mr. O'Connor's blue eyes are bright and he has two prominent dimples deep in his cheeks. His body is also trim, and I wish I could find out just how built he is right now instead of this bullshit.

"Fuck this." I stand abruptly from my seat and bend over to grab my bag.

"Leaving so soon?" His voice is like gravel, and I'm shocked when I feel his fingers gliding up my thigh. "I thought we could talk."

I slowly straighten and turn to face him, his fingers moving along with me, landing at mid-thigh. He stands and faces me, his face blank. I look at the front of his pants and notice a sizable bulge, making my core clench with need.

"Hands on the desk, Ivy."

I do as he says, bending over slightly, and watch as he walks behind me. Then he flips my skirt up and I swallow back a moan. I've been needing this all day.

"Luckily, my classroom door is one of the few that lock." His fingers dance over my panties as I watch him over my shoulder, pressing the soaked material into my sensitive flesh. "You're sure you want this?"

He pops the button on his jeans and drops the zipper slowly, his large cock springing forward. He runs his thumb over the tip, smearing the drop of pre-cum into the skin, and then popping it into his mouth.

"Yes." I finally find my voice. "Make it fucking good too."

He pulls my panties down to my knees and steps on them, dragging them to the floor. Panic seizes me for just a second as my breath gets trapped in my throat. I swallow thickly, forcing it down just in time to hear his demand.

"Step out of them." I still have my eyes on his large cock being stroked by his hand, and exhale a long breath, stepping out of my panties.

He grabs a condom out of his back pocket, rips open the wrapper, and slowly rolls it down his length.

"This is going to be fast and rough, Ivy." He lines himself up with my opening, and I feel myself clench, wanting him inside of me. "Hold on."

Then he's pushing himself in, and I whimper at the feeling of being stretched and filled with his girth. He continues to push in, and I drop my elbows onto the desk.

"Fuck," I moan and push back against him. "Fuck, Mr. O'Connor."

At the sound of his name, he pulls out and slams back in, the desk skating a few inches forward. Then he tips my hips forward further and begins a rapid rhythm of thrusts. My pussy is so wet, I can feel it dripping down my thighs.

His hand snakes around my lower stomach and his finger slips down over my mound, pressing against my clit. At the first touch, my breath catches, and I see the graying hair. My stomach rolls as I clench my eyes shut to concentrate on where I am and who's inside of me. I need to come and chase him out of my mind.

Clenching my core, I groan when Mr. O'Connor's fingers pinch my clit roughly. Stars burst behind my eyelids and my stomach tightens.

"Fuck!" I exclaim. "I'm coming."

"Cream on my dick, little girl," he growls, and my core explodes with sensations that swim through my limbs, my vision blackening for a few seconds.

As I come down, I look over my shoulder at Mr. O'Connor. He has his head thrown back and both hands on my hips, his teeth biting down into his fat bottom lip. His eyes are closed, and I know now's my chance.

I pull my phone out of my breast pocket and slide it across to the camera, taking a quick picture of his euphoric face, then replace it before he slams into me a final time and comes on a loud groan.

He pulls out of me and slaps me hard on the ass before bending to pick up my panties. Before he stands though, he leans forward and swipes his tongue through my wet folds, making me gasp.

"Monday, detention." He stands and tosses me my panties. "I'll be eating this then," he says as he sticks a finger inside me, withdraws, and sucks it into his mouth.

Fuck, he's so hot.

I get myself dressed and head for the door without a word, throwing a grin at Mr. O'Connor over my shoulder. When I walk into the hall, it's practically empty, with only a few students mingling, one of which is Carmelo.

He's standing at my locker and sporting an impressive black eye.

"Your mother and father are gonna lose their shit when they see that." I point to the bruise as I open my locker.

"How was detention?" he deflects.

"Exhilarating."

"There's a party tonight down at the wharf." He pushes off my locker so I can open it. "Coming? Or did you already do that?"

He snorts and I fight to keep the amusement out of my voice. "Who's going?"

He laughs and ruffles my hair. "Don't get yourself shipped off again. Driving to New York every other weekend is a bitch. Cam said he's going and he's bringing Amelia."

Carmelo and Cam made the trek to New York twice a month to spend a weekend with me. My mother came every weekend, but I assume that it was mostly for business with Trent.

"Fuck, he's trying to get into Amelia's pants, isn't he?" I slam my locker shut and pull my bag over my shoulder.

"I can't tell." He sounds slightly pissed off. "I usually know these things, but the asshole is being mute on this one."

"That spells trouble right there," I mumble, and we head out of the school.

He walks me to his car and pops a cigarette out of his jacket pocket. Carmelo is an off-again, on-again smoker. When he's stressed, drinking, or extremely angry, he's smoking.

"I heard Mr. O'Connor is bi, and he has a partner," he says as he takes a drag.

"Like a partner who's a man?" I ask.

"Yep." He nods.

"Then he's definitely bi."

Carmelo chokes out a laugh, and soon enough, I'm joining in. Only he can force away the shadows and make me laugh, even if it is for a short while.

"I'm serious. It was this shit that got you kicked out of

that reform school in New York," he huffs, and I roll my eyes.

He's not wrong. My English teacher, Mrs. Serrano, caught me fucking my science teacher… also her husband. Suffice to say, that didn't go over well, and here I am back in Whitsborough, completely unreformed.

"Yeah, yeah." I wave him off and get into my car. "I'll see you later."

My house is quiet when I walk inside, but I know she's home. I can feel her. My sights land on her office and the closed door as I release a sigh. She's become more distant since I've been back, and I can't help but feel a pang of guilt. I cause her so much stress.

No wonder she mostly ignores me.

I head to the kitchen and open the fridge, grabbing a Gatorade. Saxon and Dahlia won't be home for a few more hours since they both have after-school activities, and Dad usually picks them up on his way home. So, just me and the woman whose life I ruined.

I walk down the hallway, heading back to the stairs, and look at the pictures hanging on the walls. There are a few of my Great Aunt Debra and Great Uncle Scott. I know the story of how my mother came to live here with them and it's a sad one.

Her mother—my grandmother—was a single parent raising her in New York and my mother never knew her father. This is how she knew Uncle Tommy—Cameron's father— because he was originally from New York too. One night, her house burned down and her mother was inside. My mother was still a minor and had no other choice but to move here with her next of kin. Eventually, Uncle Tommy came too.

I move on to the next picture of Mother and my Uncle Emmett, her twin brother. They are identical, and if they were the same sex, no one would be able to tell them apart. Their story is a little strange and doesn't completely make sense to me.

They separated Mother and Uncle Emmett at birth, and they never knew the other existed until they were my age. Grandma Jenna always told me it was a complicated story, but no matter how deep we bury the lies, they always resurface. I never knew what she meant by that, and I've always been too afraid to ask Mother for clarification.

Uncle Emmett was raised by his older brother— Carmelo's birth father—and one day found out about Mother. He immediately came here to live with her, but unfortunately by then, both my great aunt and uncle were dead. Again… under strange circumstances.

That's repeated often in my family's history. *Under strange circumstances.*

"Ivy." Mother's voice hits me from behind. "You're home early."

I turn with a huff and look into her eyes, exactly like mine. "High school gets out earlier."

"Right." She nods and looks up at the picture I was staring at. "Is there anything you need?"

"No," I answer quickly and move around her to head up the stairs. Standing next to her feels so uncomfortable, like we have nothing to talk about.

She says nothing else, but I hear her sigh and walk back to her office. *Sorry, I'm such a fucking bother.*

I get inside my room and slam the door shut. I can't wait until high school is over and I can get the fuck out of this house. Hell, I want the fuck out of Whitsborough too.

The sharp November air cuts across the lake and I shiver into my jacket. The weather here in Ontario, Canada is fucking bipolar. Fall is warm up to a point, and with little warning, the weather turns and it's suddenly frosty. I shouldn't have worn a skirt, especially being so close to the water.

Wharf parties consist of a bunch of yachts tied together and everyone hops from one to the other. It's been just over two years since I've gone to one of these, and the last one I attended was with Charlotte. My heart squeezes at the memory of her tight curls and bright brown eyes.

"My nipples could cut ice," Carmelo grumbles beside me.

"You should've worn a jacket, shithead."

Cam's car pulls up and I huff in relief. I hate being out in the cold and he's always fucking late. As he steps out of the driver's seat, I turn and watch as he smiles.

"Fuckers!" he yells out, and Carmelo snorts beside me.

"Where's your date?" Carmelo yells back. "She couldn't sneak past the parents?"

"They're having family dinner, then she's coming by." He jogs up to us.

Family dinner? Is Neil with her? Will he come by too? The thought of seeing him again has me feeling both excited and dreadful. I can feel myself becoming curious about us, but I know he hates me, and he has every fucking right to feel that way. I can barely look at him without feeling ashamed of what I've done to him and his family.

"You fuck her yet?" Carmelo asks, and I groan.

"Cam!" I turn on him quickly. "You can't fuck Amelia."

"I haven't!" He throws his hands up. "It's not like that, I swear."

"Ivy is the only one allowed to fuck with the Jones'." As soon as it leaves Carmelo's mouth, he looks sheepishly at me. "I meant Neil, not Charlotte."

"I didn't fuck any of them." I shrug, trying to look unaffected.

We hit the first yacht and Veronica—an old friend of mine from before they sent me away—steps forward. I've been doing well the last few days avoiding her and the clique of airheads she hangs out with, but I knew it was just a matter of time before we had this conversation.

"I heard you were back." She grins at me.

Veronica Hanes. Resident bad girl, all-around cunt, and a bestie of mine at one time. She and I were the resident bad girls together two years ago, and I was also an all-around cunt. Still am, only I'm a loner cunt now.

"Your hearing is impeccable," I mutter and slide past her.

"We should catch up," she calls to my retreating back. "Amber and Tanya will want to as well."

There were four of us mean girls. There's always four, right? And then I tagged in Molly, who the rest tolerated for me. Looks like they dumped her soon after I left though. Not that I blame them, because Molly would be like that game called Which One of These Just Doesn't Belong?

"I fucked Amber last night," Carmelo cuts in. "She was asking me questions."

"Oh, yeah?" I grab a red cup and fill it up at the nearest keg. "Was it stuff like: Does it get any bigger? Are you in yet? Did you just come?"

"Oh, fuck." Cam snaps his fingers and roars.

"Fuck off." Carmelo chuckles and fills his cup. "She wanted to know why you were back so late in the school year and if you had ever gone to jail."

I should've gone to jail.

"Tell her Ivy broke out of jail and she's a fugitive." Cam snorts. "The bitch is dumb enough to believe it."

"You shouldn't be fucking one of them," I chastise Carmelo. "They'll just tell each other about your small dick, and then when you try to break shit off, they'll tell the entire school."

"He fucks Veronica all the time." Carmelo points to a gaping Cam, totally throwing him under the bus.

"Yeah?" Cam turns red, his sights landing on me and his finger pointed to my face. "You let Veronica's older sister eat you out last night!"

Right.

Riley Hanes eats pussy like a fucking champ, and I even got her number afterward. I wouldn't mind repaying the favor eventually.

"Girl's got a mouth like a Hoover though," I say as I take a drink.

Both guys laugh, and I lose myself in time with the beat of the music, letting the warmth of the beer coat my insides.

Chapter Five

"Thanks for coming to see us this week, Neil." Shay smiles as she clears away the table. "How do you think you did on your midterms?"

"Good." I nod. "I studied." I like Shay. She keeps my dad straight and raised my sister well.

"My boy is going to be hired by the Patriots," my dad boasts as he downs his fourth glass of whiskey.

Once I declared my major as sports medicine, he hasn't shut up about it, and most of the time, his drunk-ass just sounds stupid.

"I think I'm gonna head upstairs." I look at Shay. "Did you need help with the dishes?"

"No, no, I'm fine." She heads to the dishwasher.

"I'm going out for a bit," Amelia declares, and I glare

at her.

"Out where?" I demand.

"You can't go anywhere without your brother," Dad slurs, and I try to breathe out the urge to punch him in his face.

"But he is so lame!" Amelia actually stomps her foot. "He doesn't know how to have fun."

"Exactly." Dad nods and I growl.

"Ugh!" Amelia storms off to her room.

I stand up and Dad laughs. "That fixed that," he says, like he knew she wouldn't want to go out with me. Fucking prick.

Ignoring him, I head upstairs toward our rooms. Mine and Charlotte's rooms are on the left-hand side, and Amelia's is on the right. Instead of stopping at my own, I keep going and stand outside of Charlotte's. We were close at one time, but even I have to admit, the last year of her life was different. She and I were growing apart, and I attributed that to us being into different things and maturing, but now I'm realizing maybe something was wrong.

I open her bedroom door and step inside. Charlotte wasn't a regular girly-girl. She liked to watch anime, she collected key chains with her name on them, and had an obsession with old eighties and nineties movies.

She decorated her walls with posters of Rihanna, Katy Perry, and Nicki Minaj. Some even had hearts around their faces. The longer I stay in her room, the more I feel like I really didn't know her.

"Charlotte was obsessed with Rihanna," Amelia says from the doorway, surprising me.

"Yeah." I raise an eyebrow. "Looks like it."

"That summer she stayed here, the one she… you

know," Amelia stutters. The summer she died. I nod for her to continue. "Charlotte hated me," she finishes.

"No, she didn't." I'm quick to defend my sister.

"She did," Amelia insists. "She flushed all my bodywash, cut up my new clothes, and even embarrassed me in front of my friends by calling me a lesbian."

"What?" I shake my head. This doesn't sound like Charlotte. "Amelia, you were young—"

"No, Neil. There was something wrong with Charlotte." She exhales and leans against the doorjamb. "I was relieved when she was gone." Her words come out strangled with pain and guilt. "I was happy she was dead because I knew the bullying would stop. I know that's morbid and disgusting, but it was how I felt."

"Why didn't you tell me?"

"How?" she exclaims, throwing her arms wide. "You were never here. You were going to start university, and I hadn't seen you in months."

I scrub my hand down my face and let the guilt consume me for a bit. I was absent that summer for both of my sisters and that's something I can never take back.

"Where were you planning to go tonight?" I ask her, feeling myself cave.

"Wharf party." She smiles widely.

"Alright." I pull her over to me, wrapping my arms around her neck. "Let's check it out."

She squeals and her thin arms crush me in a hug.

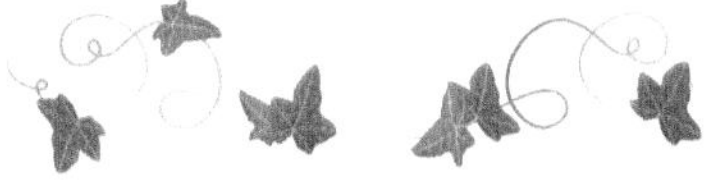

The music is pouring out of a long string of about ten yachts, and teenagers are spilling out of everywhere with red Solo cups in their hands.

"No drinking." I point at Amelia.

"I don't drink." She jumps out of my car.

That's a relief. It's another thing different from Charlotte and one less thing to worry about.

Amelia hurries ahead of me, in search of her friends, and maybe that blond asshole who was with Ivy the other night.

Ivy.

I wonder if she's here. Does she come to high school parties? She doesn't seem like the type who would waste her time with catty females or touchy guys. Fuck, what am I saying? I don't know her anymore.

A guy offers me a red cup when I step onto the first boat. I decline because I'm driving, and I rarely drink anyway. Not for a few years now, not since she took Charlotte from me. I shake my head to clear it of darkening thoughts and try to pick Amelia out in the crowd. In my search to find my sister, I find a familiar brunette a few boats over, and I lean against the side of the boat to watch her.

Ivy is alone and has a red cup in her hands—no fucking surprise—as she stares down at her phone screen. She looks angry and slightly confused as she swiftly swipes her thumb over the lit surface. Her face is slightly illuminated, and I can see the small dimple in her left cheek and gloss shining on her lips, her teeth dragging over the bottom one in frustration.

I'm hardening in my pants, and I would punch myself in the fucking dick for this reaction if I thought it wouldn't hurt so much. She's wearing a black leather jacket with gray fur along the collar, a white top underneath, and a black skirt, her long legs on display.

She shoves her phone into her jacket pocket and exhales, blowing a piece of hair out of her face. A lot of these guys have their eyes on her, and I don't fucking blame them because she's gorgeous. None of them knows what I do though. Her insides are a mess of rotting flesh, ready to destroy anyone she comes into contact with.

Why, then, am I tempted by it?

Finally, one guy watching her gets the nerve to approach, and I stand transfixed at the scene in front of me. What will she do?

He taps her arm and she turns toward him, her face now fully facing me. He leans in and says something in her ear, and I chuckle as her top lip curls up in disgust. She shakes her head at him and literally shoos him away.

Ten minutes goes by of my creepy stalking, and during that time, she looked at her phone twelve times. I wonder who is messaging her or what she's waiting for. Then another guy works up the nerve to approach her, and I chuckle in anticipation. The whole time I've been here, she hasn't looked at anyone with interest, and I find it amusing these guys want to risk it.

This time, she sees him coming before he even reaches her and shakes her head at him. I throw my head back and laugh at the guy's face because he looks so fucking dejected.

Once again, she's pulling her phone out of her pocket and staring at it with a frown on her face.

I think it's time I find out what's eating at Ivy now.

IVY

Dean: Why does Black Slaughter have me on her list, Ivy?

Dean: I told you what would happen if someone found out.

Dean: No answer?

Dean: You know the consequences.

I'm reading his messages and am shocked at what he's saying. What the fuck is Black Slaughter? And why is he acting like I told someone? I know the consequences and they are too steep to take the risk.

"You're going to have premature age lines." *No way.*

I look up from my phone to see Neil standing a few feet away, his arms crossed at his chest, and a baseball cap thrown backwards on his head.

He's wearing a brown, distressed leather jacket, a black shirt, and a pair of dark jeans. He looks good, so I give him another once-over.

"The boys are going to get jealous if they see you paying me that much attention." My guard automatically flies up when he almost sounds playful.

"What do you want?" I try to sound nonplussed.

"I want to know… What's got you looking like you want to run and hide?"

"Are you stalking me now?" I sneer at him, and he chuckles darkly.

"My only sister is around here somewhere. I need to make sure she's not in danger," he retorts, and my stomach rolls.

"Fuck you," I snarl and turn to go inside of the yacht. I need to piss and I need to get away from him.

As soon as I walk through the small door, I feel a body close at my back before a hand lands against my stomach. His scent curls around me, hugging me in a musky fragrance, and I lean into him, forgetting my initial instinct to run.

His breath hits my ear as his mouth brushes the lobe, and I suck in a breath at the foreign feeling inside me. It's not an uncontrollable lust taking over like usual. My insides are quaking for another reason, for things I want but can't describe, and I don't want his warmth to leave me.

My legs shake as I turn my face toward his, and I open my mouth to speak, but his hand clamps around it before he shoves me against the wall. My head slams into the fiberglass and I whimper at the brief shot of pain.

He crowds in around me, his mouth running a trail up my neck and stopping at my ear. "You're tempting me, bitch." His voice is harsh. "And it's pissing me off."

I feebly shake my head and dislodge his hand, but it's no use, his fingers only dig in tighter.

"I want to slit your fucking throat." Fear races through me at his words. "But I want to be inside of you before I do it."

He presses his hips into my stomach, showing me just how badly he wants it, and I once again try to shake my head. I believe him. Each word he utters, I know without a doubt, is the complete truth, and it scares the shit out of me.

His tongue slips along the shell of my ear and I shiver, not from lust but from terror. I can't move my limbs, and I'm transported back to another time when another man held me against my will. I can suddenly smell the stench of bourbon, feel the scratch of a beard, and the large swell of a cock pressing into me.

I'm no longer on the boat with Neil, instead, I have book spines digging into my back, my head throbbing from the impact of the wooden shelf, and my nails finding purchase in the soft flesh of my palms.

"Are you a virgin, Ivy?" His voice attacks my ears, and I feel the tears slip down my cheeks. *No, not this again. I can't live through this again.*

I shake with fear so potent, it pushes itself through me at a rapid speed, and I go limp at the feeling. My heart pumps faster and louder, drowning out any other words, and my throat closes around my next breath.

No, this is not happening. This is not happening, I repeat in my head just as the hand leaves my mouth and the warmth I thought I wanted steps away. Someone is speaking, but two worlds have collided inside my head and I can't determine one from the other.

I sink to the floor, wrapping my arms around my legs, and rock. I need to forget and I need to be alone. Cold air swirls around me, and I exhale the breath I've been holding, relief coursing through me.

I don't know how long I'm left here, but at some point, Carmelo appears as his arms encircle and lift me off the ground.

"It's okay, Ivy," he whispers directly in my ear. "I got you."

Chapter Six

Neil

Her cousin picks her up and carries her off the boat, but not before he throws me a menacing look. No matter how hard I try, I can't stop the guilt from eating away at me. I caused her to break down with my words and actions.

Something bad happened to Ivy and I want to know what the fuck it was. She's clearly battling with trauma, and my curiosity won't let it go. The Ivy I knew two years ago wasn't like this. She was tough and wouldn't have folded so easily like that.

If I knew this about her, would I have still done the same? Yeah, I would've. I can't help the rage and lust that envelops me every time she's near, and no matter how hard the two emotions battle it out, I'm fearful about which one will win the war.

"What's wrong with Ivy?" Amelia's frantic words hit me before she grabs my arm.

"Not sure, but I'm going to find out."

"Neil," she whispers. "Did you do something?"

I look down at my sister and she looks up at me with tears in her eyes.

"I don't think it has anything to do with Whitsborough," I tell her.

Ivy left here two years ago, completely herself and without remorse for her actions. I can still see her holding her chin high as I watched her get in a limo that would take her to New York. This girl now is traumatized, and only when she can't keep control of the strong front she puts up.

"I'm gonna need you to get me some information," I say as I watch Ivy being swept away by Carmelo and Cameron.

"No." She shakes her head emphatically. "I won't help you bring her down."

"Amelia, I'm not bringing anyone down," I lie through my fucking teeth. "I need to know what happened."

She stares into my face a while longer and finally nods. "Fine, I'll ask Cam."

"You like this kid?" I curl my fingers into fists. The thought of another little sister once again in the clutches of that family makes me angry.

"No." She laughs and pats me on the back. "It's not like that."

"Better not be," I growl and look around.

People are gathered into small groups and the tone has become hushed. It's not every day you see a Greene looking weak in this town.

I follow Amelia toward the first boat, passing a group of girls I vaguely remember from the days Charlotte and I would come here.

"The bitch has issues."

"Veronica, she looked legit sick," another replies.

"That whole family is fucked-up," Veronica snarls. "They have mountains of secrets and my nana says only money is keeping them hidden."

Well, then.

IVY

My room is pitch-black save for the illumination of my phone's screen. I'm under two thick blankets and still can't chase the cold that feels bone-deep.

By the time Carmelo brought me home, I had finally come around and declined his offer to bring me inside. I could just imagine the fuss my dad would make. We've been here before, and no matter how many times it happens, Dad worries just the same. Thankfully, they were all asleep and the house was quiet when I came in.

I'm staring at these messages, trying to decipher what they mean, and praying he's just drunk and confused. On the nights he opens the bourbon, he becomes paranoid and abrasive. What is a Black Slaughter? And what's on her list?

I hear the creak of my bedroom door and look to see Dahlia's little head poke in.

"Ivy?" Her brief whisper floats into the room.

"Yeah, Flower?"

"Can I sleep with you?" Her little lip quivers as she hurries further into the room. "I had a nightmare."

"Sure, baby." I pull back my covers and watch as she launches her little body up onto the bed.

"I was afraid you left again." She curls into my side and I nestle my face into her little brown curls.

"That was your nightmare?" I ask her as my eyes burn with tears. It kills me that my absence had this much effect on her.

"That and Mommy was sad again."

"Again?" The word is filled with disbelief as my heart

squeezes in my chest.

"When you left, Mommy cried every night." Her little voice is soft. "Even Daddy couldn't make her stop." No matter how hard I try, I can't see my mother crying about anything, especially not when it came to my actions that led to my exile.

"She cried?"

"Yes." She nods, her curls brushing my face. "Don't leave and make her sad again."

"Okay, Flower." I pull her in close. "I promise."

"Ivy." Dahlia's voice filters through my sleep. "Ivy!"

"Flower, is the house burning down?"

"No!" She giggles and bounces on the bed. "You haven't opened your eyes yet."

"Because I don't want to wake up yet."

"I want pancakes," she whispers in my ear, and I snort. "And Uncle Emmett is here!"

My eyes pop open and I stare into her bright green eyes. Dahlia looks like Dad with her deep golden skin and bright green eyes. She even has his deep dimples in both cheeks.

"He is?"

"Yup!" she squeals and jumps off the bed. "I'm gonna make him make me pancakes."

Uncle Emmett being here is slightly unsettling. He's the chief of police and I detest any fucking cop. I love him though. I just hope he's not here because of something I've done, like drinking and driving and fucking his deputy to get out of it.

When I roll out of bed, I cringe because I'm still wearing the same clothes from last night. I change quickly and leave my room, heading toward a squealing Dahlia.

I enter the kitchen and see not just Uncle Emmett, but Uncle Travis too. They have a *strange* relationship. See? There's that word again. Uncle Emmett, Uncle Travis, *and* Aunt Adri are all together. Yes, all three of them, and they have kids too.

Uncle Emmett tosses Dahlia in the air and Uncle Travis chuckles, both not noticing me right away. They look happy and stress-free, something I'm sure I'll disrupt again because my ass can't stay out of trouble.

"Ivy!" Uncle Emmett exclaims, dumping Dahlia in Uncle Travis' lap. "Can you get any more gorgeous?"

"Hi, Uncle Em." I beam as he picks me up and twirls me around.

"It's good to have you home, Ivy." Uncle Travis comes over with Dahlia in his arms and hugs me.

"Everything is better now. Ivy is home!" Dahlia's little arms strangle me.

"Thanks, guys." I grin shyly.

"Uncle Em!" Dahlia screeches, and I screw up my face at the noise. "Pancakes!"

"You're lucky your Auntie Adri isn't here to make you some," he says, and we all chuckle.

It's no secret Aunt Adri is a terrible cook, but Uncle Emmett pokes the most fun at her for it.

"What's going on here?" Dad's croaky morning voice has us all giggling.

"Uncle Em and Uncle Travis are here!" Dahlia runs to

him so he can swoop her up in his arms.

"I see that." He smothers his face into her curls, much like I do.

"Ma is home from Italy tomorrow," Uncle Travis says to him. "Rock, paper, scissors, who picks her up."

"No way, bro," Dad exclaims. "I picked her up last time."

"Nana Sharla is coming home?" I can't help the sound of dismay that filters through my words.

Nana Sharla is a brilliant woman, don't get me wrong, but she's tough and likes everything her way. All of us except one let her have it. All except Mother. She never lets Nana Sharla bowl her over, and if the woman tries, Mother just shuts her down with a few words. They love each other, you can see that, but I believe Nana has that much more respect for our mother because she doesn't back down.

The last time I saw her was this past summer, when they came to visit me for my birthday. Nana Sharla bought me a box of condoms, then lectured me about the temptation of vile high school boys who would want to impregnate me and leave me.

Dad had to sit me down after and explain that he and Uncle Travis shared the same father, and he wasn't a good man. There's not much resemblance between Uncle Travis and Dad besides the green eyes. Thankfully, I never had to witness how terrible their father was because he died a long time ago from cancer.

"Where's my sister?" Uncle Emmett asks.

"She's coming," Dad says and sits Dahlia at the table.

"E should pick up Ma," Uncle Travis says, and Dad laughs.

Uncle Travis calls Nana Sharla Ma even though she's not because his mother died in a terrible accident when he was in high school. Nana Sharla took him in after that. My family is all twisted and somehow interconnected. I still haven't figured it all out and I don't think I ever want to.

"To what do we owe the visit, assholes?" Mother says as she walks into the kitchen.

"Mommy said a bad word," Dahlia chastises and points to the swear jar by the fridge.

Mother is the only one who ends up filling it, and I can't help the grin that comes over my face at her dismay.

"Shit," she whispers.

"Heard that one too," Dahlia whispers back as a surprised laugh escapes my belly.

Mother looks at me with shock at first, but it quickly morphs into amusement.

"I'm never going to learn." She sighs. "How much do I owe the bank of Dahlia this time?"

"Five dollars." Dahlia rubs her hands together.

"Five dollars?!" Mother exclaims.

"And Daddy wants you to pick up Nana Sharla from the airport," Dahlia throws in, and I am once again laughing at the look on my mother's face.

"Like hell," she says, and Dahlia is wiggling in her seat.

"Mommy has a potty mouth, but it makes me rich." Everyone laughs, and Uncle Emmett stacks up the pancakes.

"Ivy, how does it feel to be back?" Uncle Travis inquires, sounding genuine.

That's what I love about my family, they don't judge, and even though I came home under undesirable circumstances, they would never rub it in my face.

"Not hanging out with teachers, I hope," Uncle Emmett chimes in.

Never mind, I take it back. They will totally rub it in my face.

"That teacher is lucky he was just fired," Mother snarls. "I had bigger plans."

"I can't believe he's still breathing." Uncle Emmett snorts.

"The verdict is still out, he took advantage of a minor," my mother says.

"I'll be eighteen in, like, six months, Mother." I shake my head.

"What did Ivy do?" Dahlia asks, her eyes wide with innocence.

"Ivy grew up too fast." Dad shoots me a look, and I roll my eyes.

"I'm glad." Dahlia nods as syrup runs down her chin. "I wanted her home."

I feel a lump work its way up my throat at her words, and my eyes fill quickly before I can hold them back, the tears spilling down my cheeks. I've always felt like the outsider in my family, the one being watched and always causing stress. So to hear one of them say I'm wanted brings out emotions I've tried to bury.

"I need to go get some homework done." I turn quickly before anyone can see the tears.

"Pancakes!" Uncle Emmett calls out, but I'm already

halfway to the stairs.

CHAPTER SEVEN

Ivy

"Ivy," Charlotte breaks the silence, "do you ever want to get married?"

"What?" Here I am, so fucking drunk, missing my grandma, and this is what she wants to talk about?

"Do you want to get married?"

"I don't know," I mumble.

"I want to get married." She sounds like she's sulking.

"Cool."

"Why do you only kiss me when we're alone?" she asks, and I groan into my hands.

"Charlotte!" I yell into the car. "I can't do this right now!"

My fucking grandma just died! What the fuck is wrong with her?

I roll down my window to let the cool air hit my face. I'm

angry and this night is about to go downhill.

"I know." She sniffs as I lock my jaw in frustration. "I just need to know what we are."

"We're buddies who like to make out every once in a while," I snap, then cringe when I hear her intake of breath. That was harsh.

"That's it?"

"I can't think about this right now." I shake my head. "I really can't."

I asked her to get me out of the house to take my mind off of shit, but I'm having to hear more drama.

"You're not worth it!" she screams and pounds her hand into the steering wheel. "You never really cared!"

I wake up in a cold sweat, the droplets running down my spine and dripping off my jaw. It's been a while since I've dreamed of Charlotte and it always feels so fucking real, like I'm right back there in that car with her.

I wish life was like that. You could choose when and where to go back and fix all your fuck-ups. Charlotte was my life's catalyst of fuck-ups. I wish with everything in me I could go back and reverse what happened that night.

My phone's ping sounds through my darkened room, and I reach for it off my nightstand. As soon as I see the name on the screen, my heart stops, and then gallops against my rib cage. Swiping my thumb across the phone screen opens the message instantly, and I freeze when I see a video, then my hand shakes as I press play.

"Turn around." His voice is loud in my silent bedroom.

It's me in the video and I'm completely naked, my hair hanging to mid-back in messy waves. I do as he says and turn, revealing only my upper thighs to my chest, my face thankfully out of shot.

"Touch yourself."

I remember exactly how I felt, drunk and slightly confused. Why was I doing as the old man said? I wish I could go back to this point and punch him in the face, changing the course of our relationship.

But that's not how life works. Instead, we are bound by our past decisions and forced to live a future of consequences.

I watch as my hand shakily finds my mound and my fingers slip through my folds, dry as they were. I was too afraid to feel anything, and being a virgin, I was naïve to his intentions.

The video cuts out and I'm left looking at the screen in terror. What is he planning for me? Why the fuck is he sending me this?

Dropping my phone beside me in the bed, I try my hardest not to crumble, not to give in to the desire to end it all. Instead, I think of Flower. She asked me not to leave again, and I promised her I wouldn't.

I have yet to message him back and ask what's going on. I'm playing the avoidance game, but seeing how he's escalating, I'm not sure how much longer I can let it continue. I wish I could turn to someone with this, but I can't. No one can know what happened in New York, and in the end, I always feel like I deserved it.

It's just after midnight on Sunday and I can't lie in my bed any longer. My heart is racing with anxiety, and if I don't get the fix I need soon, I know things will only get worse.

I pull up my phone and scroll to the name I'm hoping will want to see me.

Me: Meet me at the strip.

It's dark at the strip since the streetlights have long been removed. I'm waiting in my family's Mercedes, my stomach rolling and my knees twitching. I've been holding a spliff in my hand for the last ten minutes, debating on smoking it now to take the edge off or saving it for later when I want to extend my relief.

The choice is made for me when I see another set of headlights illuminating the road ahead. With an exasperated sigh, I put it back in the glove box. Later it is. The car pulls up next to mine and I roll down my window, watching as the driver in the other car rolls down theirs too.

"I was thinking you weren't going to show." I grin.

"I almost didn't." Riley smirks back. "But curiosity got the better of me."

"Get over here." I nod my head toward my passenger seat and watch as she gets out of her car.

Riley is gorgeous. There's no better way to describe her. The whole Hanes family is. Her hair shines like the golden sun, her skin is bronzed, and her face is exquisite. She looks like a sinful cherub.

She gets in my car and her perfume immediately cloys the air with the sweet scent of cupcakes. We stare at each other for a while, and I feel the corners of my mouth rise with hers.

"I don't know how to do this." She shakes her head.

"Do what?"

"Be with a girl." She looks at me through her lashes.

I lean across the seat and clasp her chin in my hand.

"Don't think about it so hard," I whisper against her lips.

Pulling her the rest of the way to me, I kiss her softly at first, not wanting to scare her off. She's wearing some sort of fruity chapstick, and I lick across her lips to taste more of it. Her mouth opens wider, so I take that opportunity to kiss her harder, deeper. She moans, and I grin against her mouth as my other hand cups her full breast.

"Take your shirt off," I say, my lips still touching hers.

She pulls back and lifts her shirt over her head, displaying her round tits in a demi-bra. Her nipples peek out over the edge, pink tightened points begging for my mouth.

"I'm going to need you in the backseat," I husk out.

She blushes a pretty pink and gets out, shutting the door, then gets into the backseat, and I get out to follow her. My mouth salivates to taste her, and my patience with being tender isn't going to last long.

I open the door and see her sitting there, tits looking fucking delectable, and her hands in her lap.

"Lie down." I sound hard, abrasive, but I'm barely keeping it together. I need to fuck the shit out of this girl.

She does as she's told and lies down, her shoes dangling outside the window. I pull off her shoes, tossing them on the floor, and reach up to undo her jeans. Her stomach is toned, and I vaguely remember Riley being a cheerleader at Precious Blood Academy a few years ago. I wonder if she continued at college. It could be a point of conversation, if we ever move past the friends with benefits stage. I pull her jeans down her legs and moan when I discover she's not wearing any underwear.

"Were you planning on killing me tonight?" I groan.

"Honestly? I didn't think we'd get this far," she whispers.

I ease her legs open and crawl in between them. It's a tight fit in the backseat, and if anyone decided to come here tonight, they'd see everything. My fingers spread open her pussy and her scent wafts into my face, her arousal is so fucking sweet. She wants me, and I'm about to show her how good a girl can eat pussy.

"You're wet for me, Riley," I taunt as I blow warm air on her.

She whimpers and scoots her ass closer to my face, wanting more, so I slowly run my tongue from her entrance to the tight bundle of nerves and back again.

"Fuck," she whispers, her fingers slipping into my hair.

I slide my tongue inside of her, the warmth enveloping me, and her musk is potent in my mouth. Fucking her slowly with my tongue, I find a rhythm in the quick sounds of her panting, then find that spot inside of her, flicking against it a few times.

"Fuck," she husks out, and I pull out of her.

Then I replace my tongue with three fingers, slamming them inside of her, and grinning when her back arches off the seat as she screams my name. Sucking her clit into my mouth, I lash my tongue across it, still pumping rapidly into her.

I bite down on her clit and she comes hard, her pussy clamping around my fingers and her juices soaking my hand. She's chanting my name again and pushing my face deeper into her folds.

"Oh my god," she continues to moan as I pump in and out of her slowly. "That was amazing."

I pull my fingers out of her and lick her cum off of them, running my tongue salaciously between each one. She tastes like the heaven she looks like she came from.

"I want to taste you again, Ivy." She sits up and practically pushes me out of the car.

Then she stands up, her bare feet on the cold pavement, and her body erupts in goose bumps.

"You need to put clothes on," I tell her.

Pulling off my sweater, I hand it to her, and she pulls it on, then reaches out to grab ahold of my breast through my tank top. I'm so fucking happy I didn't wear a bra. She pinches my nipple between her fingers and I bite into my lip, trying not to grab her throat. Riley doesn't know how rough I can be, and now's not the time for her to find out. It's our first time after all.

"I want your pants off, Ivy," she says, and I feel myself soaking through them.

I drop my pants in the middle of the fucking strip, the night air freezing, but I can't feel the sting of the cold as much as the heat building between my legs.

The clap of a slap lands across my ass cheek as I crawl into my back seat. I look over my shoulder and find Riley staring at my ass, her bottom lip crushed between her teeth. I flip onto my back and spread my legs open wide.

"Hurry," I snarl, and her eyes widen. "Or else I'm going to punish you."

She rushes forward and her blonde head disappears between my legs. When I feel the first swipe of her tongue, I lie back and exhale. This is exactly what I needed.

NEIL

It's been almost two months since I was in Whitsborough, and I am already on my way back there again. This Christmas is Dad's turn, and even though I offered to stay home, my mom would hear none of it. It's a hard time for her and faking happiness is fucking draining. I get it. She would rather wallow in her pain and think of her daughter instead of cooking and singing carols around the house.

I've spoken to Amelia over the phone at least once a week, but I have yet to ask her what she's found out for me about Ivy. I wish I could say I haven't been thinking about her, that her tortured face hasn't been popping into my head constantly, and that thinking about her no longer comes with murderous thoughts.

Don't get me wrong, I still fucking hate her and want her to pay for what she's done, but I also want to unearth all her secrets. Maybe there are a few I could use to make her disappear back to New York and far away from what's left of my family.

I pull into my dad's driveway and kill the engine. It snowed a lot the last few days and everything is now coated with a thick layer of the white shit. I hate snow, I hate the cold, and I hate Whitsborough. I get out and groan when the snow comes up above my boots, the cold, wet powder slipping inside.

Just as I turn around, I am blasted in the face with a ball of the shit.

"What the fuck?" I exclaim.

"Welcome back, big brother," Amelia calls out as I clear the snow from my eyes.

"You're done." I grin and chase after her.

She screams and tries to run back to the front door, only to slip and fall on her ass. I howl with laughter and slip right beside her, landing on my back. Both of us are laughing so hard, and when she sits up, I grab a handful of the stuff, shoving it inside of her sweater.

"Neil!" she squeals and stands to shake out the snow, only to slip back down again.

"You two are going to catch a cold out here!" Shay yells out from the door, a wide smile on her face. "How was the drive, Neil?"

Amelia and I get up, dusting off our asses, and carefully tread back to the house.

"The drive wasn't too bad."

"Come on in and get some cocoa," she says, stepping aside for us.

Thank God for Shay, otherwise, I would have my father's blood on my hands and only my mother left as family. Shay somehow puts up with him, and for that alone, I am grateful. Then she gave us Amelia, and I grew to love her for it.

"Son!" my father's booming voice calls from the family room. "Get in here."

Shay looks over her shoulder toward the sound of his voice and then back at me with a small smile.

"He's missed you." Her voice is soft.

"Yeah." I nod, fighting an eye roll.

"I'll make cocoa." Amelia heads to the kitchen. "You say hi to Dad."

Heading into the family room, I find him immersed in a football game, a bottle of whiskey beside him. I don't know how he functions enough to work, and I get the feeling the

Greenes keep him around out of pity.

"Son, come watch the game." He pats the couch cushion beside him, but I sit further down from him and watch the game in silence because he never actually wants to talk to me.

When Amelia comes into the room, her brow lifts at the silence, then she hands me a cup of hot chocolate and sits between us.

"How has school been?" she asks me, and Dad finally looks at me.

"Good." I nod and sip the warm chocolate. "How about you?"

"It's been okay." Her head dips, and I know she's lying.

I let it be for now because I know she doesn't like to upset Dad and have him storm the school. He's an embarrassment nowadays.

After finishing the cocoa, I stand, finally finding the opportunity to leave the room. "I'm gonna go get settled."

"Dinner is at eight," Dad mumbles, his eyes never straying from the TV.

"Cool." I glance at Amelia. "Come help me."

We head upstairs, and I pause at Charlotte's door before moving on down to my own. I can't lose sight of what I need to do, no matter how attractive my target is and how intrigued I am by her.

Amelia follows me in and crashes on top of my bed. "Look," she starts, "everything is fine."

"Spit it out."

"Neil…"

"Amelia." I stare down at her. "Spit. It. Out."

"I'm just upset about something stupid. I'll get over it. I see it every day at school and it pisses me off," she huffs, but I don't miss the way her face loses color. "I just can't tell you."

"Are you being bullied?" I ask as I sit beside her.

"No." She shakes her head. "Trust me, Neil, it's not that bad. Really."

"As long as you aren't hurt or anything," I tell her.

"Nothing physical, no."

"Is it a guy?"

"No." She sighs and I see what's happening.

"Is it that Cam guy? Did he get another girlfriend or something?" I would kill the fucker if he used my sister.

"No!" She looks at me wide-eyed. "I told you, we aren't like that."

Her phone pings with a message and she pulls it out. I see the notification on her lock screen: Veronica Hanes.

"Who is that?" The name sounds familiar.

"A girl from school." She shrugs. "She's been really nice to me and I've started hanging out with her group."

"Be careful," I warn her. Her eyes roll and I know she's about to ignore everything else I'm about to say, so I reference something she'll understand. "Well, what does she want? Are you guys going to make a burn book or something?"

"Please tell me you did not just reference Mean Girls?" Her brows crinkle in the center with disgust.

"Charlotte made me watch it." I shrug and wink at her.

"Charlotte had a crush on Rachel McAdams," she

scoffs, and I laugh.

"Who didn't?"

She snorts and opens her phone, reading the message, and an enormous grin takes over her face.

"What?"

"There's a party tonight at Veronica's and we have to go." She stands and does a little jump.

"No, thanks. I'm not going to another high school party." I wave her off.

"Perfect." She claps her hands. "Veronica's sister, Riley, is throwing it and she goes to college."

"Hell, no!" I shake my head emphatically. "You're not going to a college party."

"Neil!" She stomps her foot. "Do you ever have fun?"

Her words hit me in the chest and I absorb them slowly. I try to have fun, but I'm focused on my future and I promised my mom I wouldn't disappoint her. I'm all she has left. Studying is important, and partying, not so much. Besides, I partied enough through high school.

Maybe if Charlotte had me with her on her partying nights, shit wouldn't have happened, and just maybe she'd still be here. I look at Amelia, her eyes large and round, and for a split second, I see Charlotte, begging me to come to Dad's with her.

"Okay, fine," I give in. "No drinking."

"I don't drink!" she exclaims.

The house is indeed thumping with music and fucking large. I know this neighborhood because the Greenes live not too far from here, and I find myself looking around the line of cars to see if an M5 is visible.

I can't deny I want to see her, and I also can't deny I want to find out everything about her. Amelia leads us inside the monstrous house, and I cringe when I hear the loud shrill of pop music. It's not too late into the night, but some people look completely inebriated. Others look tipsy at most, and the farther into the house we go, the stronger the cloying scent of marijuana is.

"Amelia!" I turn toward the sound and find the girl I remember from the wharf party.

"Hey, Veronica." Amelia gestures to me. "This is my brother, Neil."

Veronica gives me a once-over and grins at me. *No way, little girl.*

"Hi, Neil." Her voice becomes husky.

"Yeah… no." I shake my head and walk toward the kitchen. A couple of kegs are set up against the counter and a few dudes my age are gathered around them.

"He's hot," Veronica says to Amelia before I walk out of hearing range.

Fucking jailbait.

Am I that much older than her? No. I'll be twenty in a few months, and even though it's just a couple of years, maturity is a big thing, and I have way more of it.

"Who's this Dean?"

I stop at a slightly opened door and see long, blonde hair swinging back and forth.

"No one, Riles." Ivy.

"He's constantly messaging you. Who the fuck is he, Ivy?"

"Someone in New York. He's in the past." Ivy sounds pissed.

"Then why is he messaging you?" Riley yells.

Why are they fighting like a couple? Wait. Are they a couple? I know what I saw that night at the strip, but that was just a bet, right?

"It doesn't matter." Ivy's voice is low, and I can hear the anger buried in it.

"Let me see them then." Riley sounds petulant.

"No."

"If you don't show me the messages…" Riley's voice becomes shrill. "Then we're over."

"You sure about that, sweetheart?" Ivy's voice drops, and the seduction in her words has me hardening in my pants.

"Yes." Riley doesn't sound sure. "I mean it this time."

"Then you have a pleasant life." Wow, she's fucking harsh. Then again, I already knew that because she killed my little sister.

The door swings open and reveals a crying Riley as she pushes by me. I peer into the small washroom just as Ivy sits on the closed toilet and pulls a baggie of weed out of her pocket.

As if sensing someone watching her, Ivy lifts her head, and those sea-blue eyes meet mine. For someone who just suffered a breakup, she looks pretty nonplussed. Again, I'm not surprised.

"Wow," she breathes out, her voice sarcastic. "Neil Jones back in Whitsborough." She pulls out rolling papers, and her tongue glides along the thin material, making my dick twitch in my jeans. "In or out, loser," she says as she sticks two papers together. "I don't want to share this with others."

Maybe one day I'll know the exact reason I went in instead of walking by, but I don't have the answer today.

"So, Riley is your girlfriend?" I snort.

"Was. You heard most of it." She looks up at me with her brow raised. "Are you a homophobe too?"

"N–no, I'm n–not." I stumble over my words and lock my jaw to keep from stuttering further.

"Sounds like it, Neil Jones." Her voice is taunting. "Shut the door. I need a good seal in here."

Again, I do the opposite of what I should do, and close the door, locking us inside the close confines. She sparks a lighter and brings the flame to the tip of her spliff, the cherry burning bright red under the heat. Then she takes a deep inhale and coughs, holding it out to me.

"No, thanks." I shake my head.

"You know it's going to get filled with smoke in here, right? I'm hotboxing the bathroom. You will get high." I look down at the knob and I hear her *tsk* behind me. "Can't leave now, pretty boy." I hear her inhale again. "You'll break my seal."

"Why'd your girlfriend break up with you?" Might as well get some answers while I'm in here.

"Because of some guy messaging me. Girls are jealous things." She leans back on the toilet.

She's wearing tight black jeans, rips strategically placed at the knees and upper thighs, and she has on a baggy black hoodie. Her hair is down in messy waves, the deep red hues shining under the vanity light, and her face is void of makeup. Even without makeup, Ivy is a fucking stunner.

"An ex-boyfriend?"

As she stands from the toilet, she looks up at me with a grin, then leisurely makes her way to me while taking a long drag on the spliff. She steps right up to me, nearly eye to eye, her forehead just at my chin. I like that she's tall for a girl. It's always been something I liked about her. Fuck. I try to clear my head of those thoughts, but it's foggy from inhaling the potent smoke.

She lifts her face as I bend mine, neither of us stepping away, and our lips are just centimeters apart.

"Open your mouth." Her voice sounds weird as she continues to hold her breath.

Again, I do the opposite of what I should, and open my mouth for her. She exhales a long plume of smoke, and I suck it in, eager to take whatever she's giving me. Her lips curl up as she blows out the rest, and I hold my breath, the smoke settling in my lungs.

Her mouth is still so close to mine, neither of us moving, and her eyes search mine.

"Why do you keep finding me, Neil?" she asks. "Why are you asking about my love life? And why are you in this washroom with me?"

All valid questions and yet none I want to answer at the moment. Her lips brush against mine and then she's reaching behind me to unlock the door, opening it suddenly.

"Get out, Neil," she snarls and turns her back on me.

Her sudden change in demeanor snaps me out of whatever hold her venom had on me, and I do exactly what she says, slamming the door behind me. I wish I could just slap the shit out of myself right now because I have no explanation for why I let her do these things to me. I fucking *hate* her.

Amelia is standing with a group of girls with Veronica in the center. They really resemble the fucking Mean Girls as they glare at everyone around them. I'm happy she's not being bullied, but if I find out she's bullying anyone, I will be just as pissed.

The scent of marijuana circles around my head as the washroom door opens behind me, then a loud, fake laugh sounds from the kitchen and I notice Riley hanging off a guy's arm. He looks like a footballer, tall and wide.

"Who's down for a game of Suck and Blow?" she calls out, her gaze zeroing in on Ivy.

Ivy pushes past me and into the kitchen. "Down," she states and hops up onto the island, plopping her ass there and swinging her legs.

Amelia and her group of Mean Girls laugh as I walk into the kitchen. I'm not playing this juvenile game, but I'm not leaving my sister here and risking some guy taking advantage of her either.

Riley pulls a credit card out of her purse and sucks it against her mouth. Ivy turns slightly and watches her, looking uninterested as her girlfriend—or is it ex now?—turns to the guy beside her. The guy leans forward, and just as he's about to suck the card from her mouth, Riley lets it go and crushes her lips to his. I roll my eyes at the obvious attempt to make Ivy jealous, but I can see it doesn't work, because Ivy just watches with boredom as the two suck each other's face off.

The guy finally detaches himself from Riley's clutches with a chuckle and picks up the card, sucking it to his mouth, then he leans over to Ivy on the island, and she leans forward to suck the card. Only the fucking loser plays the same dumb move Riley did and drops the card. Instead of getting a kiss though, Ivy shoves him back and rolls her eyes. I exhale with relief and once again want to slap the shit out of myself for it. I don't care who she kisses.

She picks up the card, holds it to her mouth, and sucks it on. Her eyes twinkle with mischief as she hops down from the table and starts in my direction. My heartbeat picks up and I feel myself hardening once more at the thought of her invading my space, maybe fucking dropping that card. I'm surprised though when she bypasses me and stands in front of Amelia.

Amelia blushes a bright red, giggles, and slowly leans forward. I'm holding my breath, my hands steadily curling into fists as my teeth clench tight. Why is she involving my sister?

Just as my sister's lips touch the card, Ivy reaches up and pulls the card out from between them, throwing it to the floor. The next second, her lips are on Amelia's, and she's crowding her against the wall. Ivy's hands slap the wall by my sister's head and Amelia's hands land on Ivy's ass.

I'm momentarily shocked as I hear Amelia moan while her fingers grip onto Ivy's ass. What the fuck? I'm broken from my shock as Riley comes across the kitchen, a scream erupting from her mouth as she grabs Ivy's hair, pulling her off Amelia. Ivy laughs maniacally as she slaps Riley's hands off of her and licks her lips.

"Baby Jones," Ivy purrs as she leans into my little sister's face. "Your kisses are like pure sin."

"Get out of my house!" Riley screams at no one in particular, but I take the opportunity to do just that.

I grab my sister's hand and haul her toward the front door.

"No, wait, Neil." Amelia tugs on her hand.

"We're leaving," I snap.

Anger pulses through my body, and I can't really figure out who it's for. My sister who just devoured the set of lips I've always wondered about, or the fact that Ivy blatantly acted like I didn't exist. Fuck, maybe a mixture of both.

We get outside and I drag her to the car. She's long since stopped trying to fight me, and instead, lets me push her into the passenger side. I get in the car and look at her.

She has her head down, staring at her nails, clearly avoiding me. "What the fuck was that?" My voice vibrates throughout the confined space.

"A kiss?" She looks at me, her eyes widening over my face. "Are you mad?"

"Why the fuck are you kissing Ivy Greene, Amelia?"

"Because I like her." She sounds small.

"Okay?" I throw my hands up. "But kissing her?"

"I *like* her."

Oh, fuck.

Chapter Eight

I fucked up.

I know Amelia Jones has been crushing on me for a couple weeks now, and I've ignored it for a few reasons. One, I was dating Riley, or at least trying to. Two, she's young and I couldn't be too sure how she was feeling. And three, Charlotte. She reminded me too much of her sister, and I wanted none of it.

But I fucked that all up tonight.

She's been watching me and Riley for weeks. Riley would pick me up at school and Amelia would be there, Riley would come to bring me lunch and I would catch Amelia staring. I could see she was jealous, but I chalked it up to just being curious, nothing serious, until tonight. I learned differently tonight, and I fucked it all up.

Why did I have to kiss Amelia Jones? Oh, right, I wanted to piss her brother off, and now I'm the bitch who used a young girl's feelings for my agenda... again.

Riley kicked me out of her house about an hour ago, and I've been walking around aimlessly, not wanting to go home. My house has been bustling with my family being excited about the holidays and it's depressing me even more. I hate the holidays, I hate the snow, and I hate Whitsborough, but here I am walking through it all.

My phone had been quiet for about a week, no unwanted messages, and I was just moving on, hoping he was over it. Until tonight. He sent me another video, but I am just too scared to open it. Maybe his being home with his family triggered his need to torment me, because that's what he liked, tormenting me. I don't think he'll ever stop, and I don't know what to do. I could change my number, but then I'm so afraid he'll find another way to deliver his messages.

When my feet grow numb from the cold and snow, I decide to start for home. It's well after midnight and everyone should be asleep. They should also care about where their daughter is, but seem content with my simple text responses.

Where are you? Out.

When will you be home? Later.

Are you okay? Yeah.

That's all they need to sleep at night, or call themselves parents, and conveniently brush me aside. I'm an unwanted teen pregnancy, remember?

I get to my house and stop in my tracks when an unfamiliar car is idling on the street. It's a car you wouldn't normally see around here. It looks like a Civic, and yes, I know how pretentious that sounds, but facts are facts.

The driver's side door opens and a tan Timberland boot steps out onto the asphalt. Then I see his head and I am both relieved and anxious about why he's here. He closes his door and leans against his car, waiting for me to go to him, and

I can either suck it up and do it, or freeze in the cold.

Crossing the street, I walk straight to him, forcing a brave exterior that doesn't even closely resemble my trembling insides. He's still in the same clothes and it reminds me how close I came to kissing him in that bathroom, and again in that kitchen, but thankfully, both times I remembered he hates me.

I stop a foot in front of him and lift my brow. *What the fuck are you doing here, Jones?* His arm reaches forward and he fists my jacket in his hand, turning us around, then slamming me against his car. My back absorbs the impact and then the warmth of his body presses into my front.

"Why Amelia?" he asks.

"Because I'm an asshole."

"Why Amelia?" He shakes me a bit, and I can see the conflict in his features.

Neil Jones hates me, but Neil Jones wants me too. He's pissed I've wormed my way into his sister's life, but he's also pissed I didn't try it with him. I can see everything.

I lift my hands and press them against his warm cheeks, the rough scratch of stubble scraping my palms. "I'm sorry."

He has to know I don't just mean for Amelia and that those two words are all I can offer him. I can't bring Charlotte back.

His eyes search mine, slowly losing their fire and filling with moisture. I took someone from him that can never be replaced. That void he's filling is vast, and forgiveness can never be in the cards, but he still deserves to hear it from me regardless of how he perceives it, and they aren't just words to me, they are boulders of pain.

His forehead falls and connects with mine, our breaths mingling in puffs of white. I feel his jaw flex beneath my hands and rub my fingers along their sharpened edge. Neil is beautiful.

We stay like that for a while, him letting me feel his pain and me letting it connect with my own. I wish I could take it all. I stand on my tippy-toes, and he pulls back slightly, his brows coming together in confusion. Pressing my lips against the corner of his mouth, he stiffens and drops his fist from my jacket.

"I'll stay away from Amelia," I promise as he steps away.

He just nods. There are no words needed, and I can only hope he knows I mean what I say. I slide out from between him and his car and walk toward my gate, my heart heavier with each step. Something just shifted, and I feel like no matter what I do going forward, that something will forever connect me to Neil Jones.

I chance a look at him over my shoulder. He's still standing there in the same spot, looking at the ground, and his fingers touching the spot my mouth did.

What happens now?

Chapter Nine

"Where were you last night?" I ask Carmelo as he lies across my bed.

"I had a prior engagement." He grins and his busted lip bleeds again.

"I can tell by your face."

"You should see the other guy." He chuckles.

"I actually should. Are you sure you're winning?"

"I need to take a few hits to get my blood pumping and then it's all red." He snaps his fingers. "How was the party?"

"Riley and I broke up." I roll my eyes.

"Don't look too banged up about it. Were you even really dating?"

"I think so." I shrug.

"You're still fucking your math teacher." He raises a

bandaged brow. "Shouldn't you be exclusive if you're dating?"

"We didn't set terms."

"I think when you find the right one, you'll know it. Riley was just something to pass your time." He pats my leg and stands up. "Your mother has been nagging me to let her teach me how to fight."

"Probably because she thinks you're losing." I wave at his busted face.

My mother is a trained MMA fighter, my Uncle Trent in New York is her trainer, and she still leaves some weekends to fight there. I have never seen her fight and I don't think I would want to. It would be difficult to watch someone trying to hurt her.

"Your mother is a vicious fighter." He cracks his split knuckles. "I saw videos."

"She is vicious," I agree.

"Anything else happen last night?"

I fall back to the bed with a groan. "I hotboxed Riley's bathroom…"

"Nice…"

"With Neil."

"What?!" Carmelo exclaims.

"And then made out with Amelia."

"Holy fuck!" He laughs and sits back on the bed. "How do you manage all this drama?"

"The Jones family will not leave me alone. They keep finding me."

"Some would call that fate." He stands again. "I need to get home and clean my face."

"Your parents are gonna trip." I chuckle.

"Or just call me a Torres." He shrugs. "Like father, like son, I guess."

Not only was he named after his father, looks like his father, and acts like his father, but he's reminded every day that he will never know the man. It breaks my fucking heart, and I would assume makes him the way he is.

"I'll see you in a few days," he says as he heads to the door, a slight limp in his gait.

Right… Christmas.

When I reach for my phone, I open the messages. The video is still there and my heart pounds. I need to open it and get it over with, then I need to contact him and find out what the fuck is going on.

I press on the triangle and the video plays. This time, my hands are bound behind my back with his tie and I'm face down on top of his large, oak desk. Once again, I am completely naked. He liked to do this to me, tie me up and take advantage of me.

The video zooms in on my exposed ass and pussy, my body shaking with fear. His large hand slaps my ass cheek, and I can hear myself sob quietly. A tear slips down my cheek as I watch myself just a little over a year ago, being held against my will, and awaiting the punishment I knew was coming.

By this time, I knew the patterns and just how he would ensnare me. I was utterly alone. I had no one to call and help me because my family's name was too important to sully. How could I expose this and keep my family out of it? My dad would kill him and then we would be known as a family of murderers.

No, I had to keep my mouth shut and endure it. I deserved it after all.

"Tell me, Ivy." His voice is low and barely distinguishable. "Are you ready to be punished?"

"Yes." My little voice shakes with terror.

The video stops, but the memory doesn't. That was the first time he spread my ass cheeks and fucked me there. I couldn't sit for a week, and during it all, I barely protested, because I fucking deserved it.

My body vibrates, and I know if I don't repress this shit now, I will need something extra to do it. Riley isn't here to help with that anymore, and I have no one else in this little fucking town besides my math teacher, but I don't know his number, and I really don't think he'd appreciate a call during the holidays.

Neil quickly enters my mind, but I shake it away. He would never want to touch me unless it was to kill me, and at this point, I'd probably let him.

I jump out of my bed and pace the room. I need to do something. My hands get numb and my heart skips out of my chest. Then the phantom scent of stale bourbon and cigar smoke fills my senses. I begin to feel sweaty palms on my body and then the smell of sour sweat. I retch into my hand and try to breathe, but it's no use.

I run to my washroom and open the drawer under the sink. Thankfully, my family stays the fuck away from me, making hiding drugs in here easy. I pull out a small baggie of pills that's been hiding in here untouched for well over two years and tip out two white ones. I quickly pop them into my mouth and then swallow them dry.

Please hurry, I beg, hoping they'll work fast.

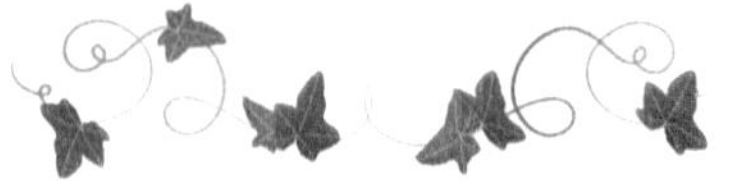

"Ivy?"

I groan and stuff my face further into my pillow.

"Ivy, I brought you some cereal. It's the only thing I know how to cook," Dahlia whispers.

I slowly open an eye and see it's once again dark outside. I slept the whole fucking day. My stomach growls loudly and I turn to face my favorite flower.

"Cereal?" I ask, my voice cracking.

"Sorry, it's the only thing I can cook," she repeats, and my heart flips. I love this little girl with my entire soul.

"Thank you, Flower." I reach for the bowl. "What's everyone doing?"

"Sax and Daddy are playing chess, and Mommy is gone for the night. Do you think she went to buy our Christmas gifts?" Her eyes widen with excitement.

"Probably." I nod.

"Hey, Dahlia?" Dad's voice breaks up our conversation. "Can you go downstairs and make sure Saxon isn't crying too much about losing to his pops?"

"Okay!" she squeals and runs out of my room, screaming Saxon's name.

"Ivy." Dad comes in and shuts the door behind him. "I need to know what's going on."

My mouth dries and my limbs stiffen as I fear he knows things. "About what?" I whisper.

"With you." He sits on the bed and pats my leg. "We've been giving you your space, but I'm thinking that's not the right route."

"I don't understand." I shake my head.

"You've been shutting us out since you got home. We let you because we know life has been tough, but you need to talk to us, kiddo. We love you."

Dad is always the one who comes for these I love you talks, always trying to get me to open up, and my heart wrenches for him because they never work. I can't open up to him, I can't tell him what my actual fucking problems are, and if he knew the real me with all my fucking issues… would he love me still?

"Sorry." I exhale and avoid his eyes. "After what happened at that school and how I got kicked out, I've been ashamed."

"Why did that happen? Why would you let a teacher take advantage of you?"

"He didn't." I finally look at him because my next words are the truth. "I took advantage of him, Dad."

"Do you have a problem with sex?"

"What?" My heart picks up again. "No!"

"You can't have sex with married men, Ivy. You shouldn't be having sex at all. I was your age once, and I understand all too well, but you cannot have sex with married men."

How do I explain that my need for sex stems from the man who took advantage of me for two years? How do I tell him I need the release sex gives me to forget the man that used it to harm me?

"I liked him, Dad." I shrug. "I now realize it was wrong."

"You're lucky your mother didn't kill him." He gives me a look, his green eyes twinkling with mirth.

"She'd be in jail." I grin.

"You'd be surprised with what she can get away with." He winks.

"Because of our money?"

"Because of how smart she is. Just like you, baby girl." He taps my nose. "Now liven up because the holidays are here and I need help with Saxon."

"Dad," I groan. "Saxon needs a therapist."

"So did your Uncle Emmett, but he turned out fine." He fluffs my hair and gets up. "When your mom is back tomorrow, let's try to have a family chat."

"Okay."

Family chat is code word for nuclear war.

Chapter Ten

Ivy

The family chat did happen the next day, which was Christmas Eve, and it needed to happen because we were having the entire family at the house for the night.

"All I'm saying is, if we're allowed to bone teachers, do I have to have a good reason?" We're sitting at the kitchen table and Saxon is looking to be murdered.

"What's boned?" Dahlia asks, and I drop my head to the table with a groan.

"Saxon." My mother's calm voice has everyone instantly quieting. "I am not above killing a child if it means I get some peace. Are we clear?"

The room is still as I slowly lift my head to look around the table. Dad has his hand over his mouth but his eyes are dancing with humor, Dahlia looks pale with her chin hitting the wooden surface, and Saxon looks like he may pass out.

Mother leans across the table to get further into his

face. "I'm not going to hear about this shit anymore, right? Because it makes me feel like I need to beat someone to a pulp."

Saxon nods and she pats him roughly on the cheek. "Perfect."

She's the only one who can reel him in, and Dad lets her because Saxon can be a bit much on a good day.

"So, no one is allowed to bone any teachers!" Dahlia claps. "Got it!"

My family is fucking strange, but they can be amusing.

"Ivy." Mother turns to me. "Tell me, how's school going?"

"Uh, it's fine." *Just boning a teacher.* "I'm pulling up my math grade." *Because I'm boning the teacher.*

"You haven't been back to New York. Is there anyone you miss?" Dad asks, his face turning sympathetic. "Best Friend? Boyfriend?"

"Girlfriend?" Mother chimes in.

"No one." I swallow thickly, hoping they let this go.

"So, you were a loser there too." Saxon snorts and Mother slaps her hand on the table in front of him, never taking her eyes off me.

Saxon jumps and Dad snorts, sounding exactly like his son.

"There's no one in New York. I wasn't in the right headspace to make friends," I whisper, and shock courses through me when Mother's eyes soften.

"And what about here?" she presses, her expression turning worried.

"Here I have Carmelo and Cameron." I shrug.

"Those are your cousins, Ivy. You need to socialize outside of the family," Mother insists.

"Sometimes family makes the best of friends." Dad covers her hand with his.

"That's true." She nods. "But you can have other friends. What about Veronica? You used to be so close."

"She's a bully now." *I also boned her sister.*

"Molly?"

"We no longer have the same interests." *And I boned her dad.*

"This will change with time, Em," Dad placates her, thankfully easing her interrogation.

"Fine, but if anyone is giving you issues, you come to me." Her eyes, the same shade as mine, bore into me.

"Okay," I agree, because what else can I say?

Then they both turn on Saxon. His grades are slipping and he's a diagnosed sociopath. He hates people, he hates authority, and I don't think I've ever seen him bring a friend home like normal people do. I wasn't kidding when I said he needed a therapist.

"Did you ask your teacher for those extra assignments we talked about?" Mother leans closer to him as Saxon nods his head.

"Yep. I've already started them too." He grins as arrogance shines from his eyes.

"Great. I'll take a look at them as soon as we're done here."

His grin falls at that and now it's my turn to snort at him.

Then they turn on sweet Dahlia and both their eyes crinkle with happiness. She really does no wrong.

"You, young lady," Dad says, "just continue doing what you do."

"Yay!" She jumps and runs around the table, plowing into Saxon.

She's the only one he softens for, the only one allowed to touch him for extended periods of time, and the one thing I think he would kill for. He hugs her back and kisses her head.

"That's right, little Miss Perfect." He doesn't say it with his usual sneer because he likes that she's perfect.

"Everyone will be here soon." Mother looks around at us, her eyes stopping on me. "Try not to make anyone cry, scream, or storm out of the house." Then she turns to Saxon. "Try to be present for longer than an hour. We are your fucking family."

"Two bad words so far, Mommy," Dahlia states, holding up her fingers.

"Right." Mother closes her eyes and breathes. "Just be with your family on Christmas. Okay, guys?"

"Got it." He nods.

"Got it," I murmur as I start to rise from the table.

"Everyone will be here in a few hours, so let's clean the house and get ready." Dad stands from his seat.

When Dad said everyone, I didn't think he meant the Jones family too. If I have to be in the same room with Charlotte's father, the guilt will literally burn me alive. Then Amelia, who I know has a crush on me, and I made out with her a few days ago, will have me swimming in regret. And finally Neil, who just fucking hates me.

My uncles, Travis and Emmett, and Aunt Adri are here too with their twins and young son. The twins are freaky with how similar they look to Mother and Uncle Emmett. Nana Sharla is also here in the kitchen, trying her best to teach Aunt Adri how to make pudding. I'm not eating it.

"Honey, I'm home!" Uncle Tommy booms from the front door, and I sigh with relief because Cameron is here.

I rush to the front to get away from the Jones' and greet them. "Hi, Uncle Tommy, Hi, Aunt Amy." I hug them both.

"Hey, Ivy." Uncle Tommy pats me on the head. He's Mother's closest friend from childhood and pretty much her actual brother.

Aunt Amy kisses my head before they both head into the kitchen. Aunt Amy is Carmelo's stepfather's sister. That's why Cameron and Carmelo are pretty much cousins. Things keep getting *stranger* around here, huh?

"Please tell me you spoke to Carmelo." I grab Cameron's arm. "He's not answering my texts."

"His phone was confiscated until after the New Year and he's not allowed out of his parent's sight." He chuckles.

Right, the last fight. They try to punish him every few months, but Carmelo is almost eighteen now. There's not much more they can do. If he wants to fight, he's going to do it.

"You look frantic." Cam smirks as he wraps his arm around my shoulders. "Is it because the Jones family is here?"

"You knew?" I look at him like the traitor he is.

"I spoke to Amelia." He laughs and drags me in for a hug. "Besides, this is an excellent opportunity to win them over with that charm."

"Cam, what fucking charm?" I hiss at him as he leads us to the family room.

He stops and looks down at me. "Ivy, you are one of the most fascinating people I know. Stop letting Neil Jones take that away. Be yourself."

His words stun me enough that I allow him to drag me back into the den of vipers with little resistance. It's hard to charm someone when their damage is so extensive. Repairing Neil's damage seems impossible, especially because I'm the one who caused it in the first place.

About an hour later, and an hour of listening to Amelia and Cam being the only two talking, the front door opens. I'm hoping it's Carmelo and his family because I need to get away from Neil's stare. If looks could fucking kill, I'd be a decaying corpse by now. All the while, Amelia keeps shooting me lusty looks like she wants to jump me. I bet that's sitting just right with Neil.

I skid into the foyer and visibly relax when Carmelo's bruised face comes into view. His mother, Marlana, sees me and smiles, opening her arms for a hug. They feel more like my family than my own because they don't hold me to an impossible standard. I rush into her arms and whimper when she crushes me tighter.

"Sorry I haven't been by since I've been back," I tell her.

"It's okay, Ivy, but don't make it a habit," Carmelo's stepfather, Charles, says as he pats my head.

I pull out of Marlana's arms and turn to give Carmelo's

younger sister, Sabrina, a hug. I see her around school sometimes, but she's in the younger grades and our schedules never mesh.

"You look so pretty," I coo as I scoop up her pink hair.

"Mom helped me." She grins.

"Whoa!" Uncle Emmett exclaims behind me. "That hair is going to be triggering." He points at Sabrina's head.

Charles and Marlana laugh, and I roll my eyes exaggeratedly at Sabrina when I see the worried look in her eyes. Uncle Emmett lacks tact.

"It looks great," I assure her as I run my fingers through the pink strands.

Then I lead them into the kitchen and stare wide-eyed when my mother bursts out laughing at Sabrina's hair. She pulls her in to soften the blow, but that reaction was rude.

"Sorry, hun." Mother snickers. "But did your mom tell you she had this exact hair color when I met her?"

"No." Sabrina shakes her head as her eyes meet her mother's.

"I had some great nicknames for her too." Mother chuckles.

"I don't think we should be saying—" Dad starts.

"I think one was bubble gum head, right?" Marlana grins.

"Cotton candy brain," Mother adds.

"Okay," Dad interjects. "Let's leave it at that."

Everyone laughs again, and I can't help but smile because I like the sound of it.

"Oh!" Aunt Adri exclaims. "I have a game we adults

can play later. Have you ever heard of saying your name backwards?"

I'm stunned when Mother spits out her wine and every one of the weird adults laugh loudly.

"Let's leave the weirdos." I grab Sabrina's arm and Carmelo follows behind us.

"Can you believe it?" I hear Marlana chuckling. "It shocked me when she came and asked me if she could dye it pink."

"Sabrina!" Sammy calls out. "Come play chess."

Sammy is one half of the twin duo and he's also the calmest. Sonja is the loud one who likes to joke around and play pranks. They're so much like Mother and Uncle Emmett but reversed. Then they have a little brother, Gabriel, and he's really smart for eleven. Next year, he'll be skipping a grade and that brings him closer to Saxon.

If my brother put as much effort into school as he does his attitude, then I know the fucker could be a genius. It actually scares me that next year he starts high school and I won't be there to tell him not to be a jerk.

He will have Sabrina and Amelia though, also Cameron will be in his final year, so that eases my mind slightly. Sonny and Sammy also start high school with him, but they mostly stay out of his way, especially at school. He needs to snap out of whatever phase he's in because I worry he'll either be bullied or become an axe murderer. It could go either way at this point.

"Is there anywhere we can go to smoke this fat-ass blunt I brought?" Carmelo whispers, and I groan.

"Thank you for small miracles. I really didn't think I'd make it out of this in one piece." I grab his hand and poke my head into the family room. "Cam, family meeting."

Cameron's head shoots up and his smile is instantaneous. Our 'family meeting' either means drugs or plotting. "I'll be back," he says to Amelia.

Both boys follow me out to the backyard, through a foot of snow, and toward the large shed in the back of the lot. It's a place we've made our own and my parents have let us take it over since we were kids. Before that, my mother said it was her uncle's man den or something. There are still a lot of rare car pictures on the walls and a sweet bar in the corner that used to house our juice, but now we hide beers in.

I punch in our code on the keypad and hear the door unlock. We open it and step inside, then immediately groan simultaneously. It's fucking freezing.

"Turn on the heater," I tell the guys. The place is insulated, but it's frigid in Whitsborough during the winters.

We huddle on the couch and Carmelo sparks the blunt, each of us taking a hit whenever it passes in front of our faces. We're quiet, contemplative of our current situations, and I'm finally feeling at ease, the anxiety slowly draining away.

"Who fucked up your face this time?" Cam breaks the silence.

"Some new kid." Carmelo passes me the blunt. "He goes to the local college and one guy brought him to the fight. He has a hard left hook."

"We gotta somehow teach you to fight without someone having to pound you into minced meat first," Cam mutters, and I snort.

"Is that funny?" Carmelo knocks my shoulder. "My face being called minced meat?"

"You're gonna end up looking ugly when you're older," I force out between chuckles.

"Whatever." Carmelo rolls his eyes. "You hit Amelia yet, bro?" He knocks Cam's shoulder next.

"How many times do I have to tell you it's not like that?" Cam huffs.

"It's really not like that," I reiterate before I can stop myself. Fucking stoned brain.

"Oh, yeah." Carmelo laughs.

"What am I missing here?" Cam looks between us.

"Fuck, you guys really aren't that tight, huh?" Carmelo taunts him.

"I made out with Amelia a few nights ago at Riley's party." Quick, like pulling off a Band-Aid.

Cam's face looks slightly confused, and Carmelo breaks out into another fit of laughter.

"She said she met someone that night…" Cam trails off. "Oh, fuck. Ivy, she was fucking talking about you?"

"I don't know." I shrug as I take another hit of the joint. "I hope not."

"Shit. She's really into you." Cam stares at me as his expression grows with apprehension.

"Did you know she was a lesbian?" I ask him.

"I had suspicions, but I never asked her. That shit is rude and none of my fucking business."

"Like Charlotte," Carmelo mutters.

After that, we all fall into another mind-numbing silence.

Yeah, it was a little too much like Charlotte.

NEIL

Family meeting? What family meeting could the three of them be having? And it's been over an hour.

"Where did they go?" Amelia mutters as she slumps down further on the couch.

"Why?" I side eye her. "Are you looking for Ivy?"

"No." Her mouth turns down into a slight frown.

"You need to get over her," I warn her as my stomach flips with jealousy.

"I know, Neil."

Our parents have long ago joined the others in the kitchen, and we are stuck here in the den with all the younger kids. It's been a while since I've seen most of them and I'm shocked at how much they've grown.

"She's toxic and fucking damaged," I continue, my words spoken under my breath.

"Neil, she's not really any of those things. She's actually sweet and maybe a little sad. You need to stop seeing her as a fucking murderer," she snaps at me, and I am stunned into momentary silence.

"She is a murderer," I grit through my teeth.

"No, I don't think she is." She shakes her head. "You need to realize Charlotte was the one damaged."

Her words are like little knives, each one slowly slicing into my heart and bleeding me dry. I need to realize Charlotte was the one damaged? What does she mean? And how can she know that?

Questioning her right now would only lead to a disagreement, so instead, I get up and decide to give myself a refresher tour of the house. I want to see the luxury Ivy grew up in, the privilege that cushioned her actions, and the wealth that made all her problems go away.

Stepping out of the family room and into the foyer, I see to the right is the kitchen, and to the left is a large oak door and the staircase. On the walls in front of me are pictures of the Greenes as children and the parents when they were younger. It's crazy that Vin and Ember met in high school and have been together ever since. No bumps, just a perfect relationship.

I turn left and stand at the foot of the stairs, the sheer opulence of the place leaving me stunned. The large mahogany staircase, a chandelier hanging in the center, and what looks to be many bedrooms on the second floor is ten times bigger than my house.

When I make sure that my sister hasn't followed me and no one is in the hallway, I make my way up the staircase and stop on the landing. To the right is one doorway and then to the left are four more. I would assume the kids' rooms are to the left.

I open the first door on the left. It's pink and filled with stuffed animals. Definitely Dahlia's room. I open the next one on the left and find what is clearly a spare bedroom, unless Saxon is incredibly dull, and I would assume not.

Moving forward to the next one on the left, I open it up and jackpot! This is definitely Ivy's room. You wouldn't be able to tell by the posters on the wall, or the skateboards lined up, and definitely not by the large, dark bed. It's her scent though, one that's uniquely hers, and I feel myself harden as I inhale deeply.

What will it take to stop having this reaction to her? I tried the girlfriend thing and sadly it takes too much effort. I tried reminding myself she killed my sister, and I even fantasized about killing her much the same way. Nothing works.

Do I need to fuck her? Is that it?

I sit on her bed and the movement sends a plume of her scent to settle all around me. Now I am rock-solid in my jeans and unable to go back downstairs if I wanted to. I think I need to fuck this girl. I imagine her lying on this bed, completely naked and her pussy glistening, primed for my cock.

A buzzing noise pulls me out of my head, and I glance at her phone on the nightstand. Another buzz comes through and I pick it up. The screen is locked, but I see message notifications. A Dean is sending her images and videos. I wonder if this is one of her boyfriends from New York. I try to open the messages, but the screen requires a password.

First I try her birthday, but that's wrong. Then I try something generic like 1234, but that's not it. Finally, and I don't even know why, I type in Charlotte's birthday and the screen unlocks. Why would she have Charlotte's birthday as her code?

"What the fuck are you doing?" Ivy's voice is a hoarse whisper as she snatches her phone out of my hands.

Her sudden presence shocks me because I didn't even hear her come in. "Sorry." I try to look chastised even though I don't give a damn. "Dean was interrupting my rest."

Her face loses its olive tone and she quickly glances down at her phone. "Did you read them?" She sounds scared. Probably a lot of dick pics.

"It took me a few tries to guess the lock screen passcode, so no." Then I slip my finger into the belt loop in her pants and pull her closer, right between my legs. "Why is Charlotte's birthday your passcode?"

"So I'll never forget what I did," she answers quietly.

My stomach flips at her words and I slip my thumb up under her shirt to rub against the soft skin of her belly. Sounds like she's remorseful, and if I'm being honest with myself, Ivy has never tried to deny what happened or lessen it at all.

"I'm having trouble," I mutter.

"With what?" Her voice sounds husky as she steps closer to me.

"Figuring out why I can't get you out of my head."

"Oh." The sound is small and insecure.

"How do I get you out of my head, Ivy? Because I'm supposed to hate you, but right now, it feels like something else."

"Don't worry, Neil." She shakes herself out of lust's hold over her. "I hate myself enough for the both of us."

Then she turns to walk away, but both of my hands fly to her waist to drag her down on top of me, both of us falling on the bed. Her eyes are wide with surprise and so fucking gorgeous. My hands glide from her waist and over her ass, dragging her against my cock.

"This isn't how," she whispers.

"What?" I grip her ass cheeks harder and groan at their fullness.

"This isn't going to get me out of your head. If anything, it will keep me firmly there, and then you'll hate me even more."

"Trust me, I can't hate you any more than I already do." I lean up and run my nose along her throat.

She moves to straddle me, sitting perfectly on top of my swollen cock, and grinds against it. Both of us make similar groans as my hands make their way up under her shirt, grazing her stomach. She lifts her shirt over her head and drops it to the bed, her black, lacy bra looking delectable against her skin. I cup their fullness in my hands, and she moans while grinding down more.

My balls tighten, and I'm shocked at how badly I want to come, need to come. I feel like a teenager again, on the brink of coming in my pants. Ivy falls forward, her hair casting a curtain around our heads and her breath fanning my face. I have one hand working the button on her jeans and the other curling along the nape of her neck, pulling her mouth to mine.

"There's no going back, Greene," I warn her. "Once I kiss you, there's no stopping."

"Okay."

That's all I need to hear before I'm dragging her mouth to mine. The instant they touch, it's like something primal comes over me, and I'm biting her bottom lip, hard. She's unbothered, grinding against my cock, and whimpering.

"Ahem."

We both freeze and pull apart, and I stare up at her wide-eyed. "Did you not shut your door?"

"Did I think you'd want to jump my fucking bones?" she growls back.

"I can hear you both," Amelia says.

Fuck, she's going to feel betrayed by this. I just know it. I've been spewing hate about Ivy, yet here I am practically fucking her.

Ivy sits up, her pussy pressing along my cock, and I have to bite my hand to keep quiet.

"Hey, Amelia." She clears her throat while looking over her shoulder.

Amelia comes into the room and shuts the door, her back hitting it with her arms crossed.

"How long?" She's looking at me.

"Just now." I grab Ivy's waist and lift her off me. "I don't know what the fuck happened."

I really fucking don't.

She looks at Ivy and raises her brow.

"What?" Ivy asks her, sounding defensive.

"You just made out with me a few nights ago and now you're all over my brother," Amelia hisses at her.

"Look, Amelia." Ivy sounds on the verge of losing her shit. "I kissed you, yes. Does that mean we're exclusively dating? No. I'm not actually dating you at all."

Amelia's cheeks go red, and she looks between the two of us, her mouth opening and shutting.

"So, you want to date him?" Amelia points at me.

"No." Ivy stands and pulls her shirt on. "I was going to fuck him. That's it. I don't do relationships."

"You were dating Riley though!" Amelia shouts. She's sounding desperate, and I want to just grab her and leave the room.

"And look how that turned out," Ivy counters. "Even if I did do relationships, I wouldn't want one with you. I'm sorry I kissed you and led you on. It wasn't my intention."

Amelia deflates against the door and nods. "I know."

"You're a good kid, but can I give you some advice?" Ivy says to her as Amelia nods once more. "Don't settle, don't take what your body is feeling seriously right now. You can't know exactly what you want. You have so much time to explore things. Take that time and fucking explore."

"What?" I interject, my face filling with heat. "Do not explore!"

"Sexuality is fleeting. One day you want one thing, the next you'll find you want another. Do not think you can only have one thing. Fuck, have it all."

"The fuck?" I snarl at Ivy. "Are you telling her to be a whore?"

"That"—she points at me—"is a prime example. Don't be single-minded, and listen to everything your body is telling you."

"Okay." Amelia nods again as she pushes off the door. "Sorry I intruded. I'll just be going."

"Take your brother with you," Ivy states as she walks into the washroom, her phone in her hands.

I stare at her retreating back until she closes the washroom door. I have never felt so fucking dismissed in my life.

"You should've told me how you were feeling," Amelia snarls to me.

"Amelia, I really had no clue, okay?" I push up off Ivy's bed.

She must see the truth in my statement because she doesn't press me further.

The rest of the night is awkward as fuck. I can practically taste it in the air and I can still taste Ivy in my mouth. It's fucking addictive, and now that I've had a taste, I won't stop until I get it all.

Chapter Eleven

The holidays are over and I am back at school, sitting at a desk without a clue of what I should be doing. The last two weeks were filled with family and Dean. His messages haven't stopped and his videos are getting worse.

Just last night, he sent me another, and once again, he was restraining me with his tie and spanking me with my science textbook. In the video, I was sobbing for him to stop and promising I'd be a good girl. I don't even remember that instance. That's how bad it was getting. Maybe I fucked my science teacher so I could get caught and come home.

Dean keeps threatening me about Black Slaughter, but I don't know what the fuck that is. Whatever it is doesn't sound good, and I am worried he's going to kill me. Can he kill me? I have no fucking idea how far his power stretches, and I'm scared for my family.

"Ivy." Mr. O'Connor's voice breaks up my thoughts. "Did you need another detention?" His smirk is doing nothing for me. Especially not after I've had a dose of Neil.

"No, sorry," I answer, and he raises his eyebrows in surprise. I bet he was expecting me to want to stay.

He carries on with the class, shooting me weird looks throughout, and when the last bell rings, his eyes meet mine. "Ivy, can you stay there for a second?"

Rolling my eyes, I nod. I don't want to fuck him today, and honestly, I haven't been able to get Neil out of my head. It's a fucking shame we couldn't finish what we started, and now he's back at school in Toronto, probably fucking a bunch of college girls.

The students leave, and I can say with one-hundred-percent certainty, I know maybe one or two of their names. I hate school and I feel confined, forced to learn shit that will do absolutely nothing for me later on in life.

"Is everything okay, Ivy?" Mr. O'Connor comes toward my desk.

"Yes." My voice is saturated with boredom as my face falls into my hand.

He sits on the edge of my desk and runs his fingers along my hand. "Are you sure?"

I snatch my hand back and get up from my seat. "Yes, I'm sure. Can I go?"

"Do I need to remind you about the repercussions of what we've done and if it got out?"

"Look,"—I grab my bag—"it was good while it lasted, but shit's getting boring."

His eyes widen and he barks out a laugh. "What?"

"You heard me." I pass by him. "And I won't say shit. I wanted it after all."

He doesn't say anything, just continues to watch me leave. I head to my locker and bypass Molly on the way. She has her head stuck inside hers and her shoulders are shaking. Is she crying? Fuck. Do I have to talk to her? I look around for someone and then remember this girl eats her fucking lunch in the bathroom. There's no one else who will help her.

"Molly?"

Her body stiffens as she blows her nose. "What?" Her voice is muffled by the locker.

"Is everything okay?"

She finally pulls her head out and looks at me over her shoulder. "Why do you care?"

"Not sure." I shrug, deciding to go with the truth.

"My mom is leaving my dad," she wails, and I look uncomfortably around the hall.

"That sucks."

"He cheated," she continues to cry. "Mom found hotel charges on his credit card."

The fucker really is dumb. He blackmailed me, and instead, got himself caught.

"Let me take you home," I offer, knowing she usually takes the bus.

"Really?" She sounds shocked and somewhat hopeful. I know I'll have to cut her off later, but right now, I want to cause a little chaos in Officer Van Dyke's life for being a shitty lay.

The ride to Molly's is excruciating. She drones on and on about how she's getting her braces off next year and she's going to get a car. Oh! And also, she's convincing her dad to get her a cat. She told me her mother is leaving and moving to Toronto with her parents, so she'll be the only woman in the house. Her dad and her brother ignore her and she's going to be so bored.

"Do you think you'll want to come over and bake?" she squeals. "Like we used to do?"

This is not worth it. "That was an Easy Bake Oven, Molly," I huff.

"Well, I learned how to bake with the big oven. I'll teach you too." Then she claps. *Fucking stab me, someone.*

I pull into her driveway, and sure enough, there's a moving van. Molly once again deflates as a large tear runs down her cheeks.

"Hey," I say to her, "I'll come inside with you."

"Okay." She nods as she sniffs back the snot dripping from her nose.

As soon as we step out of the car, the sounds of her parents' shouts fill the air. It's a wonder neighbors aren't out watching the drama unfold. We step around the van and find Mrs. Van Dyke headed our way, rolling a suitcase behind her.

"I will see you in Hell, Adam!" she screeches, and then stops short when she sees Molly and me.

"Ivy Greene?"

"Hi, Mrs. Van Dyke." I give a little wave.

"Molly, sweetie, I will be back on the weekend and we will go out for Froyo." Then she pushes past us and toward the van.

"Sandra!" Adam steps to the porch. "If you leave now, don't you ever come back."

His eyes land on me and the fucker pales. I toss him a grin and then run to Sandra, helping her lift the suitcase to the van. She smiles at me appreciatively.

"Don't ever get married, Ivy. Men are pigs."

"Apparently, so are cops," I retort, and she bursts out laughing.

"What are you two talking about?" Adam demands, suddenly behind us.

"Daddy, leave Ivy alone," Molly whines.

"Talking about how men are pigs," I tell him, and Sandra snorts. "It's a shame you ruined a perfectly good family." I *tsk* and Sandra hums behind me.

"You don't know what's going on," Adam snarls.

"Oh, no?" I bat my eyes as he pales further. "I'm sure I could figure it out."

He takes a menacing step toward me, a growl escaping his lips.

"Adam!" Sandra steps between us. "What are you doing?"

"Nothing." He looks shameful.

"Yikes." My tone is heavy with sarcasm. "I better get out of here." I walk toward my car and look back at Molly. "See you at school." She nods, but she's too engrossed in yet another screaming match her parents are having.

This just made my day.

Chapter Twelve

"I love you, Ivy." She sobs as her tears drip off her chin and soak her shirt. "I fucking love you!" Her fist hits the steering wheel.

"Listen." I touch her arm and she shrugs me off. "Can we talk about this another time?" My fucking Grandma just died!

"No!" she screams, the shrill noise startling me.

"Charlotte, this shit is crazy." I breathe out.

"Crazy?" Her voice becomes deathly calm and my heart pounds inside my chest.

We skid around a narrow corner, the tires squealing, but she doesn't let up on the gas. What the fuck did I do? Why would I ask her to take me for a drive during this time and right after Grandma Jenna died?

"Charlotte." I keep my voice steady. "Please, pull over."

She doesn't listen to me and makes a sharp right-hand turn down a small, residential street. I don't know where we are right now, but it's no longer in Whitsborough. We fly down the street at an alarming speed, and I begin to sweat, my sobriety fully intact now.

"I have loved you for a year. Did you know that?" She sounds crazy. I drove my best friend crazy.

"No," I whisper, and she growls, punching the steering wheel again. "Please, slow down."

"You kissed me at the wharf party last month, and I thought that was it, you were finally feeling the same." Her words catch on a sob. "It wasn't fucking it, was it?"

"Charlotte, I care about you," I plead. "Please, slow down."

"A week later, we were making out every chance we got. Is that just a friendship to you?" she grits through her teeth. "Now, you won't even hold my hand?"

"Okay." I reach for her again. "I'll hold your hand."

"Don't touch me!" she screeches.

"Okay, fine." I hold my hands in the air like a criminal. "No touching."

"Just last week, you had your mouth on me, your fingers inside of me, and now what, you don't love me?"

"I do love you, Charlotte." I try to placate her, because I really do, just not how she wants me to.

"Not like I love you!" she bellows, and the car swerves. She rights us but keeps going at a breakneck speed.

I try to envision Mother, Dad, Saxon, and my little flower because I feel like I may never see them again. This moment feels like an ending, yet instead of being terrified, I am almost serene.

"You need to pull over before you get us killed," I tell her, keeping my eyes on the road as it rushes past us.

"Then you will have to be with me forever, won't you?" She looks at me, her eyes off the road. "If I can't have you, I guess no one can."

I wake up with a scream lodged in my throat and I swear I can still smell the gasoline fumes. I can't help but think I'm dreaming about Charlotte because of Neil. She promised me I would have no other, and since then, she has kept her end of the promise. I haven't had any other and I can't keep another as well. The night she died, so did a part of me.

I think she took my soul right along with hers and left me here to roam the Earth as an empty carcass. She made sure the rest of my days were filled with misery, and each painful day would be my constant reminder of what I did to her.

Sitting up in bed, I cringe when I peel my soaked T-shirt off my body, letting it slap to the floor. Every nightmare feels like I'm right back in that car with her, simultaneously pleading for our lives and breaking her heart.

I grab another shirt from my dresser, putting it on before heading down to the kitchen for a drink. My throat is dry and feels like I was once again screaming for her not to leave me, just like that night.

After gulping down two glasses, I drag my feet back upstairs and mindlessly head back to my bedroom.

"You were screaming Charlotte's name." Saxon's voice startles me. "I was going to come in and wake you up."

"Oh." I swallow thickly. "Thanks."

"You were screaming for her to slow down, Ivy." He narrows his eyes on me. "Something doesn't add up because you said you were driving." My face drains of blood and my throat seizes. I stand there silently for a few minutes, just looking at him, and finally, he breaks the hold. "Anyway,"—he steps back into his room—"night."

Fuck, this is bad. Saxon is unpredictable, so I don't know what the fuck he'll do with that information.

Chapter Thirteen

Neil

"Then I had a puppy named Benji. He was the sweetest little sheepdog and so fluffy." Her voice is pitched too high and her eyes are too dark, nothing like the clear, blue Caribbean Sea. I curse myself and scrub my hand down my face.

"Is everything okay?" Paula leans across the table and takes my hand.

"Yeah, sorry." I smile at her. "It's been a long week."

It hasn't been a long week. We just finished exams and I have the week off before the next semester starts, but she doesn't question me. No, Paula is sweet and so very trusting, a good girl all around. She doesn't race her car and then spreads her pussy open in front of everyone when she wins. Paula is loyal, looking to commit and start a life, and yet, she's doing nothing for me.

My stomach doesn't flip at the mention of her name, my dick doesn't harden at the sound of her voice, and I don't feel an overwhelming need to see her whenever I can. Fuck, it's not going to work out with Paula and she's the second girl I've dated this month.

"How about I get you home?" I offer as her face falls. I'm not here to lead anyone on.

"Okay," she whispers.

About ten minutes later, we pull up to her sorority, and I turn in my seat to face her, readying myself to break it off.

"It's okay, Neil." She gives me a sad smile. "You don't have to say it."

"I'm sorry, Paula."

"Tell the one you're thinking about that they're so lucky." Before I can attempt to deny it, she's out of my car and hurrying to her front door.

Neither of us are lucky in this scenario.

"How's Dad?" My dorm room is a mess, and I began to feel homesick because my mom makes sure my laundry is off the floor and my bed is made. So, that's why I called Amelia.

"He's the same." Amelia exhales into the phone, which means it's bad. "Mom wants to put him in a rehab facility."

"Make the Greenes pay for it," I snarl as she huffs.

"Neil, we both know he's always had this problem."

"How's everything else?" I change the subject.

"If you want to ask about her, just do it." Her tone is laced with humor.

"Who?" I play the idiot, which obviously fails.

"You're a loser." She chuckles. "She looks okay, but I don't think she actually is."

"What does that even mean?"

"Why don't you come home next weekend?" she suggests, and I can hear the exhaustion in her words.

"Okay, sis. I'll see you next weekend."

Another trip to Whitsborough. For a guy who hates the place, I'm fucking there an awful lot.

The following weekend, I get my ass moving and drive to Whitsborough. This is the most I've been here since Charlotte and I were kids, and I can admit it's because of a certain dark-haired girl. I need to settle this beef with Ivy once and for all. Either I fuck her and get her out of my head, or decide to forgive her and move on from the hatred.

Maybe both.

Forgiveness feels like the hardest thing to do and a betrayal to Charlotte. She didn't deserve to die, and she should be the one making her way here to hang out with the family she loved and all her friends.

My dad's house is dark when I arrive. The clock on my dashboard says its just after midnight. It's Friday night, so I would assume everyone is sleeping. I pull out my phone to text Amelia, but instead, hover over Ivy's name.

Yes, I have her number. Yes, I want to text her. And yes again, I stole it from my sister's phone.

Me: You up?

After a few minutes and no reply, I make my way to her house. I pull up and park on the side, trying to peer through the hedges in front of the fence. The gate is obviously shut tight, so I can't just drive up to surprise her. I rest my head on the wheel and breathe through my irritation.

Then my phone pings beside me and I scramble to pick it up.

Ivy: Who is this?

Right, she doesn't have my number. I should've thought of that. She's probably thinking it's one of her rotations, hoping for a late-night meetup. I groan at my thoughts and again try to breathe out the irritation. What am I even doing here?

Before I can even turn the car around, my phone pings again.

Ivy: Leave me alone.

Huh?

Me: It's Neil.

Why the fuck did I do that? The phone pings again.

Ivy: Neil Jones?

Me: No, another Neil.

I laugh when she sends me the middle finger emoji.

Ivy: What do you want?

Me: Who are you telling to leave you alone?

Ivy: You?

I snort and scrub my hand down my face.

Me: Do you want me to leave you alone?

Am I fucking flirting with the girl who murdered my sister?

Ivy: Not at all.

Me: Good. I wasn't planning on it.

Yes, I fucking am.

Ivy: How's work at the hotel?

Me: I took this weekend off.

Ivy: Sweet.

Me: Come outside.

I don't know why my heart races after I send that, and my palms are suddenly sweaty. What if she doesn't come out? Ten minutes goes by without a reply and I start to regret sending that stalkerish text. I turn the key in the ignition but stop when the gate opens.

Ivy: Come up.

I pull into her driveway and drive up to the house, which is also dark, and I feel a pang of guilt. Maybe I woke her.

She's standing on her porch, hopping from side to side in nothing but an oversized sweater and fluffy slippers. My cock hardens like steel, and I groan. This has been the reaction I've been looking for all over campus and I can only find it in the girl I should despise.

I get out of the car, uncaring that I'm wearing track pants, and still uncaring if she can see her effect on me. I'm so fucking tired of fighting this. Running up to the porch, I stop and stand in front of her, then slowly walk her backwards inside, my body just barely touching hers.

"It's good to know the cold doesn't have that same shrinkage effect on you," she mutters, and I snort.

"Everyone asleep?" I look around the darkened foyer as she steps away to shut the door.

"Only Saxon and I are home. Everyone else went to New York for the weekend."

"You didn't want to go back and see your friends?" I press her.

"I haven't had a single friend since Charlotte, Neil." She sounds just as tired about this as I do.

"Why not?" I ask as she leads us into the kitchen.

"Because I never, ever wanted to be in that position again." She opens the fridge and throws me a can of beer, then opens one for herself.

"What about this Dean?" I grin at her over my can.

"Not a friend." She's quick to answer, her face falling. Definitely not.

We drink in silence for a few minutes as she stares at me from ten feet away.

"What?" I finally give in.

"Why are you here?" Good question.

"I was driving home to see Amelia for the weekend," I begin, running my finger over the sweat on the beer can. "The house was dark, and I don't know, I ended up here."

"Oh." She takes a sip. "I see."

"Do you?" I demand, standing from my seat and walking toward her.

She swallows, her throat working hard, and the vein there pulses rapidly. I reach down, wrapping my hands around her waist before plopping her up on the table. Then I wedge myself between her legs and brush her hair off her face.

"Well?" I continue, rubbing my thumb across her bottom lip. "Do you?"

She moans quietly, breathy and soft, and her eyes are wide and staring into mine, those lips slightly open. I bend, my hands dropping to the table on either side of her, then bump her nose with mine.

"What do you see, Ivy?"

"I see you here… with me," she answers, her voice husky, the sound shooting straight to my cock.

Swooping in, I claim her mouth with my own. My hand snares into her hair and I angle her head to get better access. She opens on a moan after I swiped my tongue along the seam of her lips. I only got a taste last time, and I couldn't forget it, but I'm truly fucked now because I'm drowning in her.

Her tongue tangles with mine as I wrap my arm around her waist, pulling her in against me. She wraps her legs around me and rubs herself along my cock over my pants.

I pull back from her mouth and yank the sweater up over her head, groaning when I see she's just in a pair of boy-cut shorts.

"Are you fucking serious?" I whisper, leaning forward and taking one of her dusty rose nipples into my mouth.

When I pinch the other, I find a bar. I release her nipple with a pop and pull the pierced one into my mouth, then tug on it with my teeth, and she moans loudly.

"Tell me Saxon is a heavy sleeper because I'm about to have you screaming," I tell her, hoping my words are true and my dick doesn't fail me, because I'm about to come as it is.

"Even if he hears it, he won't give a shit," she rasps.

I press my hand against her chest and force her to lie back on the table.

"Are you going to fuck me on the table my family eats dinner off of?" She grins at me.

I run my finger over her panties, the wetness soaking all the way through, as her chest heaves with every breath. Then I hook my finger into the waistband and drag them down, exposing her a bit at a time, and losing myself more with every inch revealed. I drop the panties to the floor and stand there, just looking at her glistening for me.

Then the panic sets in.

IVY

He's just standing there, completely still and completely clothed. The indecisiveness is etched into the features of his face as the battle wages on silently inside of him. His feelings for me, lust and hatred battling it out, and I'm just foolishly lying here waiting for whichever one wins.

I sit up and reach for my sweater.

"Wait." His voice sounds pained.

"Neil, just go home." I push my arm through.

He yanks the sweater away and chucks it behind him, then his mouth is back on mine. Once again, I'm lost in his kiss. It's aggressive and fucking perfect. His tongue pushes its way inside my mouth, its rough surface skating across mine, and his hand finally between my legs.

"You're so wet," he says against my mouth.

"Don't fucking waste it, Jones," I retort.

His finger pushes into my core, and I gasp against his lips. It feels like forever since I've had sex. I haven't touched anyone since before Christmas, since before I kissed Neil in my bedroom.

Neil breaks our kiss and continues his way down my chest, licking my skin, dragging his tongue along every dip and groove. Then he's between my legs, his breath fanning my wet skin and his eyes looking at me. He pulls his finger out and uses both hands to spread me wide before taking a deep inhale of my arousal.

"Neil, please," I beg. I'm not above it because I want his mouth on me so fucking bad.

His tongue tentatively licks through my folds, and I sink back onto the table with a moan. He's soft but deliberate in his swipes. I'm used to having sex a bit more on the rougher side, and I know this sweet making love shit won't cut it for me.

His eyes meet mine as I pop up on my elbow.

"I won't break, Neil. I need a fucking, not a love session."

His eyes darken and he stands up tall, pulling his pants down by the waistband. His black boxer briefs do nothing to hide his size as my mouth fills with saliva.

"I want to suck your cock," I declare. "But I can't right now because I need you inside of me."

He pulls down his boxers and then curses. "Give me one minute."

I growl in frustration as he runs to the front door, but laugh when I see his pants still around his thighs. What the fuck is he doing? He opens it and rushes outside. It's fucking cold. Is he dipping out on me?

I sit up completely and hear his car door shut. *No way.* I'm about to get off the table when he rushes back in, a square wrapper in his mouth and his pants still wrapped around his thighs.

"The fuck you doing?" he asks as he pushes me back down. *"Don't waste it, Jones,"* he mocks me before pulling his pants and boxers the rest of the way down.

Then he yanks his sweater off, and I'm stunned silent when I see all the tats decorating his chest and stomach. His stomach! It looks like I could scrub my laundry clean on it and worry about the fabric fraying. That's how defined he is. My gaze lowers as I fall back to the table with a sigh. Thank God for *large* miracles. As long as he knows what to do with it.

The sound of him sucking his fingers into his mouth has my gaze moving from his cock back to his face. He pulls them out slowly before running them over my clit, then sinking them deep inside of me. My eyes are slipping shut as I gasp, because he's pulling them out to rub my wetness over his cock before sliding the condom on.

"I hate condoms and I wanted to feel you," he groans as he pulls my ass off the table and lines himself up.

I want to feel him too, but I agree we need the protection because as much as we know each other, we don't actually know each other.

He pushes himself in, and I grunt at the stretch. His fingers dig into my ass cheeks and then he gives one good push, jamming himself in deep.

"Fuck!" I yell and then groan when he pulls back out.

"That's right." He leans over me, his hands landing on either side of my head. "Tell me what it feels like."

He begins to piston in and out of me and it's becoming hard to form words.

"Feels so good." My back drags along the wooden surface as I moan, his thrusts becoming harder and deeper.

I can feel the familiar tug at the base of my stomach, the tightening that comes before my release. Opening my eyes, I find him watching me closely, like I'm precious or fleeting. He leans forward slowly and sucks my bottom lip into his mouth, his thrusts now slow and languid.

His growl is my only warning as he devours my mouth and begins to fuck me hard, my pussy weeping all over him and the table. The table my family fucking eats off of. I don't know what's wrong with me because I come apart right then, my pussy clamping around his cock and my body jerking with each pulse. I have never come like this before.

My body is throbbing with the aftershocks, my thoughts

erratic, and my vision blacked out.

"My name sounds good screaming from your mouth," he says as his thrusts become sloppy.

I said his name?

Then he slams into me, jarring my head against the wood, and groaning my name, his cock jerking inside of me. My vision comes back in time to see his features as the bliss takes over his face, and something warms inside my chest, something I don't want to acknowledge, and certainly not ready to feel. His eyes open, connecting with mine, and his lazy smile slowly disappears.

Yeah, this is the part where we become awkward and go back to hating one another.

Neil eases out of me and walks to the powder room to clean himself off. I hope he flushes the condom, or else I'm telling my parents Saxon had a friend over. Better him than me.

I hop off the table and find my sweater, pulling it on. Then I find my panties, deciding to pocket them since they're wet and couldn't be bothered anyway. I lean against the table as he comes out of the bathroom, his boxers and pants back on.

He hasn't really made eye contact as I continue to watch him pulling his sweater back on, his muscles bunching.

"I should… ah… probably get home," he mutters.

"Yeah."

His eyes meet mine as the confusion and lust in him becomes clear. I wonder which emotion is winning. Then I turn and walk out of the kitchen, leading him to the front door, my chest growing heavy with each step. This was his one fuck to get me out of his system, right? Maybe now he can leave me well enough alone.

My heart drops to my stomach with that thought, and

for the first time in my life, I don't want to be left alone.

I open the front door and look at the floor as he walks by me.

"Ivy…" he begins, but I cut him off.

"Good night, Neil." Then I shut the door softly in his face.

I just shoved my feelings into another box, locking away the last piece of my heart.

Chapter Fourteen

Neil

I wanted to tell her I'd call or text, but she just shut the door. Now I can't sleep and I'm lying here in my bed, still smelling her on my skin and wondering if she gave me the chance to say it… would it have been the truth?

The answer to that question is complicated. I want to say I am truly done with Ivy now that I had my fill and can let her go, but I didn't fucking get my fill because I am still lying here, thinking about her, uncomfortably hard, and remembering her silky warmth around my cock. No, I am not done with Ivy, and that fucking scares me.

Charlotte, what's happening?

I feel the pressure building inside my chest and my eyes begin to burn. Have I failed my sister? Have I gone against everything I promised her? Because me fucking Ivy wasn't fucking at all, I was pouring my soul into that, and I will never be the same. I fucking failed Charlotte.

When it becomes obvious sleep will be impossible, I

get up out of bed and head down to the kitchen. Shay is already up and making coffee, her face looking drawn and tired.

"Neil." She smiles. "I thought I saw your car pull up last night. It's good to have you home." She looks like the stress is beginning to get to her. Amelia is right, it's time to seek out treatment.

"Yeah, thought I'd check in on everyone."

"I think we may have to have a chat about your dad." She lets loose a long sigh. "He's getting worse."

"Amelia said as much." I lean against the counter and scrub a hand down my face. "Maybe we need to look into facilities."

A tear slips down her cheek and I pull her in for a hug. The woman has been a godsend to our family, but my father is too far gone in his addiction and taking it all for granted.

"We'll get him some help," I promise her.

I'm sitting in a small mom-and-pop diner that has servers on rollerblades. This shit is so weird, but Amelia swears by the milkshakes.

"Have you spoken to Ivy?" she asks me while looking over her milkshake glass.

"Not really." I shrug.

"What exactly is going on there?" She drops her hands to the table. "How are you feeling?"

"Can we drop the whole Ivy thing and talk about Dad?"

She rolls her eyes and nods. "Fine."

"What's happened since Christmas?"

"He's been getting angrier when he drinks, and he ends up breaking things," she says quietly. "A few nights ago, he told Mom that Charlotte was a problem child, and he was getting ready to ship her to boarding school when the accident happened."

"What?" I straighten in my seat. That's fucking weird.

"Neil, I told you. When Charlotte died, there was a lot going on. She was angry often and had these random outbursts. She was mean." I try to comb over my memories of my sister, but I can't think of a time she was unnecessarily angry. "Seriously." Amelia leans forward. "Dad thought there might've been drugs involved."

I can't dispute that because we refused an autopsy on Charlotte. It was obvious how she died, and the thought of her being cut up only hurt us more.

"But why is he talking about Charlotte?"

"I think each time he drinks, he's regressing and thinking of the times he is most ashamed of." She shakes her head. "He has a lot of regrets about you and Charlotte."

"Dad didn't have it easy when he was younger," I tell her one of the stories Mom told me. "He partied, sold some drugs, and ran with the wrong crowd. Then he landed in jail and that's when Ember came along. He tried to raise me and Charlotte with my mom, but once he ended up in jail, she got out."

There's no doubt he has regrets, especially because he wanted to be a father to us, and I know if he doesn't get the help he needs, that list will just keep getting longer.

"We need to do an intervention." Amelia nods.

"Let's do it after dinner today," I agree.

Chapter Fifteen

His car pulls into my driveway as I watch it through the security app on my phone. I forgot to close the gate last night. Fuck, I really wish I remembered that. The closer he comes to my house, the more I feel like I might toss up my dinner.

Neil parks behind my car and sits in his seat like he's waiting for something, or maybe trying to talk himself out of being here, and I'm hoping he decides to leave. There are things he may want to discuss, about feelings and shit, and I'm not good with all of that.

The driver's side door opens and he steps out of his vehicle tentatively, making my stomach flip. He has on a puffy, black winter coat, dark jeans, and a baseball cap pulled low on his head. He looks so hot and a little dangerous. I feel myself already growing wet just thinking about the things we did on my kitchen table.

He gets to my porch and scratches his fingers on his scruffy goatee, still looking undecided. Eventually, his hand comes out and presses the doorbell. Even though I saw him do it, I still jump from the noise as it echoes throughout the house.

"Who is it?" Saxon calls from his room.

"A friend!" I yell back and listen until his bedroom door clicks shut again.

I run to the front door and open it to stare into his golden eyes. He looks sad and tired.

"Hey." His voice is scratchy, like he has been screaming all day, but so fucking sexy all the same.

"Hey." I open the door wider, inviting him in.

"Sorry for just showing up here." He steps inside and looks at his feet, then takes off his boots. "I just had nowhere else to go and I needed someone to talk to."

"What's going on?"

"Fuck, that sounded bad." He grabs my chin and pulls me in, his other hand snaking around my waist. "I can't stop thinking about you and I'm here because I wanted to talk to you."

I suck in a gasp from his confession and feel my face heat. What do I say to that? How the fuck do I do this?

"Oh."

Oh?!

"I know I was a dick last night. I'm just used to hating you, and I don't know how to be any other way." He's feeling guilty for what we did, and I get why. I do too.

"It's okay," I whisper, still feeling awkward and not knowing what the fuck to say.

"Can I kiss you?"

That's new. No one has ever asked my permission before. "Yes."

He tips my head back and then his lips are on mine, soft and warm. It quickly becomes aggressive, and it's like with just a simple taste, we can't control ourselves. I end up pushed against the wall, lifted in his arms, and our teeth drawing blood.

Vicious in our attacks, we don't notice our surroundings until it's too late.

"Don't mind me," Saxon purrs as he walks by, causing Neil to nearly drop me. "Just getting a drink. Make sure you disinfect that wall and the kitchen table when you're done."

Oh, damn. I can't help it when I look into Neil's stricken face and burst out laughing.

"It's not funny," he hisses at me. "Your brother saw us last night."

"I doubt he saw anything, more like heard it." I shrug, not bothered in the slightest.

Saxon walks back by us and heads up the stairs. "Neil, your hatred has manifested in the strangest way. I like it." And then he disappears.

I burst out laughing again, and then Neil joins in. "I needed that." He shakes his head.

"You said you needed someone to talk to?" I lead him to the family room and sit on a couch opposite from him. The more space, the better.

"We had an intervention for Dad earlier."

"Rodney?" I gasp. "What's wrong?"

"He's always enjoyed a few drinks, but lately it's spiraled out of control. He's becoming an angry drunk and I worry about the girls in that house with him."

"What are you going to do about it?"

"He's leaving for a rehab facility tonight, and I couldn't stay there to see him go. He's pretty pissed at me right now." I feel his pain as he bows his head. It's hard to disappoint your parents.

"You did the right thing," I whisper as he nods.

"I'll be staying in Whitsborough for a while." His words light up my chest and give me anxiety at the same time. "I will defer this semester so I can help with Shay and Amelia. I need a job though. Any chance your dad is hiring?"

"You'd want to work with my family?" With my brow raised, I look at him.

"I need a job."

"I'll ask him." It's a promise I'm not sure I'll fulfill. Do I want Neil in that close proximity?

Neil is moving here, to Whitsborough, and even though I'm excited, I'm also fucking scared. What are we even doing? Does he still hate me? Why wouldn't he?

"I should get back." He stands and I stand with him.

"Okay."

I follow him to the door and watch as he bends to put his boots on, his jacket pulling up and revealing the muscles at the bottom of his back. He's also tattooed back there. He opens the front door and steps out onto the porch as the frigid air sweeps around my face.

"Come for a drive with me." He turns quickly, shocking me.

"A drive?" My heart drums out a quick staccato inside my chest. It feels a little like déjà vu, like it's Charlotte standing there and not her brother.

"Yeah." He raises a brow.

Suddenly, his face falls, finally understanding my hesitation, or maybe not so much understanding it as he's realizing it.

"You know what?" I stuff my feet in my boots and grab my jacket off the hook. "I'll come."

"Cool." He smiles, even though it's slightly strained.

I follow him out to the car and hop into the passenger seat, snapping my seat belt on and grabbing my phone to text Saxon. As soon as we pull out of the driveway, I close the gates behind us, and Neil heads in the wharf's direction.

We're quiet as he drives. It's not an uncomfortable silence, but it's not comfortable either. Somewhere in the middle, which perfectly sums us up too.

He parks in front of the wharf and we both sit back in our seats, watching the slightly frozen water. I remember Charlotte daring me to run on the ice when we were younger, and thinking about her once again brings back the doubts. How can he stand to be in this car with me? After everything I've done?

"You look like you're in pain," he murmurs, and I snap out of my thoughts.

"I'm okay." I shake my head, not wanting to upset him, especially since he's the one who drove us here.

Fuck, I should've offered to drive.

He reaches over and tucks an unruly wave behind my ear, slowly skimming his fingers down my neck. My skin breaks out with goose bumps, and I shiver. He chuckles, leaning in slowly to replace his fingers with his lips.

I tip my head to the side, giving him better access, and moan when I feel his tongue glide along the column of my neck. Then he nips my earlobe before kissing my cheek. I turn my head to the side and brush my lips against his. There's a single moment when neither of us knows what we should do next, so we stare at each other as we breathe the same air, and just feel.

That moment is fleeting, because the very next moment, we are ramming our tongues down each other's throats and ripping our jackets off. I'm pulling off my leggings and crawling over the console just as he pops his seat back. It's like we feel the impending doom but can't do a single thing to stop the destruction. We just have to ride it out.

You better believe I am riding the fuck out of it.

I slip my hands up under his shirt and he rips mine off over my head, groaning when he sees I'm not wearing a bra… again. I fucking hate them, and they always catch on my piercing. Neil leans forward and bites my pierced nipple, making me cry out as he pinches the other. It's rough and I wouldn't want it any other way.

He pushes me away to undo his jeans, growling when it takes a few tries. I can already tell this is going to be quick and fucking messy. He slides his pants down and his hard cock springs up between us, red and angry at the tip. I glide my wet pussy along its length and Neil tips his head back with a moan.

"Your pussy is so good." He gives my ass a quick squeeze and then he's reaching into the center console, pulling out a condom. Thank God one of us is prepared and fucking thinking straight. He rolls the condom on and then wastes no time lifting me up before impaling me on his cock.

It's so deep like this as I continue to grind into him, sucking him in those last few inches.

"Fuck," I groan.

He's stretching me in the most perfect way, not quite

painful, but it takes a minute for me to accommodate his size. He gives it to me, focusing on my breasts, sucking on my nipples, and pinching them. Then his arm comes up behind my back, hooks onto my shoulder as he pulls out, slamming me back down on him.

I scream at the assault, yet he doesn't let up, just continues to batter my pussy, my juices coating both of our thighs.

"Ivy," he pants, "touch yourself."

My pussy pulses at his words and we both groan. I reach between us and begin to furiously rub my clit, chasing the orgasm I so desperately need. I feel myself tightening, on the verge of snapping, my body bowing as my pussy clenches. Then I'm flung over the edge, free-falling into a pool of sensation. My body erupts with tingles as Neil keeps pounding up into me, his cock dragging out my release.

"Fuck, Ivy," he snarls. "Fuck!"

His cock jerks inside of me as his face pushes into the crook of my neck. I relax, my body becoming fluid as I sink down on him to rest my forehead on his shoulder. We're both panting and our chests are heaving like we just ran a marathon.

"Tell me you've had it better than this before. I dare you," he murmurs against my skin.

I don't say anything because I can't. I haven't had it this good, and I can't explain to him why. I can't tell him I was raped many times over two years and every sexual encounter after that was to chase away those demons. So I stay quiet and grin when he chuckles into my neck.

"Thought so." *Smug bastard.*

I lift myself off of him and crawl back over to the passenger side, slowly dressing as he does the same. We're quiet again, but this time it's a comfortable silence.

It's been a week since I've heard from Neil, but it's not like we're dating. I really shouldn't be so weird about it, right?

It's Saturday night and I have Carmelo in my room, scrolling through my Netflix and trying to convince me to hit up a house party. It's Pat's house, so I'm not sure I want to deal with the drama of stealing his girl after I beat him down at the strip a few months ago. I say I'm not sure, but I can't deny the appeal of rubbing it in any guy's face that I stole their straight girlfriend.

"Come on, cuz," he whines. "I need to get out of the house and there's no fight tonight."

"So call Cam." I roll my eyes.

"He's chilling with Amelia, not fucking, because she only wants pussy."

I chuckle and he joins in because that's fucking funny. I don't want to admit I'm feeling down because I haven't heard from Neil, and if I'm going out, I want him to be there. Pathetic, I know.

"I won't let Pat do shit to you." He cracks his knuckles. "But if you want to start a little shit for your favorite cousin, I won't stop you."

"That's why I don't want to go," I stress. "You're needing a fight and that's why you're going."

"Nah." He lies back on the bed. "I need pussy and I'm betting you need dick. It's been how long now?"

To blow his mind or not blow his mind? *Ah, fuck it.* "I'm good, actually. I fucked Neil both Saturday and Sunday last week."

The room is quiet, and it feels something like the eye of the storm, calm before the chaos.

"I'm sorry." He chuckles. "I really thought I heard you say you fucked your worst enemy."

"He's not my worst enemy, trust me."

"You really fucked Neil?" He jackknifes up on the bed. "How?"

"Uh." I give him a confused look. "I really think you should ask your mommy and daddy those questions."

"Oh, fuck off." He whips one of my pillows at my head. "How did it happen?"

"It just did." I shrug and effectively dodge it at the same time.

"There's serious voodoo shit goin' on around here," he mutters and stands up. "Get ready. We leave in five."

I'm two beers in when Riley shows up to the party. She's clearly still mad at me because she attempts to make me jealous by making out with Pat. What she doesn't know is that I feel sorry for her. She's lost in a sea of toxic people, and I am one of them.

"How does it feel to watch your ex-girlfriend make out with her ex-boyfriend?" Carmelo asks and then laughs.

"Relieving." I snort and he laughs again.

"Let's do shots." He drags me by the arm over to a bar setup.

"Carmelo!" A guy fist-bumps him. "I saw your fight the other night. You're fucking insane."

"Thanks, bro." Carmelo beams. "My cousin and I want some shots. What you got?"

Three tequila shots and a whole-ass boring conversation later, I slip away from Carmelo and his groupies, and head outside. My face is hot from the liquor and the cold air feels good.

Pulling out my phone, I frown at the lack of messages. I really thought Neil would've at least texted me by now. I thought there was no better than what we had, so where the fuck is he?

Fuck it, I bring up his contact and hit send before I chicken out.

"Hello?" He sounds so fucking good. "Ivy? Did you just moan into the phone? Is everything okay?"

"I don't know," I huff. "You tell me."

"Is it about work?" he asks, and I roll my eyes. He's been working with my dad for the last few days.

"Why haven't you called? Did you finally work me out of your system?"

"Are you drunk?" he exclaims.

"Are you horny?" I counter, in what I hope is my sexy voice. He's silent, and I suddenly feel ridiculous. "Never mind."

"No, wait." He takes a deep breath. "I've wanted to call, but what is there to talk about? I can't just fuck you all the time and leave."

"Why not?" I retort.

"Because it's wrong." He chuckles, the deep tenor ripping through me.

"It's only wrong if I don't want it. I'm not relationship material, Neil," I whine. "Can you just come get me and fuck me, please?"

"Where are you?" His voice drops, and I clench my thighs to stave off the sudden arousal.

"Pat's house."

"I need an address, Ivy." He sounds just as impatient as me now.

I give him the address and then attempt to text Carmelo what I'm doing. He can get himself home fine.

Neil takes less than ten minutes to turn onto the street, and as soon as I'm in the car, I have my arms around his neck and my lips fused to his.

"Get us somewhere private," I growl just before sticking my tongue down his throat.

"Jesus," he groans as he pulls away and adjusts himself in his track pants.

And now I'm fixated. I reach out and rub my hand along his hard length.

"Ivy, I'm trying to drive… Oh, fuck." His moan is loud in the confined space as I pull him out and lean forward toward his lap.

I've been wondering what Neil tastes like and didn't get the chance to find out the last two times we've been together. I lick the tip of his wide head and we both gasp at the contact. His skin is smooth and he tastes like perfection.

Slackening my jaw, I slurp him into my mouth, sucking on him like he's a melting popsicle. I let my saliva run down his length and then suck the tip as my hand works his shaft. I get a good rhythm going of sucking him in tandem with stroking him when he suddenly swerves off the road, cutting the ignition.

Neil pulls my head off of him and yanks me over onto his lap. Thankfully, I'm wearing a skirt. His fingers slip inside my skirt and he yanks my thong aside, claiming my mouth in a possessive kiss.

"I'm sorry I didn't call. I'm a jerk," he says against my lips. "I missed this pussy."

Then he's pulling my core down over his cock and we both moan at the feeling of him filling me. His skin feels like velvet as he slips into my wet pussy and I grind into him.

"Shit." He pushes up inside me. "We need a condom."

"It feels so good though," I pant out and lift myself up, slamming back down.

"Fuck," he breathes out.

I lock my mouth back onto his and continue riding him, my juices making each movement loud inside the car.

"I'm so wet." My fingers find my clit, rubbing the swollen bundle of nerves.

"You're soaking my fucking cock." He angles his hips up and grabs my waist in his hands. "Hang on." His grin is devastating as he begins to furiously pump up into me.

"I'm coming," I moan as my pussy tightens and the warmth pools in my belly.

"Come all over me." He thrusts up into me harder.

Tossing my head back, I scream his name as my pussy convulses around his thick length. Then his thrusts become shallow before he slams me down onto him, groaning my name as he comes inside of me. I slowly grind on his cock, riding out the aftershocks of my release and enjoying the small noises he's making.

"Is it okay that I came in you?" he asks.

"Yes, please." I fall back over into the passenger seat.

"I think you need your bed and some aspirin." He chuckles.

"Yes, please," I repeat, exhaustion coming over me.

I ask Neil to drop me at the gate instead of my front door to avoid questions and head up my driveway. I'm so fucking satisfied right now, I'm practically purring.

As soon as I step into the house, the sounds of a game on the TV filters out of the family room.

"Ivy?" Dad calls out.

"Yeah." I wonder if I sound drunk?

"You good?"

"Just gonna go to bed," I call back and rush up the stairs. "Night!"

When no one comes to check on me, I shut the door and exhale with relief. I don't want to hear a lecture about drinking. I crawl into my bed and moan as the soft blankets envelop me in their warmth.

My cell phone rings and I smile as I swipe to answer it. "Miss me already?"

"Excruciatingly so."

My body slams forward at his voice, and I automatically begin to quake. "Dean."

"I've been texting you. Are you avoiding me?" His voice is level, but I know him well enough to know he's been drinking.

"Why are you sending me those things?" I press him. "I haven't told anyone."

"It's hard to believe because your uncle is on my ass and I know he knows the Black Slaughter."

"My uncle?" I shake my head. "Black Slaughter?"

"Your Uncle Trent here in New York. He paid me a visit a few weeks ago."

"I haven't told anyone anything." My voice is trembling as a tear slips down my cheek. "I just want you to go away."

"I reformed you, made you into a perfectly obedient student." He chuckles, and the sound sends waves of nausea through me. "Did I not?"

"Y–yes, you d–did," I sob. "I didn't tell anyone."

"I believe you," he croons into the phone.

"You do?"

"Of course, but I need you to prove it," he says.

"How?"

"Call your uncle off, tell him I am an upstanding citizen and you flourished under my teachings. It's not a lie exactly, is it?"

"No, Dean," I comply. "It's not a lie."

"I expect him to disappear by the end of next week," he continues. "And when do I get to see my Ivy?"

I never want to see him again, but I can't tell him that because he has too much on me, and if my family found out, they would disown me in an instant.

"I don't know when I'll be in New York again," I whisper.

"Your mother is here often, no?"

"Yes, sir." My voice betrays my anxiety as I whimper.

"I'm sure you will figure it all out. I bought a new red tie and I want to see if it is indeed a match for human blood. Good night." He hangs up the phone.

I am stunned with the phone still to my ear and my heart pounding. How the fuck do I get out of this one?

Chapter Sixteen

I fucked her raw.

I've never fucked a woman raw before. I've always been meticulous about that shit because I know what it's like being raised in a broken home. I never wanted to carry on that cycle. I need to make sure she's protected, and if she's not, we need to get her the morning-after pill.

When I slap myself on the forehead, I groan into my pillow. Ivy gets me so worked up that I lose all fucking common sense. That can never happen again. I have a future planned, which doesn't involve kids before I'm married.

Worrying about it now will do nothing. What's done is done, and if she doesn't agree to a pill, then I'll respect that. But I need her to agree to a pill because she isn't looking for a fucking relationship. Do I want a fucking relationship? Do I want one with Ivy?

Fuck, I don't know. I'm still hung up on Charlotte and what happened to her. It's conflicting and confusing, every emotion that is associated with Ivy Greene. Life is so fucking complicated.

"So…" Amelia smirks from across the table. "Where did you run off to last night?"

"Just went for a drive." I shrug.

"We really appreciate you being here with us, Neil." Shay pats my hand.

I actually want to be in Whitsborough for the first time since I was thirteen years old, and it has everything to do with one fiery girl who sets my soul ablaze.

"You were out pretty late," Amelia continues pressing, and I shoot her a look.

"Amelia, stop it. Neil is a grown man. He can come and go as he pleases," Shay chastises her.

"I think Neil has a girlfriend," she taunts, and my chest tightens.

"Really?" Shay looks at me with a wide smile.

"Nope, your daughter has some strange ideas." I shake my head.

"Amelia is bored, clearly." Shay *tsks* as she stands from the table.

"Were you with Ivy last night?" Amelia leans across the table to whisper to me.

"No." I roll my eyes.

"Are you two together now?"

"Amelia, stop," I implore.

I get up from the table and head to my room, but stop at Charlotte's. I open the door, walk in, and softly close it behind me. In this room, I feel closer to my sister, but it doesn't help the pain settling itself once more inside my chest.

I can't take back my decisions, and even if I could, I don't think I want to. It's time to admit to myself that I want Ivy Greene, and what better place to do that than in the girl's room I promised to avenge? I miss Charlotte and I love her, but holding onto anger for so long is damaging.

It changes a person, sends them down a darkened path, and it's hard to navigate your way back out. Right now, my heart feels loyal to Charlotte, but there's also something growing for Ivy, and I can't deny it much longer.

Sitting on Charlotte's bed, I look around her clean room, trying to bring back my memories of her and pick apart the points that coincide with what Amelia was saying. Dad thought she was on drugs and Amelia called her a mean girl, but I just can't picture any of it. Charlotte was sweet with me, always ready for an adventure, and always wanting to be by Ivy's side.

"Charlotte, forgive me," I whisper into her room. "I need to know you forgive me."

The door opens and Amelia steps in. "I thought I heard someone in here."

"I feel lost." I shake my head.

"I think we all did at one point," she reveals. "But Charlotte is gone, Neil. She's not here to dictate your life, and I would like to believe she'd want you to be happy."

I want to believe that too. I hope she's accepting

everything that's happening, and somehow, I have her approval. It's hard to move on without it. The guilt is tearing me up inside, and it will come between Ivy and me eventually. Charlotte will come between us if we don't figure shit out.

"You can't live your life for your dead sister," Amelia says, and even though the words are harsh, I understand their meaning.

She's right, of course. I need to live life for myself and to let go of my grief for my sister. Before I can do that though, I want to speak to the other people who knew her. I clearly have a distorted image of Charlotte and it needs to be reconciled. It's not to paint her in a poor light, it's putting her in her own light and seeing her for who she really was. I'll love her regardless.

"You need to talk to Ivy about Charlotte," Amelia states, like she's reading my mind. "She knew her best, I would think."

That's a hard dig, but again, not something I can deny. Charlotte grew from a child to a teenager with Ivy, and I would also assume she knew her best.

"How about you tell me more about how she was with you?" I look at Amelia as her face pinches.

"There's a lot of bad there," she confesses as pain seeps into her eyes. "Are you sure you want to hear that?"

"I need to hear it," I correct her.

I need to know all about my sister, the good and the bad.

IVY

I've been sent on a mission because Flower wants authentic maple syrup for her pancakes. She'll get it because she's a fucking angel, and I would do pretty much anything she asks of me. Mother and Dad are making the pancakes, and both stressed I have literally ten minutes to get back.

It feels like I'm on one of those reality TV shows, racing all over Whitsborough, and the grand prize is a stack of pancakes. I pull into the grocery store parking lot and park across three lanes. Whatever, it's a fucking emergency.

Rushing inside, I nearly plow down Adam Van Dyke, knocking one of his bags out of his hands and watching as a cucumber rolls to my feet. I pick it up and hand it back to him, his eyes narrowing on me and his mouth flattening into a line.

"I would suggest starting with that sucker in the bedroom next time." As I pass, I pat him on the shoulder. "The woman will be less disappointed."

I hear his growl of frustration, but I don't have the time to criticize Adam's anatomy—or lack thereof—because my time is running short, like the very anatomy I'm talking about.

Jogging through the aisles, I grab the syrup she asked for and get back to my car in five minutes. That leaves me two to get home, and with my driving, that's more than doable. I pass by Adam's patrol car and give him a wave before speeding off. He wouldn't dare run me a ticket with the knowledge I possess about his micro weenie.

I'm home in three minutes, and I blame the fucking old lady crossing at the crosswalk in her fucking old person walker.

I run in the door and Dad begins to *tsk*. "Two minutes late, Ivy."

"What?" I huff out. "One minute."

"It was only one minute," Mother agrees, and I stick my tongue out at Dad.

"You still win." Dahlia grins. "Because you got my favorite syrup."

"Don't side with them." Dad swings his finger between Mother and me. "I'll ask Aunt Adri to come over and cook your pancakes next time."

"Oh, no." Dahlia's eyes widen, looking truly terrified.

Mother and I burst out laughing, but Dad keeps a straight face. "Oh, yes." He nods. "I bet her pancakes would be to *die* for."

"I'm too young to die," Dahlia squeals, and we all break out into laughter.

"I can never sleep in on a Sunday." Saxon comes into the kitchen yawning.

"Pancakes!" Dahlia exclaims, and he smiles at her.

"With your favorite syrup too." He ruffles her hair.

"Ivy got it for me." She nods.

"She's a good big sister," Saxon says as he sits.

I'm shocked momentarily by his admission because this is Saxon, and compliments or sentiments aren't his thing. Not because he's mean, but because he really doesn't feel them or see a need for them.

"Thanks," I mutter as I sit down beside him.

"Someone needs to tell you something good because I'm afraid you're gonna drown in all the bad shit." He shrugs and grabs some pancakes.

See what I mean?

"Ivy is a great big sister," Dad agrees, and Mother nods at the griddle.

"She's the best big sister," Dahlia gushes around a mouthful of pancakes.

"All right, all right." I wave them off and grab a pancake off the stack.

I'm looking over my homework later that evening when my phone pings, sending my heart back into my stomach. I pick it up and smile when I see it's Neil.

Neil: My dick's in my hand because I can't seem to forget what you felt like last night.

Right, we fucked last night without a condom, and even though it was irresponsible, I'm not really stressing about it. I'll grab a morning-after pill tomorrow.

Me: About that, I am taking care of it. No more trysts without a condom though.

Neil: You sure? I can grab whatever it is you need.

He's sweet, and it makes me wary because it wasn't too long ago the guy hated me. He probably always will in a way.

Me: I'm good. Now tell me more about what's in your hand.

He sends me a few videos, and before long, I'm sliding my hand down my pants, imagining he's there.

Chapter Seventeen

"What the hell does that mean, Charlotte?" I stare right back at her.

"It means,"—she takes another sharp corner and the tail end of the car swings out—"that if you don't give us a chance, there will be no others."

"You need to pull over, right now!" I scream at her, no longer able to keep up with my calm facade.

She laughs maniacally and shakes her head. "Why, Ivy?"

"Why, what?" I grip the door as she pulls a U-turn.

"Why have you been doing all this stuff with me? Kissing me and touching me?"

"Because you are beautiful!" I exclaim.

"So, I'm just a pretty face?" Then she snorts, and we're flying around another sharp turn. "If only my daddy knew that all his warnings would be for a girl and not a guy."

Her head tips back and she laughs, the car swinging into the *oncoming traffic lane. Thank God there's no traffic this late at night.*

"Watch the road!" I grab the wheel and bring us back into the proper lane. "Pull over, Charlotte, before you do something you will regret."

"I already regret so much!" she shrieks. "I regret coming to Whitsborough, I regret the pills, and I regret you!"

That last one stings because Charlotte has been my best friend since we've been in diapers. I try to tell myself she's angry and they're just words, but I can feel the anger rolling off of her.

"You can't mean that." My voice sounds small, and I feel like I am once again losing someone I love.

"There's a thin line between love and hate, Ivy."

Chapter Eighteen

I hate Mondays so much.

It doesn't help that I barely slept last night, and these dreams of Charlotte are getting more consistent. Digging myself out of the hole after each one is so fucking difficult.

The day drags on and then math takes the fucking cherry off the cake.

"Ivy," Mr. O'Connor calls me. "Did you hand in your work from this weekend?"

He is sitting at his desk and the room is quiet, everyone turning to look at me curiously. I'm the girl who ignores everyone, and I'm rarely called upon by teachers.

"Sure did," I answer. What the fuck is wrong with him? He saw me hand it in.

"I don't have it here," he states, and I screw up my face in confusion.

"It has to be there," I counter.

"See me after class, Miss Greene."

That's his plan? Hide my work so I have to stay late after? Is he that desperate to fuck his students? *Whatever.* I lay my head on the wooden top of my desk and wait for the end-of-day bell. My knee starts bouncing with anxiety as the bell finally rings. I'll wait patiently for the asshole to make his move, and then I can turn him the fuck down.

A few minutes after the last student leaves, he's still sitting at his desk, and I slap the wood on mine. "What is going on?" I lose my patience. "I handed in my shit and you know it!"

The classroom door opens and Mr. Pratt from phys ed comes into the room. Then he leans over Mr. O'Connor's desk and kisses him passionately. What the fuck is happening?

"Ivy looks confused," Mr. O'Connor states.

"Why am I here?" I ask as my heart spears up into my throat. Mr O'Connor hasn't tried anything with me since the last time I shot him down, but this feels different.

"I thought I would introduce you to my partner," Mr. O'Connor says.

Suddenly, I'm feeling scared and cornered and it's reminding me of Dean. They must see the look on my face because they try to backtrack.

"I thought it would be fun." Mr. O'Connor's eyebrows lift in surprise.

My heart thrums inside my chest and their voices sound like they are floating away. Why would he think I'd want to join in with them both?

I stand quickly, my chair flying back and crashing to the floor.

"Whoa." Mr. Pratt looks a little green. "I thought

you said she'd be into it?" He stares at Mr. O'Connor, who's watching me hastily grab my bag.

"Let me out." My voice shakes. I can't be trapped in here with them both.

I thought it would be fun, Dean's voice booms in my ear, along with the phantom clap of a leather belt.

"Move!" I scream, and both men back up against the blackboard, their hands in the air.

"Ivy, we're not here to hurt you," Mr. Pratt tries to placate me, but I'm already yanking the classroom door open and running down the hallway.

My brain snaps to autopilot as I run for the car and jump inside the driver's seat, locking the doors behind me. A lot of my anxiety is coming from the fact that I have to somehow stop Uncle Trent from looking into Dean and avoid ever seeing him again. I'm fucking done with teachers. What the hell was I thinking getting involved with Mr. O'Connor?

There's a banging on my window and I startle, a scream escaping my mouth. I look and see my Aunt Adri standing there, her hands on her hips, so I start the car and press the button to roll down the window.

"Oh, hey, Aunt Adri." My voice cracks and she raises a brow.

"You okay, kiddo?" She looks around the parking lot. "I was in my car when I saw you run by."

"Oh." I clear my throat. "Yeah, I'm okay. I just need to get home for dinner with Dahlia."

It sounds suspect. It's not even three in the afternoon and she knows my family has dinner at seven, but I don't have anything else coming to mind.

"Okay, as long as you're good." She looks over her

shoulder as Mr. Pratt opens the main doors and sees us together. I can see his eyes widen from here, and Aunt Adri turns away from him, looking at me again.

"I'll see you tomorrow, okay?" She stands back up. "I love you, Ivy."

"I love you too, Aunt Adri." I nod and then she walks slowly back to her car, watching Mr. Pratt until he turns back inside the school.

Fuck.

I've been in my bed since I came home, uniform still on and the blankets pulled up around my ears. There's a soft knock on the door and I assume it's Dahlia coming to check on me.

"Come in!" I call out.

The door opens but there's no little squeal or footsteps. When I feel the bed dip with weight, I lift the blanket off my face to see my mother.

"Hey," she says softly, pulling the covers further away.

"Hey." My voice comes out as a squeak.

"How was school?" Her hand smooths back the hair on my head and I almost cry from her touch.

"Fine," I croak.

"You know..." She looks like she's struggling to piece together what she wants to say. "My childhood was happy but difficult. My teenage years were filled with anger and violence. I want to say my adult life has been amazing and being a mother has been a breeze."

I sit up at her words because I can feel her struggling to speak about her feelings, and I have this problem too.

"Being your mother has been hard. You gave me the roughest go at parenthood." My heart sinks. "I couldn't figure out how to parent you. Your independence scared the shit out of me. You would scream at me if I tried to tie your shoes. You were that adamant you could do it on your own." A tear slips down her cheek and I am stunned to my spot on the bed.

"You have this fire inside of you, Ivy, and I just don't know how to hold you close without being burned. Saxon will tolerate me, even let me love him without walls, and Dahlia is just eager to please everyone, even at the expense of her own happiness. But you had to figure everything out on your own and you wanted to do it with no one interfering, and I wanted that for you." She exhales and gives me a sad smile. "My mother used to tell me I was hard to love, that I was more a parent than I was a child, and I never understood what she meant until you. You are the most like me, and it scares me."

"Scares you?"

"Yes." She nods as a chuckle escapes her lips. "I'm not the best to be like. I am irrational, I like to be in complete control, and I would rather do things on my own, regardless if asking for help would make it easier."

I am all of those things.

"I'm weak in the sense that my happiness relies on others." She takes my hand. "And when I feel like I'm not needed, I hide myself away." Dad has always told me Mother was the glue to our family, that she brought everyone together and fought to keep them safe. "I leave you be because I don't want to take away your control, but I fucked up," she admits. "I'm on your side, Ivy. There's nothing you could say or do that would change that. I would do everything I can to keep you safe and I would do it gladly."

"You didn't fuck up." I shake my head. "I just always felt like maybe I was a mistake."

She laughs, a deep melodic sound, and I feel my lips curling up in response. "You weren't planned," she confesses. "But when I found out I was carrying a piece of your father inside of me, I was so fucking excited. I could see a child with his endless patience, complete acceptance, and loving nature. I couldn't see a child like me, and to be honest, I hoped like hell you would be nothing like me."

"Why?"

"There are many things you don't know." Her face falls as her smile slowly fades. "Between your father and me, he is the good one, so pure. Then you were born, and even in labor, you did things your own way. You came a month early, and when doctors were telling me to hunker down for a long labor, you said fuck that. You were born within twenty minutes of my water breaking."

I smile because my mother has never taken the time to tell me all these things.

"You came out and the doctor told me I had a girl. I could feel the fear rush through me." She nods. "It was like I knew you before I even met you. I knew at that moment I just had my greatest achievement, but you would also be my most complicated task. I was scared when he put you in my arms and your eyes opened, so much like mine. Your face was all me, and it solidified it when you stared at me and squawked. Not a cry, more like a yell. The doctors and your father laughed, but I was fucking petrified."

She pulls me in and wraps her arms around me, hugging me tight. I breathe in her scent and feel her rapid heartbeat against my ear.

"I was petrified because I knew there would be no other I could love more, and even though you were everything I feared, I was still completely at your mercy. I wanted you to grow into your own, to be the greatest you could be, and I couldn't be prouder, Ivy. You are strong and you are so much more than I could ever be." She pulls away and looks down at me. "But I will always be behind you, watching you succeed, and destroying anything that tries to harm you."

Her words are everything I needed to hear, and I wrap my arms around her, finally letting her in. "I'm sorry about Charlotte," I whisper.

"So am I, baby." She kisses my head. "But no matter how hard you try, you can't save everyone."

"I screwed up at Johnstone Reformatory." I sniff.

"I see it like a necessary screwup, although I still want to kill that teacher, but it brought you home."

"I'll try to be a better person."

"Live your life and learn along the way. That's the only thing I can tell you. To me, you are perfect, but my opinion doesn't matter. The only opinion that matters is your own. I will always be here to help you if you need it."

"Thank you, Mom."

She kisses the top of my head and stands. "I need to now have a talk with Saxon and explain that telling his teacher she should lose weight is not helpful."

I snort loudly and we both laugh. Then she leaves my room, and as much as I wish I felt lighter, I don't. I still have to figure out Dean, and now I have Mr. O'Connor and his creepy boyfriend to deal with.

It's Thursday and a huge storm has canceled race night at the strip. As much as that pisses me off, it's nothing near to how I'm feeling about Neil ghosting me yet again. I texted him a few times over the week and got no reply. So, if I see him around town, he's getting a fucking kick in the dick.

Bright side to this week? Mr. O'Connor and Mr. Pratt have taken a vacation. It eases a bit of the stress that's been threatening to completely overwhelm me, but Neil's attitude is just the cherry on top.

"Hey, hey." Aunt Adri strides into math class. Right… downside? Principal Greene has taken over teaching this class until a substitute is found.

She starts with attendance and then assigns us a chapter to review for an upcoming test.

"Do you find it strange Mr. O'Connor has just disappeared?" a girl to my left asks a guy sitting beside her.

"Who cares? The guy was beyond creepy, and all you females were heated for him." He's not wrong.

The last bell rings and everyone stands to pack away their things.

"Have a good evening, everyone," Aunt Adri calls out as students fly out of the classroom.

I slowly make my way to the front, waiting for the kids to all leave, then stand in front of the desk.

"Aunt Adri?"

"Yes, Ivy?" Her deep brown eyes look up at me. Aunt

Adri is classically beautiful with dark features and olive skin. She rarely wears makeup.

"What happened to Mr. O'Connor?"

"He's on vacation with his partner, Mr. Pratt." Her eyes never wander from mine, but I can sense a lie. She's just gotten good at covering them up. "Why? Do you have anything to tell me about them?"

"No." I shake my head. "But Mr. O'Connor didn't mention a vacation."

"Must have been impromptu." She shrugs. "Are you worried about my teaching skills?" Her grin is wide and I give her one back.

"No."

"All right, I'll see you tomorrow." She chuckles and goes back to grading.

"Good night!" I yell as I leave the classroom.

I get to my locker and find Carmelo has Cam in a headlock. "Heathens." I kick Carmelo in his ass as I walk by them. They break apart, laughing and swatting at each other, as I open my locker.

"Your teacher buddy is gone," Carmelo says as he leans against a locker, trying to catch his breath.

"So is his boyfriend," Cam chirps from my other side.

"And?" I ask them.

"Did you get him fired?" Carmelo presses as I shut my locker door.

"I didn't. Why? What have you heard?" I look at Cam because he's always been the eyes and ears.

"All right." He stands up straight. "Here's the thing. My

friend, Andrew, lives two houses down from Mr. Pratt, okay? Andrew says Mr. Pratt is a little strange and that girl scouts don't knock on his door."

"What the fuck does that have to do with a vacation?" I huff.

"Hear me out." He raises his hands. "So, he watches his house because Andrew is a fucking loser and only has me as a friend."

"Also a loser." Carmelo laughs when Cam gives him the finger.

"Andrew says Mr. Pratt's car didn't come home last night. Not weird, right? He could've been at Mr. O'Connor's place having a romantic night of chocolate-dipped strawberries and chocolate-flavored lube… I digress."

"I'm slightly turned on," Carmelo mutters.

"Same," I agree. "Mr. O'Connor would suck the chocolate off those strawberries with precision."

We're all fucked.

"Moving on," Cam continues as we walk out of the school. "Andrew is somewhat of an insomniac and says he heard Mr. Pratt's car arrive home late in the night, like two in the morning."

"So?" Carmelo snorts. "Was he covered in chocolate?"

"That's the weird part." Cam stops and looks at us. "A woman got out of the car and went into Mr. Pratt's house."

"That is strange," Carmelo states.

"Right?" Cam nods. "If he's catching home runs from Mr. O'Connor's bat, then why is there a woman?"

"Can you not?" I stare at him.

"Sorry." He shrugs.

"Did Andrew see what she looked like?" Carmelo asks.

"Nah, dressed in black, went into the house, and never came out."

"So, she's still in there?" I ask.

"I doubt it. Maybe she went out the back," Cam guesses as we resume walking to our cars.

"This shit is weird," I murmur.

"Whatever." Carmelo shakes it off. "I have a fight tonight and you both are coming to watch."

"I hate watching you fight," I whine. "You always take such a beating. Plus, there's going to be a storm."

"You love driving in the snow. Stop giving me excuses, and it's at the strip." His smile is wide. "The word is getting around and there's going to be a huge turnout."

"You're fighting in the fucking snow?" I hiss at him.

"Should help with the swelling." Cam high-fives him.

"You're both losers." I unlock my car door.

"Ten tonight." Carmelo kisses my cheek. "Don't be late."

Chapter Nineteen

"Neil!" Amelia skids into the kitchen. "There's going to be a fight at the strip tonight and you're taking me."

"I'm fucking tired." I shake my head. "I can't tonight."

Vincent Greene, Ivy's dad, has been riding my ass all week by having me drive all over the place and being an all-around gopher. I get home every night, put some food in my stomach, and die in my bed. Only to do it all over again the next day.

"Carmelo is fighting." She stomps her foot. "He's really good."

"Ivy's cousin?" I ask her.

Ivy. I haven't spoken to her in a few days, and even though I miss her, I had to put the brakes on our hooking up, because I don't want to carry on any further without figuring out where we stand. I refuse to be that guy.

"Yeah!" Her eyes light up like she's convinced me.

"Nah, I'm good." I stand up from the table. "I'm seriously tired."

"Fine." She walks out of the kitchen. "I'll just drive myself."

I try to ignore the words, knowing exactly what game she's playing, and attempt to just get my ass to bed. But nope, big brother conscience steps in and clocks me on the chin.

"Fuck," I curse and walk out behind her. "We are not staying late. I have to be up early tomorrow morning."

"Okay!" she squeals and grabs our jackets.

By the time we get to the strip, snowflakes are coming down in thick white puffs, and the ground already has a few centimeters gathered. It's not frigid cold though, which means we can chill outside to watch two guys beat the shit out of each other.

Humanity has come a long way.

"There's Cam!" Amelia exclaims, grabbing my hand and dragging me over to Cam and Ivy.

Cam scoops Amelia up into a big hug while I stand off to the side, my eyes on Ivy. She glances at me, then gives me a slight nod of her head, but that's it. I guess I deserve that. She looks just as tempting as always in a black puffer jacket, loose beanie, and furry boots. Her hair is loose around her shoulders and her cheeks are rosy from the cold.

The sight makes me want to pull her into my arms and give her my warmth. See? This is the shit that happens whenever I see her, every bit of my intuition leaves me. I lean against a light post, waiting for these guys to start the fight so I can go home and sleep. It's been a long week and it's not even over yet.

"Did your phone blow up in your face?" Ivy husks as she leans on the other side of the post.

"No." My heart begins to pound as I decide to be honest. There are a million excuses I could use, and yet, I don't want to do that to her.

"Pity."

I chuckle and reach over to flick her nose. "I am dead tired because your father is a workaholic, and honestly, I'm just trying to work through my feelings."

"You could've just told me that," she huffs.

"I guess, but then I wouldn't be a typical guy." I grin at her.

"You're not a typical guy, Neil." She smiles and turns back to watch her cousin.

She doesn't think I'm a typical guy, so what does that mean? What does she think of me? Am I more than a hookup she calls when she's drunk and wants dick? Does she see a relationship with me eventually? Even though she said she doesn't want one?

The crowd roars when a guy steps out onto the road in front of Carmelo. He's bigger and meaner looking.

"Who's the guy?" I ask Ivy.

"Some guy from the next town over." She brushes the hair out of her face. "I don't even want to watch this." She turns her head to look at me. "Want to go fuck in your car instead?"

I groan so loud that people nearest to us look over curiously. "Yes." Then I narrow my eyes on her. "But no."

"I figured." She blows out her breath and it wisps in

front of her face before dissipating.

"You're the typical guy between the two of us." I tug at the ends of her hair, unable to stop myself from touching her. "You know that, right?"

"I've heard it a few times." She grins, then sucks her bottom lip into her mouth.

She's so fucking gorgeous that I am just about to change my mind about fucking her when the crowd roars. I look over in time to see Carmelo taking three quick raps to the face and then falling onto his ass.

"Is he any good at this?" My eyes widen as he rolls over onto his stomach.

"Yes?" She makes it sound like a question, and we both cringe when Carmelo takes a kick to the ribs.

Then, Carmelo pops to his feet and starts swinging hard blows at the other guy, who has his arms up around his face. Carmelo's punches to his opponent's body are precise and solid, bringing the guy to his knees. The sudden turnaround leaves me shocked and I begin to see why he wins but leaves a match bruised and bloody.

Carmelo's face is completely covered in blood, and he spits a bright red wad onto the snow, the color stark against the white fluff. There's a blank look in his eyes, like he sealed up his humanity and let his body finish the fight. It's the look I would imagine on a soldier's face just before he pulls the trigger.

Carmelo pulls his right arm back and slams his fist forward, right into the other guy's temple. It effectively knocks him out, his body falling forward and his eyes rolling into the back of his head.

"Come get your boy!" Carmelo calls out to a small group gathered off to the side. "He'll freeze in the snow."

At least he has decency.

"That was quick, thank god," Ivy mumbles and then looks at me. "I should go check on him… Take care."

She starts to walk away but I grab her arm, pulling her toward me and wrapping my arms around her shoulders. Then I tuck her head against my chest and rest my chin on top, her arms finally coming around me.

"Give me a little time," I whisper and feel her head nod. "I'll text you when I get home."

"Okay." Her voice is small and muffled.

She pulls back and smiles up at me, her eyes watering. I lean down and press a quick, chaste kiss to her mouth, then pull away before I lose all willpower.

"Good night, Neil," she rasps as she backs up.

"Good night, Ivy."

She turns and walks away, her boots pressing into the snow. With each crunch, my heart drops, like it knows she's pulling away and I'm letting her.

"Let's get you home, old man." Amelia pats my back, giving me a knowing smile.

IVY

The red and blue lights flash in my rearview and I glance up, seeing a police car behind me. I check my speed and see I'm just under the speed limit. It's a fucking blizzard. Why am I getting pulled over?

I ease onto the shoulder and pull out my license and registration. The snow is coming down hard now, so I don't see the figure until he's practically up on my window.

Adam Van Dyke.

He bends and motions for me to put down my window. Apprehension skates along my neck and down my spine as I push the button to drop my window down halfway.

"Hey," he says, his voice even. "I noticed your rear right tire is pretty low. Are you feeling drag when turning?"

"No." I exhale the breath I'm holding, hoping it eases the tension inside my chest. "I haven't really checked them though."

"I have a pump in the car. I'll grab it." He turns back and walks toward his car.

I get out and head to the rear, trying to see the tires through the whiteout of snow. Without warning, a body slams into my back and I'm shoved up against the trunk.

"What the fuck?" I scream as my heart pummels my ribs and my widened eyes try to make out anything through the thick, falling snow.

"You little bitch," Adam snarls into my ear. "You little fucking whore."

"Get off of me, you pig!" I struggle and both of us slip in the wet snow at our feet.

"How about now?" I feel the icy sting of metal against my temple and freeze. "That's right. Now you're going to do everything I say, clear?" When I don't answer him, he taps the barrel of the gun to my forehead and I nod. "Good little whore." He chuckles. "Take off your clothes."

"What?" He can't mean for me to get naked in this fucking blizzard.

"You heard me." The gun once again hits me on the side of my head. "Now."

I should be terrified right now, I know that, but instead, I'm numb and having what feels like an out-of-body experience. My brain already knows what's coming because my body has endured it many times before. It knows its coping mechanisms. Adam Van Dyke won't get the pleasure of a scared and crying girl.

My clothes hit the snow one by one and I'm stepping out of my boots to pull off my pants. Finally, I'm standing in my bra and socks, my brow flicking upward as I taunt him to get this over with.

"You can leave your bra and socks on," he sneers. "It's cold." Then he undoes his belt buckle and the zing of his zipper hits my ears. "Bend over, Ivy, just like the whore you are."

I do as he says and pray this is over quickly. I swallow thickly at the feel of burning in my eyes. I don't want to cry, but being here in this situation again, and once more at the mercy of a predator, feels like more than just bad luck.

His hands spread me open and his foot kicks apart my legs, my feet slightly frozen to the icy snow. I feel his fingers, wet with his saliva, coat my dry pussy, and then he's shoving himself inside of me. It's painful and humiliating, but I've been down this road many times. I know what I have to do to make it easier for myself.

The shock tears through me when I feel a metal cuff clasp around my right hand before he yanks my left behind me, cuffing them together. He lifts my arms up and shoves me face down onto the trunk's metal, the cold surface cutting through my skin.

Then he's yanking on the cuffs, pulling me harder into his thrusts, and a whimper escapes me. It feels too much like Dean and his many ties, and I'm having a hard time keeping it together.

"Maybe I should've brought that cucumber to fuck your asshole with. Bet you regret saying that shit to me now, bitch."

I don't regret it. What I do regret is how naïve I was to get out of the fucking car in the first place. Everything that's happening right now is because I'm way too trusting of fucking monsters. He picks up the force of his thrusts and his movements are smoother now that there's some wetness, but judging from the pain, it's most likely blood. Bet that will get him off later when he sees it coating his little dick.

I concentrate on the cold metal of the car touching my cheek, the large snowflakes dropping on my face, and wiggle my toes to make sure they're not frostbitten. Doing these things also distracts me from the pain being inflicted between my legs.

He jars my face across the trunk with his last few thrusts and groans loudly, spilling himself inside of me. Then he pulls out and steps away while humming a fucking song.

"I–It's c–cold, Adam." My words are choppy from the chattering of my teeth. "U–undo t–the c–cuffs."

"Oh, it's cold, is it?" His sarcastic tone and menacing laugh has my heart dropping into my stomach. "Let me help you with that."

I stand up, holding my hands out behind me, waiting

for him to unlock the cuffs. The first splashes of warm liquid hitting my thighs confuses me, and I turn my head to see what's happening. Adam has his dick in his hand and he's pissing all over my ass and legs. Humiliation and shock keep me locked in place until he's done, tucking himself into his pants before striding forward.

"I think we have an understanding now, right?" He's back to sounding like Officer Van Dyke, as if nothing fucking happened. "You will stay away from me and my family. If you come around any of us ever again, I'll pay you another visit."

He doesn't scare me because I learn from my fucking mistakes, and I adapt really fucking fast. He will never get me alone again. He undoes the cuffs and I stand stone-still, not wanting to engage or enrage him further. I just want him to leave.

"You reek of piss," he tuts as his voice fades. "You should shower."

I bend down to pick up my clothes, grabbing my pants and hauling them on, the pain making me wince. His car starts, the rumble loud in the silence around us as I quickly step into my boots, using my sweater to cover my chest. He passes me and sounds his sirens for a second, the noise jolting me into action. I need to get home.

I throw on my jacket and run to my driver's seat, the car still running, and slam the door shut, locking it immediately. The scent of ammonia taints the car as I finally let myself break down, my sobs filling the car's interior.

Chapter Twenty

Neil

It's been a few days of texting Ivy without getting a response. I guess she's giving me a taste of my own medicine and I'm finding it hard to fucking swallow. I almost broke down and asked her own father where she's been, but I didn't want to have to answer questions I don't even know the answers to.

Today is Monday and I've asked Mr. Greene to let me go early. He obliged, so here I am, sitting in my car in the parking lot of Precious Blood Academy. Weird fucking name for a school. I don't see her car here, but maybe she rode with her cousin.

High schools all look the same: tall, dark, and looming. Not welcoming, and certainly not always a safe place. My high school life consisted of mean cliques and a few drugged-up jocks. This school looks no different, just filled with richer kids who could possibly be even worse.

The ring of the bell brings me out of my thoughts, and I watch as students rush out. Some to cars and others to waiting school buses, but none of them are my girl.

I get out and lean against my car, hoping she's late and that my assumption about her schedule isn't wrong. Does she have last period off? Maybe she gets out earlier than the others? I breathe a sigh of relief when I see her cousin strolling to his car.

"Hey," I call out to him. "Carmelo!"

He turns, and I wince at the motley of bruising on his face.

"What's up?" he asks as he stops to give me a scrutinizing look.

"I'm looking for Ivy." My hands slip into the pockets of my jeans as I feel myself wither under his glare.

"She's been home sick for a few days," he says. "What do you need from her that you haven't already taken?"

Well, I guess I deserve that.

"Just checking in on her." He stares me down for a few more seconds, his eyes two fiery orbs.

"She's fine," he finally snaps, and I get the feeling things aren't fine.

"I'll have to drop by her house then." I shrug and turn toward my car.

"Her mother would eat you alive," he huffs, his words hitting my back. "That would make things for Ivy worse."

"Worse how?" I turn to look at him, my brows coming together with assumptions.

"She has these episodes." He runs his hand through his hair. "Sometimes depression hits her hard and she doesn't want to leave her room."

"When did that start?" I fear I already know the answer

but I need to hear it anyway.

"When her grandma died… and then Charlotte." He looks uncomfortable as he avoids my eyes for the first time.

"I don't want to cause problems," I swear to him. "I just want to see her."

"So do I." He exhales. "She's my best friend, but it's hard to get through to her right now. We just have to wait it out."

Fuck that.

"All right." I nod, letting him think I'm taking his advice. "Your face looks like shit."

"Thanks." He grins widely and heads back to his car.

"Neil?" I hear Amelia and turn to see her with the group of mean girls.

"Hey." My eyes narrow in on her as her expression grows sheepish.

Her friend, Vanessa, is salivating at the mouth, and I have the overwhelming urge to tell her to fuck off.

"What are you doing here?" Amelia asks.

"Need a ride?"

"No, I'm riding with Veronica." Right, Veronica, not Vanessa.

"Cool." I turn and open the door. "See you at home."

"Okay." She bites her lip and looks slightly worried.

"Everything is fine."

She nods and the tension leaves her body. It's not like me to show up at her school, and the last time I did it was when our parents were at the hospital identifying our sister's body.

"Is your brother single?" I hear Veronica ask as I'm shutting the door.

Not a chance, bitch.

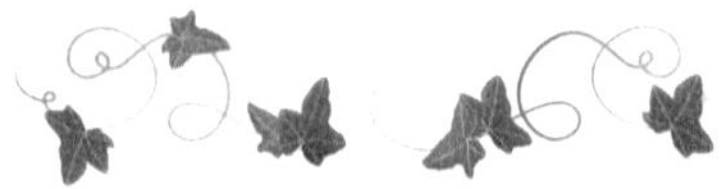

I hate that Ivy's house is locked up like Fort Knox. I've been parked on the street by her gate for hours and just saw her dad pull in. Maybe I could text Mr. Greene and tell him I have a question about a car, but that sounds stupid.

The gates open, and I look for the car that's exiting, only to see a tiny figure walking toward the road. Ivy walks slowly, her hoodie pulled up on her head, and approaches my car. My heart is beating wildly and I'm craving for a look at her face.

She opens the passenger door and slowly sits in the seat, lightly closing the door behind her.

"My family thinks you're stalking me," she states quietly, her voice void of any emotion. "We can see you on the cameras."

Well, shit.

"I've been trying to get ahold of you. I was worried."

"I'm fine." Robotic.

"Are you?" I reach out and touch her arm, but she pulls away and sucks in a breath. It's as though my touch scorches her skin and it makes my heart sink down into my stomach.

"I just haven't been feeling well."

"All right." I pull my hand back and scratch my head. "Did your phone blow up in your face?"

"Nope," she answers, but I see a slight curve on her lips.

"Pity."

"I'm just not feeling well lately. I need some time to forget," she whispers.

"Forget what?"

"Forget life." She turns to open the car door, but I stop her with my hand on her arm.

"I'm not asking you to explain to me what's going on," I twist a lock of her hair around my finger. "But could you please just answer a text? Once a day?"

"I don't know where my phone is." She sounds on the verge of tears, and I don't know how to handle this. I've never seen Ivy looking distraught. "I think I lost it."

"In your house?" I just want her to look at me, I want her to see how worried I am for her.

"No." She sucks in a large breath. "At the strip maybe."

It sounds like a lie, but I don't know which part exactly.

"Okay. I'll send you a new phone."

Her eyes finally turn and land on mine, and air escapes me when I see the depth of their despair.

"You're going to buy me a new phone?" She sounds skeptical.

"Mr. Greene works me hard, but he pays me really well." I smile at her but I get no reaction. "Just receive the package and answer a text a day."

"I'll try," she rasps, her voice breaking.

Then she gets out of my car and slowly walks back through the gates, the sound of them closing behind her deafening.

What happened after I saw her at the strip? What triggered this?

Chapter Twenty-One

It's been a week and I still can't bear to be around people. Seeing Neil a few days ago almost sent me right back into the black depth I've been slowly clawing my way out of.

This would happen every few months in New York—usually after Dean took my punishments to depraved levels. Being pissed on is a new level for me.

I received a new phone from Neil yesterday and it's still sitting on my bed, in its box. I've been trying to work myself up to open it and see what his texts say.

"I helped him set it up," Saxon states from my doorway. Number one rule while I'm in my depressive state: my room door stays open at all times. So, I have no choice but to endure my family. "It's to replace your old phone. What happened to it?" he asks.

"Lost it." My voice croaks from misuse. All my collection of photos is lost with it. Everything I filed away to remind myself I made my own choices... Gone.

"He's persistent, so I don't know how much more time you have until he's banging our front door down." Then Saxon leaves my doorway, and I hear his door open and shut. At least he can close his door. My parents are scared of how despondent I become, and after all the strange things that have happened to our family, my mother is a little paranoid.

Grabbing the box off the top of a pile of textbooks, I open it, my heart picking up speed for the first time this week. Aunt Adri has been dropping off my homework all week, but I haven't even cracked the cover of one textbook. I pull the phone out and there's a little folded-up piece of paper under it. I unfold it and feel the corners of my mouth twitch.

Don't waste it, Greene.

I swipe my thumb across the screen and see it has indeed been hooked up to my old number. I have a few messages from Carmelo, Cam, and there's Neil's number, but the name says Hotter than Sin. What a loser.

I open his messages first and the twitching in my lips turns into a small smile. There are three.

Hotter than Sin: This phone cost me a small fortune. Tell your father I need a raise.

Hotter than Sin: Today I went with your father to pick up a Ford Thunderbolt. I fell in love for the first time.

I snort at that one because I know the feeling of seeing those cars for the first time.

Hotter than Sin: You've broken the rules and now I need to figure out how to break into your house.

A small giggle escapes me as I type him a message.

Me: Hey.

That's all I got right now. I just feel so tired, and mentally, I'm drained.

Hotter than Sin: You owe me three messages. That one doesn't count, Greene.

Me: I smell terrible.

Hotter than Sin: Ew. WTF?

I giggle again.

Me: I have a mountain of homework.

Hotter than Sin: Delinquent.

The smile on my face is hurting my cheeks. It's been that long since the muscles were used.

Me: And I hate when this happens.

I'm not sure what makes me tell him that, but it's there and I don't want to take it back.

Hotter than Sin: Until tomorrow, Greene.

He doesn't pry information out of me, and it's refreshing. Besides, I wouldn't say shit anyway, so he probably figured that.

I really do fucking smell and it's seeping into my bedsheets and blankets. I crinkle my nose and sit up gradually. It's just a shower, I can do it.

The pain I experienced between my legs from Adam's assault is now just a dull ache and my body—especially my hair—is screaming to be cleaned. The weight of my body causes my legs to shake when I get out of bed.

Shuffling slowly to the bathroom, I stop in front of the mirror and nearly collapse at the sight. I look like hell. Dark circles are thick under my eyes from lack of sleep, my eyes themselves have red lines throughout, and my skin looks sallow and green. Why did I let my mind consume me again?

"Ivy?" Mother's voice calls from my room door.

"Bathroom."

I hear her padding over my carpet and then she's standing at the bathroom door. She's giving me a once-over and I can only imagine what she's thinking.

"What triggered it?" she asks. "Was it a bad dream about Charlotte? Saxon says you've been having them." Of course he told her, but it's a better explanation than the truth.

"Yeah."

"Do we need to go see Dr. Kahale?" She looks worried.

"I'm okay now," I try to assure her. "I'm going to take a shower and start some homework."

Her eyes brighten a bit as she runs her knuckles over my cheek. "I left you some soup on the table by your bed."

"Thanks, Mom."

Neil: I bet you changed my name back, huh?

His message comes through the next day as I'm sitting on my bed, poring over homework.

Neil: Don't use up your answer on that one. It doesn't matter.

Neil: What's your favorite color?

What the fuck is he doing? I'm once again smiling at the screen of my phone.

Me: Green.

Neil: Makes sense.

I snort and throw my phone back on my bed. My chest is feeling lighter and my head a little clearer. Soon, the idea of leaving my house won't feel like the end of the world. Anger is slowly replacing my devastation and I want nothing more than to hurt Adam Van Dyke for even thinking he could get away with what he did to me.

"I ordered pizza since Mom, Dad, and Dahlia are gone to New York for the weekend," Saxon says from the doorway.

"Why didn't you go?"

"Someone needs to be here in case you decide to kill yourself." Then he's walking back down the hallway.

Typical Saxon.

Neil: I had a dream last night.

Neil: I dreamed an angel came to me and gifted me glasses that would give me the power to see a person's soul.

Neil: I saw my sister's soul. It was so damn dark. I woke up really sad and couldn't go back to sleep.

Neil: What is your favorite food?

Me: Charlotte's soul was prismatic, shining in pristine technicolor. Pizza.

He doesn't answer me back and I leave it alone. I know Neil is struggling to come to terms with his sister's death and my role in it. One day, we will have to talk about it, and I will have to tell him the truth because he deserves it, and I need to tell it at least once.

I wonder if it was my soul he saw in his dream and not Charlotte's?

Neil: If I tell you I'm outside, would you let me in?

It's Saturday evening and even though I'm feeling better, I don't want to be near anyone. At the same time, if it weren't for Neil, I would still be wrapped up in my bed, stinking like a rotting corpse.

Neil: Don't mind me, I'm not freaking out waiting for your answer.

Shit.

Me: You're here?

Shit.

Neil: Yeah. Well, on your street again, like a stalker.

Shit!

Neil: No pressure. I can leave.

Me: Wait.

The part that wants to see his face wins out over the anxiety of being around people. I pull on a hoodie, opening the gate with the app on my phone.

Me: Come up.

I'm watching the video surveillance on my phone, and the second I see the hood of his car, my heart is in my throat. Just when I thought I must be having a heart attack, he steps out and my heart pounds harder, reverberating through my ears. He looks good, happy, and I'm petrified I might have to pretend to be those things too.

I open my front door and then back up to sit on the stairs as he comes up the porch. He looks at me and gives me a small smile as he steps into the house, closing the door behind him. He doesn't say anything, just reaches down to remove his boots and then hangs his jacket on the hook.

"Your dad said something about being in New York this weekend, and he may have asked if I'd be stalking you."

"Dad asked you to come by?" I'm a little shocked by that.

"Just asked if I'd be stalking." He shrugs. "Figured I wouldn't let him down."

There it is again, the slight quirk of my mouth, and then the overwhelming need to cry. Not because I'm sad, but because, for the first time, someone has reached me through my fog of depression and slowly drawn me out.

"Oh!" He snaps his fingers and reaches into his jacket. "I brought a list of movies I like and thought we could try to have a marathon. I assume you have Netflix?" He looks at me over his shoulder. I nod. "Great. I ordered pizza. You can have the Hawaiian because I think it's blasphemy to put pineapples on pizza. Saxon and I will have the meat lovers."

"Saxon?" My voice is raspy.

"He's been my spy inside." He winks at me and I nearly melt into a puddle. "We're besties now."

"Besties sound like something adolescent girls scream at slumber parties." Saxon's monotone words hit me from behind.

"You're an adolescent." Neil raises his brow.

"Are we going to paint our nails and sing Taylor Swift songs too?" Saxon reaches the step I'm sitting on and pats my head.

"I like Taylor Swift." Neil gives Saxon a confused look as he passes him and goes to the family room.

"Figured as much," Saxon retorts.

"He's fucking mean." Neil looks at me with shock and a chuckle escapes me.

"Yeah, he can be." I stand from the stairs as he holds his hand out. The thought of touching him sends shards of ice up my spine, but the thought of not touching him makes my stomach sour. So I take his hand and exhale when it feels warm and safe.

About half an hour later, our pizzas arrive and the three of us settle in to watch Transformers, the first movie on Neil's list. There are six of these movies and Neil says we have to watch all of them.

By the third movie, I am nudging a sleeping Saxon and telling him to go to bed. Neil is also looking tired, but I'm wide awake and used to little sleep.

Saxon gets up and drags his feet out of the room, heading to bed, and Neil restarts the movie. When Neil and I were kids, and Charlotte too, we would always watch movies. They were my first friends outside of family and the three of us had a bond until Neil matured, refusing to chill with us girls anymore.

Sitting here with him, watching movies, and eating pizza, is both heartwarming and heartbreaking. I miss Charlotte and I can feel something solidifying between Neil and me.

He senses my eyes on him and turns to look at me, quirking a brow. "What?" he asks.

"Do you have full-sleeve tattoos too?"

"Nah." He shakes his head and runs a hand over his mouth. "Ma would kill me. Just my chest and back so I can cover them when I'm a doctor."

"You still want to be a surgeon?" I'm surprised because

I remember him saying that when we were younger.

"No." He chuckles, his plush mouth curving upward. "Sports medicine now."

"Wow, that's impressive."

"What about you, Ivy? What do you want to be when you grow up?"

"Race car driver," I reply.

"Still?" He has a huge smile on his face.

"Yeah, but Mom says I have to go to college for something. So I'm going to major in business." I shrug.

"Nice." He smiles.

"What are they?"

"Huh?"

"Your tattoos. I saw them briefly… before…" I gesture toward the kitchen and then feel my face heat when he grins.

"I have a lot of things for my family on my chest and then my back is a full dragon."

"That's cool." I nod.

We settle back into the movie and by the fifth one, he's snoring softly beside me. I turn off the TV and stand from the couch, nudging him with my foot.

"Sorry." His eyes slowly open as he stretches, his shirt crawling up his stomach.

I panic a little because what if he thinks this is like his last few visits and he wants a quick fuck before he leaves? I can feel the blood drain from my face as my chest tightens in fear.

He stands and his brows come together when he looks over my face.

"You look like you're going to be sick, Ivy." He reaches out to touch my face and I stumble back a few steps.

"I can't sleep with you right now," I blurt out and then slap my hands over my mouth.

"What?" He looks confused. "I didn't come here for that. Is that why you think I'm here?"

"I just…" I shake my head and my vision blurs as my eyes fill with tears.

"I'm going to text you when I get home." He walks by me and heads to the front door. "Then I'm going to text you tomorrow. Answer me, okay?"

"Okay," I whisper as he puts on his boots and jacket.

"Good night, Ivy. Make sure you close the gate behind me."

Then he's out of the house and I feel like I can breathe once again.

NEIL

Ivy was triggered by the thought of physical touch.

It's plain in all of her reactions, and it's difficult because all I want to do is hold her. I can't tell if it's something that happened recently or an older incident, but Ivy is showing classic signs of PTSD. This isn't regular depression.

I get home and the house is quiet. Shay and Amelia must be sleeping. I shoot a quick text to my mom and then head up to my room. Once I'm in bed, I fire off what will be the beginning of my efforts in getting Ivy to open up to me.

Me: When we were younger, Charlotte and I begged Mom for a dog.

Me: After months of bothering her, Mom agreed and we got a puppy. It was from the shelter, so we didn't know what type it was.

Me: But this puppy got BIG. He also had a vicious streak with his food.

Ivy: I remember him. His name was Hippo.

I'm glad she remembers because I'm hoping she can somehow connect to this story and open up to me.

Me: Yeah, Hippo. Charlotte named him that. He bit me one day when I was feeding him. I still have the scars on my wrist.

Ivy: I remember Charlotte saying you had to get rid of the dog.

Me: I'm still afraid of dogs.

She doesn't immediately text me back and I hope she realizes what I am trying to get at. That I can see she has a fear of something, or someone, and it's obvious no one else knows about it, because as much as I've talked shit about the Greenes since Charlotte's death, they really care about their own.

I settle into bed and decide to let her stew. I'll talk to her again tomorrow. Just as I'm about to fall asleep, my phone pings. I reach over and grab it, anxiously swiping it open to read her message.

Ivy: Once bitten, twice shy.

Sundays are always lazy days for me, but I have a certain brunette with ocean eyes on my mind, and I won't be able to relax until I speak to her. I've come to accept I have feelings for Ivy, the type that could grow into something more if I let them, and I want to believe Charlotte would be happy for me.

On my quest to find out about Charlotte in the last few months of her life, I've spoken to Amelia, and some things she's told me are brutal. She says Charlotte was extremely moody, anger being the most prevalent mood, and physically violent if triggered.

Amelia showed me a scar on her calf when Charlotte threw a toy at her and it lodged into her skin. She also pulled out papers she had kept that Charlotte used to slip under her door.

Ugly whore.

Lesbian bitch.

Die, lesbian.

All furious, deep pressed pen strokes into the paper, and nothing like the Charlotte I knew. As much as I want to believe my sister could never do such things, I also see the lasting effects it's having on Amelia, so I can't disbelieve her anymore.

She says my dad was adamant Charlotte was doing drugs, but unsure how he found out. Only that they fought a lot about it and he was worried when she'd go back home to me and Mom. Was she getting drugs from our high school? It's possible, because if you asked the right person, you could get your hands on anything.

Amelia says she heard him asking her to give him the pills frequently, which would make the most sense because Charlotte didn't smoke and was petrified of needles. Then again, what the fuck do I actually know about my sister?

There is someone who would know everything, but Ivy is fucking fragile right now and I don't want her pushed over the edge. I also can't keep pushing it off too much longer. I want to show Ivy I can help her be relationship material, but first I need to reconcile all the things I didn't know about Charlotte.

Only when I know the complete truth will I be able to move on, and I want to move on with Ivy.

Chapter Twenty-Two

Ivy

Neil: Have you done anything harder than weed?

Me: I'm assuming you mean recreationally?

Neil: Yeah.

Me: Once. After my grandma died.

It was the worst experience of my life and that night ended with a catastrophic event. That's why I want to swear off the hard stuff and stick to the mild shit like weed.

Neil: What was it?

Am I being interrogated? And what do I say if he asks where I got it from? What's making him even ask these questions?

Me: Oxy.

There, it's out, but if he asks where and how I got it, I'm not answering him. I breathe with relief when the line of questioning stops.

"Ivy!" Flower's little voice sounds as the front door opens. "Saxon! Did you guys miss me?"

I step out of my room at the same time Saxon does, and we both head down the stairs.

"Mommy and Daddy found another old car!" She giggles when I pick her up and kiss her cheek.

"Cool," Saxon says and ruffles her hair. I put Dahlia down and she stands beside Saxon, linking her hand with his.

Mother and Dad come into the house and give us both hugs, then Mother heads straight upstairs to her room. She looks exhausted, and there's what looks to be a bruise on the edge of her jaw.

"Did she have a fight this weekend?" I ask Dad.

"Nah," Dad replies, his eyes following her up the stairs. "She took a hit while sparring with Uncle Trent."

Uncle Trent never gets the jump on Mom, and I see his jaw clenching, telling me he's not being completely honest.

"Thanks for sticking a stalker on me this weekend." I smirk, changing the subject.

"Neil's a good kid." He smiles at me. "You guys used to be tight. Thought you could help each other forget the hard things you're going through for a short time."

"He wants to bone her," Saxon states.

"What the fuck?" I turn on him.

"Oh!" Dahlia squeals. "Five dollars, Ivy!"

"What do you know about boning?" My dad chuckles as he locks Saxon into a headlock, which has him letting go of Dahlia. "Let's go discuss it further."

I laugh as Dad drags Saxon into the family room.

"Why are we talking about boning again?" Dahlia asks me, her eyes wide and innocent. "Can someone finally tell me what that is?"

Stepping out of my car, I stare across the parking lot toward Precious Blood Academy. I decided I was ready to come back to school despite feeling nauseous this morning and wanting to crawl back into bed.

This recent bout of depression has taken its toll more so than the others. I'm tired and my body feels like lead, but it was time to drag myself out into the real world.

I walk through the large wooden doors and head to my locker. My bag is stuffed with ten textbooks and there's no way I'm carrying this around. Lucky me, Veronica, Amber, and Tanya are standing in a small group as I'm making my way by.

"Oh, look," Veronica sneers. "She didn't kill anyone else after all."

I stop at the vitriol in her words and turn to look at her. "What's up, Veronica?" I drop my bag. "Not enough attention from me since I've been back?"

"My sister got enough of that," she huffs. "You ruined her."

"Veronica…" Tanya tries to grab her arm, but Veronica moves it out of the way. "Don't."

"Ruined her? How?" I ask, this time getting right up in her face.

"You turned her into something like you." Her spit flies with the force of her words.

"Like me?"

"Stop!" Tanya yanks Veronica back. "You can't say shit like that."

"My parents hate Riley now!" Veronica screams.

"Because she dated a girl?" I *tsk*.

"It's your fault!" Veronica screams at me, and I laugh.

"Girl, homosexuality isn't contagious." My eyes land on Tanya. "Ask her."

Tanya's mouth falls open and her face turns a bright red.

"What?" Veronica looks at one of her oldest friends with shock.

"She kissed me the first year of high school and then dated *tons* of boys." I slowly clap. "She's normal."

Then I pick up my backpack and look back at the three of them. Tanya looks like she might faint and the other two are staring at her like she may very well be contagious. Stupid assholes.

The day drags on. By the time I get to Math class, I see we have a new teacher. Not a substitute, an actual new teacher, and she's here for the rest of the semester. When the final bell rings, I'm out of there just as quickly as the others, eager to ask Aunt Adri about the situation.

Aunt Adri's office is enormous with large floor-to-ceiling oak bookcases, which is eerily similar to Dean's. That's why I tend not to go in there and usually have her secretary go get her.

"Hey, Ivy." Aunt Adri's voice is sweet and soothing as she steps out of her office and walks toward me. "Great to have you back."

"Thank you for bringing me my work all week." I smile.

"No biggie. What's up?"

"Mr. O'Connor has been replaced?" I drop my voice so the secretary can't hear.

"Yes, he resigned last week," she tells me. "Something about finding better opportunities."

I guess that's good, right? One less thing I have to stress over, and this way, he's not trying to corner me into threesomes. I just can't shake the lingering tendrils of doubt, and I wonder if there isn't more to it. I brush it off, because honestly, I have enough shit on my fucking plate, and this is a gift.

"Okay." I grin. "Thanks!"

"Have a good night, sweetie." She blows me a kiss and heads back into her office.

Good riddance, Mr. O'Connor. Wherever the hell you are.

NEIL

Me: Your favorite subject at school?

Yesterday I asked her about drugs and when she answered with Oxy, my stomach landed at my feet.

Mom has had terrible back pain for twelve years now because of a severe car accident. She even had surgery, but she is prescribed Oxycodone for days when her pain is unbearable. She doesn't like to take them and waits until the pain nearly renders her immobile before she gives in. Charlotte had every opportunity to take those pills, and Mom trusted us enough to never actually track them.

Charlotte could've been the one to bring Ivy the Oxy, and Charlotte herself could've been taking them. It makes me so fucking sick that I didn't see it.

As I'm slowly piecing together the life of my sister before she died, I am learning more and more about the family I was surrounded with daily, and the things I'm learning are heartbreaking. Charlotte severely bullied Amelia, Charlotte took drugs, and Dad began to drink himself to oblivion when his daughter died

Ivy: Science.

I stand staring at my phone, trying to think of anything else to ask her, something to continue the conversation, but my mind is still trying to wrap around the inner workings of my dead sister's mind. I slide my phone back into my pocket and bring lunch Mr. Greene ordered back to the office.

The old community center in Whitsborough has been changed into a shelter for abused children and Travis Greene runs it. Behind that building, Vincent Greene built the headquarters for his business, so that way they work closely together. I sometimes see Ember Greene go between them when she's visiting her husband and his brother.

This family is tight, and they keep a lot of information just to their inner circle. I would be lying if I said I didn't want to be in that inner circle. Dad tried to get in there, but apparently those walls are impenetrable. I want to learn how to be that successful, to have that drive and make something of it. The more time I spend working for Vincent, the more I love it, and the cars are a bonus.

All of these cars are rare, like only a hundred ever produced, or have custom factory paint jobs, and I fucking foam at the mouth for all of them. I heard Vincent tell Travis his son, Saxon, doesn't have a love of cars, Ivy loves them but doesn't want the business, and his only hope of passing on the family business was to Dahlia, who likes her Princess Barbie car. So he feels there's a chance.

I want to tell him to take a chance on me, that I love everything about this business and would love to be his protégé. Sports medicine was a dream I had years ago, but after working with Vin, I'm beginning to realize I really like this business. I'm just waiting to prove myself. I look up to the man because he's a straight shooter and works fucking hard. He's not a CEO who sits and lets everyone else work for him. He's driving all over the country and even other countries for these classic cars.

I bring lunch into the boardroom and find Travis, Emmett, and Ember in deep conversation with Vincent.

"Sorry to interrupt," I mumble and set the bag on the table.

"Well, if it isn't Neil Jones." Ember smiles at me and it makes my breath catch. Ivy could be her fucking clone.

"Hello, Mrs. Greene." I nod as I slowly back toward the door.

"Oh shit, no, don't do that. Call me Ember." She

waves me off and then raises her eyebrow. "Stick around for a minute."

"Okay," I agree quickly, but I don't think I could ever call her Ember.

"Thanks for checking in on Ivy and Saxon this weekend," Vincent adds as he opens the bag of deli sandwiches.

"No problem." Sweat begins to gather along my forehead as the bright fluorescents above my head heat my skin.

"Saxon is taking a liking to you, even if he thinks you want to bone my daughter." Ember's eyes are twinkling with humor, but I'm choking on her words.

"I… No… It's not… Shit."

They all laugh at my stuttering and coughing as Emmett leans back in his chair. "Ivy is complicated." He scratches the hair on his chin. "She acts tough, but it's a facade, she's soft as a marshmallow and just needs someone to love her right."

"Like someone else we know." Travis coughs into his hand.

"Yeah." Ember smacks the back of Travis' head. "My daughter is a lot like me." She looks up at me, her eyes shining with pride. "She's loyal in every way, even if it means she takes the fall. She'll do it happily."

Her eyes bore into mine as her words echo in my mind. Is she referring to Charlotte's death? How did Ivy take the fall if it was her fault?

I nod because I have nothing to say that would work in my favor, and besides, I'm not looking to disrespect anyone.

"Thanks for grabbing lunch, Neil." Vincent smiles.

"I checked in on your dad today at the facility," Ember

cuts in, her tone softening. "He's asking for you."

"Thank you for doing that." I turn and reach for the door.

"Parents aren't perfect." Her voice hits my back. "We know that better than anyone, but if they are willing to make their lives better and turn themselves around, that's something to admire."

I don't reply any further and step out of the boardroom, releasing the breath I was holding as I shut the door behind me. I don't want to talk about my dad right now, and seeing him would only make things worse. He found solace in alcohol after Charlotte's death while the rest of his family struggled, and he was okay with that.

My phone pings and I pull it out of my pocket.

Mom: How's my boy?

I want to tell her I know her teenage daughter was dipping into her prescription, I want to scream at her for not paying more attention, and I want to bash my head into a wall for all the same reasons.

Me: Everything is good, Mom.

I put my phone away and head to my small office. The rest of my day will be scouring resale websites for lemons worth a small fortune.

Chapter Twenty-Three

Dean: Serrano hasn't been in touch for two weeks.

No, no, no.

I haven't heard from him in three weeks and things were looking up. I thought—or at least I'd hoped—he had moved on, but I was so fucking wrong.

Dean: Looks like maybe the Black Slaughter got to him.

What the fuck is a Black Slaughter? I Googled it and found nothing. I don't know what the hell he's talking about. I haven't engaged with him about it so far, but I think it's time I do.

Me: I have nothing to do with any of this. I just want you to leave me alone.

He sends another video, and I press play before I can even think about it. This is one of me spread wide, bent over his desk, and he's finger fucking me. My pussy was wet with arousal, betraying my internal torture at his actions. I can hear my muffled voice, and by the sound of it, this was one of the times I was gagged with my own panties.

Dean: Looks like you were enjoying our visit that day.

Me: What do you want from me?

He doesn't answer me and the anxiety I'm feeling has my heart rattling my ribs apart. If he continues to feel threatened, he will release those videos, and I will have to explain everything to my family. I don't think I could come back from that. They will never see me the same again.

If I change my number, he will contact me another way, and it worries me he'll take the path of my parents. My anxiety ramps up at that notion and a powerful wave of nausea hits me. I barely make it to the toilet before I'm throwing up my dinner. This is getting worse, and I can't see how the fuck I can do anything to stop it.

I can't go see him, and talking to my Uncle Trent about it will only cause more suspicion. I plant my ass on the floor in front of the toilet and let the tears I've been holding in saturate my cheeks. It's fucking hopeless.

The ping of my phone sounds from my room as I sob, but I can't deal with it anymore tonight, so I curl up on the floor beside the toilet and cry myself to sleep.

"Ivy." Saxon's voice echoes around me, pulling me from my sleep. "Who the fuck sleeps in the bathroom?"

"Huh?" I open my eyes and see the porcelain of the toilet in front of my face. "Fuck."

"Are you sick? Like more than just your mental problems?" Asshole.

"I was feeling nauseous earlier," I admit to him.

"Your phone was ringing. How did you not hear it?"

Then it all rushes back, the reality I tried to bury with blissful sleep, and I groan back into the bathroom mat.

"Can you get off the floor of the room you shit in?" Saxon pleads as he pulls on my arm. "You're making *me* nauseous." I let him pull me up and stumble into my bedroom, planting face-first onto my bed. "Get some sleep, you have school tomorrow, and brush your fucking teeth." I hear the shudder in his voice as he leaves my room.

"Yes, *Dad*," I mumble sarcastically.

I grab my phone off the bed and stare at the screen. There are three missed calls from Neil, and I quickly sit up because he never calls me. The last missed call was ten minutes ago, and it's after midnight. Suddenly, I'm worried and rush to call him back.

"Hey," he croaks into the phone, and I gasp at the sound of his sadness.

"What happened?" I get up and prepare myself to go wherever the hell he is.

"I need to know if it was Charlotte who gave you that pill."

When it rains, it really fucking pours.

"I…"

"Ivy, I've been cruel and don't really deserve any truth from you, but you were the person who was involved in my sister's death. I hated you. I still hate that it was you there with her that night, but I need to know if she was on drugs." He's pleading with me, and I don't know what to say because my loyalty will always be to Charlotte.

"Neil, I don't know if she was on drugs that night. As for where I got the pills? Someone at school." It's a blatant lie, but I'm hoping he buys it.

He needs to let his sister rest in peace and not dredge up her past. What difference would it make at this point? And to be fair, I really don't know what Charlotte was taking in the days before she died because I was consumed with my grandma's illness and then her death.

He's quiet, and I lie there in silence with him. I can't bring his sister back, no matter how hard I wish for it, because I've fucking tried. I offered whatever god was up there to take me instead. I didn't deserve to live and I wanted to leave this Earth anyway, but I never get what I pray for.

"Sorry I bothered you," he finally says, and my heart breaks.

"You're not a bother."

"Good night," he whispers and hangs up the phone.

What has made him turn his sights onto his sister like this and dig through her life? What has he found out that's making him see something he didn't see before? I don't want him to dig because if he finds out the one secret I've been keeping safe for over two years, then he will hate me more, along with everyone else, and then everything I endured at the hands of Dean will all be for nothing.

It can't ever be all for nothing. I couldn't live with that thought because the demons I keep locked away will surely find their way out. I need to find out what he's searching for and then I need to keep him away from it, because I don't want him to ever drown in regret.

Amelia may be my key in all of this, but I need to make

it clear to her I'm into her brother and probably always have been. I have a feeling she's been telling Neil just how crazy Charlotte was becoming, and I can't let that come out.

None of it was her fault.

Precious Blood academy is bustling with Friday excitement. The students in the halls are chirping and everyone is talking about parties they're hitting up. I have one person I need to find as I zone out all others in my line of sight.

"Ivy?" Her voice has me stopping dead in my tracks and my arms breaking out into goose bumps. "I haven't been able to catch up with you. I heard you were sick?"

I turn and stare into Molly's eyes. It takes everything in me not to claw them out. I know she's not her father and she has nothing to do with what he did to me, but her face is fucking pissing me off.

"I can't talk right now, Molly." Trying to calm my quaking insides, I breathe deeply. "How's your dad?"

"Oh, he's okay. I think Mom is coming back home." She looks at me with a slightly confused look.

"Tell him I say hi." I turn and then storm off. I'm not sure what made me say that, and I'm not really thinking about the repercussions. Regardless of the fear I should be feeling, right now it's all rage.

I finally spot Amelia's dark, curly hair standing at her locker, in the company of Veronica, Tanya, and Amber. When the fuck did she start chilling with them?

I shove myself between them and stand in Amelia's

face. "We need to talk."

Her eyes widen as Veronica clears her throat, but I just turn my head and glare at her over my shoulder. "Not right now, bitch."

She looks stunned and then turns on her heel to stomp off down the hall. My gaze finds Tanya and Amber, and I shoo them away with my hands before they quickly chase after their ringleader.

"Fuck, that was hot," Amelia whispers.

"Keep those panties dry, brat." I slap the locker beside her head, making her jump. "I'm here to ask about your brother."

"Of course you are." She grins and leans back against her locker. "What do you need to know?"

"Why has he been asking about Charlotte?" She stands straight at that and looks up and down the hallway. "Knock it off, no one here knows Charlotte," I hiss. "Tell me what he's asking."

"It's not so much what he's asking as it's what I'm telling him." She takes a tiny step back from me as her eyes fill with trepidation.

"What do you mean?" I step closer to her.

"Charlotte was a bitch to me, Ivy," she whimpers, tears coating her eyes. "She was constantly yelling at me about being a lesbian when we both knew she was one herself, even if she didn't want to admit it." Oh, she admitted it. "She was taking something those last few months. Apparently, Dad found out." She relaxes against her locker again. "He confronted her about it the night that... you know." Of course I fucking know. I was there. "Then she stormed out of the house, your grandma died, and shit just went chaotic."

"That's one way of putting it," I murmur. "He's asking me about her drug use."

"Tell him what you know because he deserves the truth. He's holding on to this fairy tale version of his sister and it wasn't reality," she sneers.

"Does he really need to know?" I raise a brow. "What difference would it make? It looks like you need to forgive your sister for her demons because she's no longer here to ask for it. She wasn't herself, Amelia, and eventually, she would've been better. I just took that chance away from her. Forgive her and stop trying to tarnish her further in death."

She drops her eyes and blows out a breath. "It was hell with her, Ivy." Her voice shakes. "It's all I can remember, and right now, forgiveness feels impossible."

"Make it possible because you will never get closure from her now, and stop fucking up your brother by ripping away the happy memories he has of her. You're the one becoming a monster now."

It's harsh, I know, but she needs to hear it. Defaming her sister in death is doing nothing but poisoning her insides with hatred, and there will be no apologies from the dead for their actions when they were alive.

She huffs out her breath and tears roll down her cheeks. "Fuck."

"Let her faults rest with her. None of us know the full story, and you're doing more damage than good, okay?" I pull her in for a hug and pat her back.

She's young and still carrying anger that feels like the end of the world. I don't want her getting older with regret in her heart.

"Thanks, Ivy," she rasps and pulls away. "I'll try."

That's all I can ask for.

It's been nearly three years since I've driven to this house, and it strikes me how close it is to Molly's house. Adam Van Dyke, the rapist, lives a street over from Rodney and Shay Jones. Being here is creeping me out way more now.

Amelia let me know Neil called in sick today and was still in bed when she left the house this morning. I know Shay isn't home because she owns the only gym in Whitsborough, which means working six days a week. I'm sitting in the Jones' driveway, trying to muster the nerve to get out of this vehicle and knock on his front door. I know he's home because his car is here.

I take a deep breath and hop out quickly before I can change my mind, jogging up to his porch, then ring the doorbell and wait. It takes the guy five minutes to get to the door, and when he opens it, he looks like utter shit.

"You really are sick." My eyes rove all over his face.

He cracks a ghost of a smile and leans against the door. "You worried about me, Ivy Greene?"

"Yes." I go with honesty. "And hungry, so I ordered myself a Hawaiian pizza and a Meat Lover's pizza for you because anyone capable of eating that much meat on a pizza is a psychopath."

His thick arm reaches up and grips the top of his head as he laughs, his shirt riding up, revealing his abs. "Come in then." He opens the door wider. "I'm glad you're here."

"I skipped classes today for you." I slip off my shoes. "You better be glad."

He chuckles again and then stops abruptly to haul me into his arms. He tightens his hold around my shoulders as his nose hits my hair, inhaling deep. I stand completely still for a second, waiting to see if my anxiety will rush me at his touch, and then relax when it doesn't, wrapping my arms around his waist.

"I'm not sick," he whispers.

"I know."

"How do you know?" he asks, his chin moving against the crown of my head.

"Because I looked the same way when I was grieving for your sister."

He tenses for a second and then I feel him nod. "Only you didn't have someone to order you pizza and check up on you."

"No," I agree.

I didn't have anyone checking up on me. I was stuck in a court-ordered boarding school, being ridiculed every day, and enduring abuse a few times a week. I certainly didn't get pizza.

He presses his lips to my forehead, and any lingering doubts about my anxiety disappears when I feel my chest warming up to him. His touch doesn't freak me out and his scent makes me feel safe.

"I brought a list of movies. I assume you have Netflix?"

Once again, his head tips back, his laugh loud in the empty house, as he leads me into his family room. "Yeah, we have Netflix."

We've watched Mean Girls, Hocus Pocus, and Dirty Dancing. We're both nearly half asleep from a pizza coma when the front door opens.

"Neil?" Amelia's voice calls out.

"In here," he replies.

Amelia pops her head in and sees me nestled into Neil's side, his arm around my shoulders.

"Hey." She looks at me. "I didn't know you would be coming by."

"Why would you?" I raise a brow. "I came to see your brother."

I hate being rude to her, but honestly, I'm not fucking sure what she's trying to prove. She's becoming annoying and I can honestly say it's because of the shit she's running Charlotte's name through. Also, she seems to think I need to tell her when I'm visiting her brother.

"Right." She takes a deep breath and blows her hair out of her face. "Well, you two have fun." Then she disappears back around the corner.

"I think those long claws you have can be retracted now." Neil snorts as his fingers draw lazy circles on my shoulder.

"Sorry." I smile at him, not meaning it at all.

"Let's go to my room. Shay should be home soon too." He stands and then freezes. "Unless you want to stay here. It's up to you."

"It's fine." I wave him ahead of me.

He leads me up the stairs and past what I remember to be Charlotte's bedroom, my chest growing tight. I miss her so much. I continue following Neil to his bedroom, and as soon as I step inside, I inhale his scent. It's soothing and all male.

"Your room is clean." I look around.

"Yeah, yours isn't," he retorts as he shuts the bedroom door.

"You were in there one time." I roll my eyes.

"And it was a fucking pigsty."

I laugh and he joins in, sitting on the chair by the bed. I take a seat on the mattress and feel the air in the room change. We need to talk.

"About that phone call last night…" I begin.

"Yeah, I'm sorry—"

"Why?" I cut him off. "Why all the questions?"

"Amelia told me our father caught Charlotte with drugs." He leans forward, his elbows resting on his knees. "And I couldn't believe it. That's not how I remember her."

"Okay." I nod for him to continue.

"Amelia knew it was something about pills, but she was too young to remember all the information." My heart speeds up with the word pills. "So, I figured you were her best friend. If she was doing it, then you must've done it with her."

"That's stupid." I sound calm, but I am far from it.

"Then when I asked you that question and you said Oxy, I knew there was something there," he states, looking me in the eyes.

Why the fuck did I answer him honestly?

"You see…" He sits back again, his eyes intent on my face. "Our mother was in a pretty terrible car accident and injured her back. She went through a few surgeries, but some of the damage couldn't be repaired."

I nod because I know all of this.

"She was prescribed Oxycodone for the days the pain became unbearable."

I drop my chin to my chest and groan. I don't want to

lie to him, so I make the decision to give him some peace.

"Yes, Charlotte brought me that pill." I lift my head and look at him. "If you're asking me if she had a problem, my truthful answer is I have no idea. She was only here every other weekend."

"Okay." It's his turn to nod me on.

"I had a problem at that age though. I was drinking and smoking a lot of marijuana. Charlotte would join me in drinking but not the weed until a few months before she died. She brought me that pill. She said she wanted to try it with me. We did it and I hated it. After that, it was never brought up again."

"Did her behavior change? Was she angrier?" His questions stir feelings inside me I've tried to suppress.

"We fought more," I answer him. "She wanted… certain things."

"What things?"

I feel the first tear drop and hit my kilt, the wet patch spreading. "Charlotte claimed to be in love with me."

"Seriously?"

"Yes." I shake my head. "I didn't feel the same. We were fooling around, and for me, it was just fun, but for her, it was real."

"Charlotte was a lesbian?"

"Am I a lesbian?" I raise my brow and smile when he looks confused. "I don't know what she was, Neil. We didn't discuss that."

"Okay." He looks more confused than when we started, and I feel sorry for him.

"I think I should go now." I stand from the bed.

"Okay," he says again and leads me out of his room.

As I walk by Charlotte's door, I run my hand along the wood and tell her I miss her. No matter how things ended, she will always be my best friend.

We get to the front door and I pull on my boots, then my jacket.

"Thanks for having me," I tell him and reach for the door handle.

"Wait." His hand lands on my arm and he pulls me into his, then his finger lifts my chin until he's staring down into my eyes. "Can I kiss you?"

I nod and almost swoon. It'll never get old, him asking for permission.

His lips gently connect with mine and he tightens his hold on me, our bodies pressing closer. When my chest squeezes, I pull back and smile up at him. It's not that I don't want to kiss him, I do, I just can't let it go further, and the longer his mouth is on mine, the more sure I am that it will.

"Thanks for checking on me." He kisses my cheek and I nod as I step outside.

When the door shuts behind me, I find it easier to fill my lungs with air and calm myself from the panic attack I could feel coming on. I head to my car and pull out of his driveway. I feel sad for Neil, but I'm hoping he can move on from obsessing over Charlotte and let her rest in peace.

A police cruiser crosses the intersection in front of me as I pull up to a stop sign. My blood pounds throughout my body, the sound ringing in my ears, and my mouth dries when I see it's Adam, his eyes lasered onto my face.

He raises his pointer finger as he passes, and I feel like it's a bullet straight to my heart before nausea courses its way up my throat. I only move when his vehicle is completely out of sight, yet I can't even remember how I got home, ending up back in my bed.

I'm back at square one.

Chapter Twenty-Four

I let myself have the weekend to wallow, even avoiding Carmelo and his begging to come see me. He has a fight coming up next weekend and wants me there. After the last one, I'm not even wanting to think of a fight night, and I know what happened isn't his fault, but it's hard to separate the two right now.

It's Monday and I am back at school, and hit with a sudden hunger. I head to the cafe to grab something to eat because I never eat breakfast. As soon as I step in, the collective scent of different foods sends me into a severe case of nausea and bile burns its way up my throat.

I race back out and head all the way back down the hall, getting as far away as I can. With a few breaths, I try to control the rolling of my stomach. I'm pretty sure I'm coming down with something and I don't think I will make it through this day. On top of everything, I can feel the beginnings of a migraine too.

I head to Aunt Adri's office and ask the secretary to call Mother, telling her I don't feel well.

"You look green, honey," the secretary states as she calls my mother.

After assuring Mother I can drive home, I head outside and run into Amelia on her way in.

"Leaving?" she asks.

"I don't feel so great. I think I'm coming down with the flu."

I continue to walk without listening to what she says, just wanting to get home and curl up in my bed. As soon as I'm in the car, my phone rings.

"Hello?"

"You're sick?"

"Neil?" I ask, sounding so stupid because obviously it's Neil.

"Yeah, baby." Him calling me baby makes my stomach flip and he sounds so good, making me miss him so much. "Do you need anything?"

"Can you come be with me today?" I know I sound like a baby, but I want someone to take care of me.

"Yeah, I'll be by soon. You want some soup?"

The thought of food makes me want to gag even though I was really hungry not too long ago. "No."

"I'll see you soon." And then he hangs up.

It must be all the stress I'm under lately, making me sick and so damn tired.

Once I'm home, I hit the couch as I wait for Neil to get here. My stomach is still queasy and my head is pounding.

When the doorbell finally rings, it takes all my energy to get off the couch and walk to the door. I open it and see Neil's concerned face, his eyes giving me a once-over. Grabbing his jacket, I pull him in, wrapping my arms around his waist, then I sink my nose into his chest and breathe in his cologne, something musky and spicy.

He kicks the door closed and lifts me up into his arms before slipping off his boots.

"Let's go rest, okay?"

I wrap my arms around his neck and nod. I just want him with me. He walks us up to my room, opens the door, and sets me down carefully on my bed. Then he drops his jacket on the chair at my desk and crawls beside me, pulling me against his chest.

"What time do I have to sneak out of here?" he asks into my hair.

"Never," I murmur, already falling asleep.

"You asked for it."

That's what I think he says anyway.

There is an intense heat along my back, like someone is holding a heater right to my skin, and I can feel it seeping through my muscles. I try to move away from it, but something large and heavy is holding me in place. I open my eyes just as the panic causes my heart to drum rapidly.

"Relax," Neil rasps into the back of my neck. "It's just me."

I relax and sink back into him, overheating be damned.

"What time is it?" I ask him.

He shifts around, and when he searches for his phone, his knuckles brush along my thigh, exposed by my flipped-up kilt.

"Just after noon."

His hand lands back on my waist and his fingers lightly massages me over my shirt.

"Are you feeling better?"

"Yes," I reply and press my ass into his erection.

"Ivy." His fingers clench and he stalls my movements.

"Don't you want me?"

"That's fucking dumb of you." He shoves his steel cock against my ass. "What the fuck do you think?"

My core clenches and I can feel myself burning up for a completely different reason. I don't want to ignore my body when it tells me I'm ready to move on, especially when I'm ready to forget.

I bring his hand up from my waist and cup it around my tit as I continue to grind my ass into his hardness.

"Fuck," he groans as he squeezes me roughly.

Then he pushes me onto my back and hovers over me, ensuring he's not touching me. He leans down and kisses me softly, but the touch of his lips drives me into a frenzy. I missed this feeling, the feeling of wanting release and waiting to fucking soar.

He drops his body weight, and he's instantly everywhere I want him, all his rough edges against my soft curves. I arch up into him and practically purr when he thrusts his cock at my core.

Our tongues are rough as we seek each other's mouths, and our teeth clash just as we try to get closer.

He pulls back and I grab the sides of his face, trying to drag him back down to me. "Wait." He chuckles breathlessly. "I want something else."

He slowly moves down my body, opening up my dress shirt and lavishing my breasts over my bra. Then he pulls down the bra and my nipple is between his teeth, the peak being lashed with his tongue. Liquid lava pools in my panties and I am nearing the edge with no attention on my pussy. That's how long it's been.

His tongue dips into my belly button and I arch my back off the bed, trying to move him exactly where I need him. Fuck the belly button. He laughs again and then he's flipping up my skirt, nipping me through my boy cut shorts. His finger runs up my seam and lands on my clit, rubbing me through the material.

"You're soaked right through." He leans in and inhales me. "You smell amazing."

He continues to rub my clit, sucking and licking my inner thighs, and whispering profanities as I grow wetter. Finally, he slides his finger under my panties, and I nearly come off the bed when our skin touches. He slowly slides one finger inside of me and then brings it back out, sucking my juices off with a groan.

"Neil." His name rumbles from my mouth in warning. If he doesn't hurry up, I will sit on his face, smothering him until I come.

"Okay, baby." He pulls down my shorts, kneeling to take them off fully, and tosses them behind him.

Then he winks at me, licks his lips, and dives back down. He starts by sucking my pussy lips into his mouth and nibbling his way from the bottom to the top. His tongue strokes my clit a few times before he's sliding it inside of me, propping my ass up with his hands, and tongue fucking me in rapid motions.

Then he moves up and latches onto my clit, his fingers now replacing his tongue. He sucks my clit into his mouth and runs his tongue over it, and I can feel my juices running down to my asshole—I am that turned on and ready to fucking fall apart.

"Give it to me, Ivy," he growls against my pussy. "Come all over me."

I suck in a breath as my body erupts in sensation, all moving outward from my core as my pussy clamps down hard. I black out from the force of my orgasm, my eyes bursting with colors behind my eyelids and his name stuck in my throat on a silent scream.

My orgasm stretches as he continues to suck on my clit, my body and pussy convulsing in tandem.

"You taste so good," he groans as he sucks up every fucking drop. Not forgetting the juices pooling at my asshole, he licks and sucks that dry too.

I finally come back to myself, panting heavily and moaning random noises. Exhaustion settles in and I yawn, losing my breath.

Neil comes up beside me and tucks me back under his chin. "Sleep."

"But you…" I try to pull away.

"Next time." He kisses the top of my head and I drift off immediately, cocooned in his scent.

NEIL

Leaving her is hard, but I don't want to wake her because she's finally sleeping so soundly. My cock swells again as I lick my lips, and I curse softly. Her taste is still fresh.

There's one more errand I need to get done today, and I'm not looking forward to it, but I force myself out of her bed because I've decided to finally visit my father and talk to him about Charlotte. It took a lot of convincing for my father's counselor to agree to let me see him and I had to explain it was a bit of an emergency. I'm ready to let her rest, but first I need to know what happened before she died. It won't change my opinion about her though because she'll always be my sister, and I love her without question.

Ivy's mother will be home soon, and I'd rather not be here when she does. I'm not ready to put a label on whatever it is that's brewing between me and her daughter, and I don't think Ivy is either.

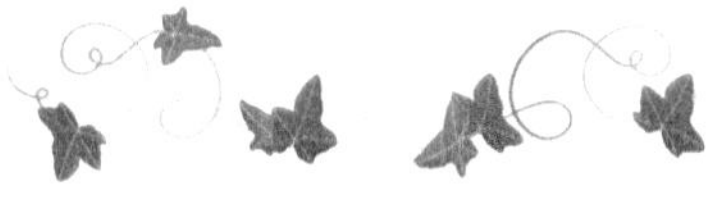

An hour later, I'm pulling up to the rehab facility in Toronto. I walk inside and see two nurses at the desk, both perking up when they notice me. This would've been my time to flirt, wink a little, and grab both their numbers, hoping for a threesome. Now, I just want this done so I can go home and talk to Ivy.

I'm not stupid. I know what the fuck is happening here and I'm nearly ready to tell her how I feel. I just have one more obstacle to overcome.

"I'm here to see Rodney Jones," I tell them.

"And you are?" The blonde flutters her obviously fake eyelashes.

"His son, Neil Jones. I'm a contact on his paperwork." She begins tapping the keyboard, taking her time as I shift from foot to foot.

"It's after visiting hours, Neil Jones, but I'll make an exception," she purrs, her eyelids growing heavy as she bites into her lip.

"I already checked in and made the appointment with his counselor. He said he would make a note of it. Is it not there?" I quirk my brow as she swallows thickly, her co-worker leaning in to read the computer screen before snorting.

The blonde's eyes close briefly as the girl beside her chokes on a laugh. "Straight down the hall, room twenty-three." She doesn't look back up at me.

"Thank you." I politely nod and head to where she directed without a backward glance.

I'm nervous to see my father because it feels like a long time since I've seen or spoken to him while he was sober. It's been two years of him drowning in alcohol, so I'm not sure who he is anymore.

I knock on the door and hear his voice call out to come in. He sounds clear, no slur, and when I open the door, his eyes widen in shock.

"Neil?" He stands from his chair and crosses the room to hug me. "Son, I can't believe you're here."

"Me either." I pull out of his embrace, the close proximity making me uncomfortable. "You look good." His eyes are focused, his skin looks healthier, and his voice is strong.

"I feel good." He looks at his desk of papers. "I have an assignment this week to write out all the wrongs I did while drinking, and I think I'm going to need more paper."

"I feel sorry for all those trees," I mumble as he laughs.

"Your name appears quite a bit on these papers… and Charlotte's too." His eyes gather moisture. "I can't even tell her how sorry I am for all the things I messed up with her those last few months."

"Like what?" I sit on his small twin bed as he leans against his desk.

"Charlotte was complicated. She had no real plan for her future and was angry a lot. I chalked it up to adolescence, but eventually, it became clear something else was going on." He sits at the desk and pulls out a paper. "She asked to come live with me and Shay because she said you and your mother were never around. I told her no because I didn't want to do that to your mother. She's a good woman and I wasn't looking to start a war."

A swift pang hits me in the chest. I wasn't around because I was hustling with a few part-time jobs to make ends meet, and Mom was working when she could, which wasn't often after her accident. Besides all that, child support was meager since Dad didn't have a great job.

"Mom wouldn't have let that happen," I tell him. It's the truth. There would've been a huge custody battle.

"There were some issues with her at school." He bows his head as he exhales. "She was expelled that week before the… accident."

This is the first I'm hearing of her being expelled, and if this was a few months ago, him calling Charlotte's death an accident would've sent me into a rage. I always referred to Charlotte's death as a murder.

"Expelled? For what?"

"Selling drugs." He looks at me like I'm crazy. "Your mother said you knew."

"I didn't." I shake my head. Why wouldn't Mom tell me? And why would she lie and say I knew?

"She was caught with two bottles of Oxy in her locker and some kids confessed that Charlotte was selling them on school grounds. So she was sent to stay with me for two weeks because your mother had had enough."

This is all news to me. I was in my first year of university when Charlotte was starting her second year of high school, and even though the workload was hefty, I was still at home. Well, unless I was working at the hotel, and even then, I was only doing part-time hours.

"This really makes no sense." I shake my head. "I actually came here to talk to you about Charlotte because Amelia told me some terrible things."

"Yes." His eyes cloud over as he scrubs a hand down his face. "She took her bullying to extremes with Amelia. I always thought it was jealousy, but now I think the drugs had something to do with it."

"Bullying Amelia about her sexuality wouldn't stem from drugs, Dad."

"No, but it would come from her anger toward her own situation. She wanted to live with us and go to school with Ivy, like Amelia did. Sometimes, I felt like her interest in Ivy was borderline obsessive."

Borderline obsessive. Why though?

He sees the confused look on my face and his softens. "Even through all of that, Charlotte was a good girl. She loved hard and she would've been fine if the drugs weren't in the picture. I don't think she was hateful."

No, she wasn't hateful, but it's clear Charlotte was having issues at home. I need to talk to Mom. It really doesn't make sense that Mom would hide this from me. I feel like I'm on a trail of breadcrumbs and chasing them down is tiring.

"Then there's you." He pulls out another paper. "I pushed you too hard. I made you feel like you had to be the man of the house for your mother and sister when your mom and I split up. I never told you enough how much I appreciated everything you did in my absence."

Well, this is unexpected, but I'm not in the right headspace to get emotional with him, as much as I've always wanted to hear him say these things.

"Thanks, Dad." I pat his shoulder awkwardly and stand, digging my hands into my jacket pockets. "I'm proud of you for all of this, and when you're out, I really want to hear all of it."

"Really?" His eyes brighten.

"Yes." I can forgive him for the grief he had for his daughter. I understand not wanting to feel the pain of losing a child.

The overwhelming need to get back to the house and call Mom before her next shift at the diner comes over me. I have questions about Charlotte and she's going to tell me exactly why I was kept in the dark, but before I leave, I need a bit of clarification.

"Why would you say Charlotte was obsessed with Ivy?" I ask Dad as his brows come together in thought.

"Because she always wanted to be with her."

"They were best friends. Girls are like that."

"This was more of a need to know where Ivy was, even when she wasn't in Whitsborough, calling me to ask Vin where his daughter was, things like that. I also found a few letters in her room that looked like love letters addressed to Ivy. I chalked it up to being a joke, but I'm not so sure." He scrubs his hand along his scalp.

"Maybe I'll talk to Ivy," I murmur.

"Ivy is a good girl," my father states. "I never blamed her for Charlotte because I was never convinced of her story."

"She admitted Charlotte's death was her fault," I argue.

"I also knew at the time Charlotte was troubled and under the influence." He stares at me. "What do you think?"

My breath is lodged somewhere in my lungs and I'm finding it hard to breathe. What do I think? I think Ivy is the type to cover for her best friend, even at the cost of being sent away. Then Ember Greene's words come back to me. *She's loyal in every way, even if it means she takes the fall. She'll do it happily.*

"I think I need to talk to Mom."

"Okay, son. Take it easy on her. Being a single mother is never easy."

I nod and head to the door, my visit short and nearly devastating.

"I'll see you when you get out," I promise him.

"I can't wait." He laughs as I leave his room.

I head back out to my car and pull out my phone. Mom better have the answers I need.

Chapter Twenty-Five

I'm back in front of the toilet and staring at my bile in horror. This isn't normal. When I woke up, the room spun and my stomach heaved almost instantly. I just made it to the toilet and even though I had nothing to throw up, I couldn't stop heaving.

It's not stress that's causing this and I don't think it's a bug. My stomach rolls again with my thoughts and I'm back in the toilet, bile burning my throat. I think back over my calendar and realize two fucking things.

One: I stupidly had unprotected sex with Neil when I was drunk, forgetting the morning-after pill after my run-in with Mr. O'Connor. And two: I was raped by Adam and I'm not sure if he used a condom. That was the furthest of my concerns when his gun was pressed to my head.

I am at least two weeks late for my period, and as I look at the swirling bile in the toilet, I realize I'm in serious shit. How the fuck do I fix this? Can I go through with an abortion? What do I tell Neil? I fall back to my ass as sobs tear through my chest, shattering the silence in the washroom. I am in so much shit.

I need to go to the pharmacy and buy some tests, then take it from there. I just don't know where to take it from there. What do I do? I get up slowly and sob again when the room spins. My family is going to kill me, and I could never admit what Adam did to me.

I quickly change out of my school uniform and make my way downstairs. No one is home yet, so I can leave with no questions being asked. I can't fucking deal with questions right now.

The drive into town is filled with tears, and my body feels like I'm walking through quicksand. I can barely breathe. The pharmacy is thankfully empty, and I thank whoever the fuck it was that invented self-checkout. I leave the place with five tests and somehow get my ass back home in one piece.

After sitting on the toilet and peeing on two of the five tests, I pace my bedroom for the two minutes needed. Two minutes of pure torture and the worst kind of anxiety I have ever felt. I run over every scenario in my head, and I know without a doubt, if I'm pregnant, I will have to terminate it. If there is even a slim chance of it being Adam's, I could never raise it. I wouldn't be able to love it like it deserved.

My walk back to the washroom feels like the end of my life as I know it. If I am pregnant, there's a chance this child is Neil's, and terminating that feels impossible. I don't know when it happened or how, but my heart belongs to him, and having his child would be amazing. Am I ready right now to have children? Of course not, but I could make it work, and even though my family would be disappointed, they would help me, and I know Neil would be a great dad.

It's heartbreaking to think I would destroy that. Could I destroy that?

I walk to the counter and close my eyes, calming my

breathing. Whatever the little plastic stick says is going to change me forever, I know it. I open them, and what I see sends me straight to my knees.

NEIL

She didn't want to worry me. My mom thought by holding back all the problems she was having with Charlotte and keeping me in the dark would mean one less child to argue with. That's exactly what she said to me, and it broke my heart.

I could've helped Charlotte, convinced her that being home with Mom was for the best, and I could've focused on being a better brother. I could've stopped her from going to Whitsborough by being with her more often, and just maybe she'd still be alive. Mom said Charlotte was stealing her pills, and she had an idea for a while but didn't want to believe it.

My fist hits the steering wheel and a string of curses are screamed into the interior of my car. I could've been the one person that changed the course of the Jones family history. That also means I would've never reconnected with Ivy and the feelings I have right now wouldn't exist. I can't imagine them never existing.

My phone pings and my heart clenches, knowing it's her.

Ivy: Hey. Can we meet up?

Me: Miss me?

Ivy: It's important.

The serious tone of her message has me sitting up straight, and I wonder if she's finally ready to admit everything about Charlotte.

Me: Where?

Ivy: The strip.

Something doesn't feel right, and I have a terrible sense of foreboding as I start my car. The drive back into Whitsborough will be a quick one.

Chapter Twenty-Six

Ivy

February in Whitsborough is usually a mix of semi-spring weather and bitter winter cold. Today is milder than usual, the air holding the scent of Spring. It's a tease though, because we'll be buried in snow many times over by the time Spring finally arrives.

The rumble of an approaching car breaks me out of my thoughts, and I watch as Neil pulls up beside me, his forehead wrinkled in concern. I get out of the car as he gets out of his, meeting each other in the middle.

He tugs me in and wraps his arms around me, his scent a soothing balm to my anxious insides. The overwhelming need to touch him has me unzipping his puffy jacket to bury my nose against his chest. My hands slide up under his shirt and he shivers from the icy feel of them.

"Are you okay?" he whispers into my ear.

"I just need to feel you right now," I murmur against his chest.

He pulls me in tighter and I can feel him hardening against my stomach. I know I shouldn't be doing this, but I want him. Just one more time before he goes back to hating me. I know it'll be the last time, so I'm about to make it count.

I run my hand between us and my fingers skim over his abs, skating down to his fly.

"Ivy." His voice turns raspy with the warning. "Don't start something you can't finish."

What he doesn't understand is that I need to finish, and I want to do it while he's so fucking deep inside of me.

My hand continues south, and when his hard length presses into my palm, I grip it tight. He groans and I'm suddenly pushed against my car, his cock grinding into me.

He grabs my chin roughly and tips my head back. "It's fucking chilly," he growls as he undoes his pants. "I can't be blamed for any shrinkage."

I open my mouth to laugh, but his lips catch the sound as his tongue thrusts inside. It ignites something hot in my core, stealing any conscious thought from my mind. I shove his hands away and finish dropping his fly, then switch our positions, shoving him against the car.

"Whoa," he breathes out but grins. The only thing I need is for him to replace the last asshole who forced himself inside of me.

I undo my jacket, ripping it off my arms and throwing it to the ground. His golden eyes alight with flame as my core clenches in anticipation.

Thank God for track pants. I sigh with relief as I drop them around my ankles and stand in front of Neil, completely bare. He's stroking himself in long, languid motions, panting heavily, his breath coming out in wispy puffs.

Neil's cock is beautiful, so thick and so fucking long. The way he stretches me is so exquisite, I want that but I want it rough. I flip around and bend forward, placing my hands on the hood of his car as the heat from the motor running keeps my fingers from freezing. I look over my shoulder and raise my brow.

"Make it hurt, Jones." Then I toss him a grin and add, "Don't fucking waste it."

He's behind me in seconds, one hand between my shoulder blades, pushing me down, and the other to line himself up. He slams himself in as far as he can go and I scream, the sound echoing back at us.

"So fucking tight," he groans as he pulls out a bit and then roughly thrusts back in.

"More," I pant, needing to feel the pain but knowing it's coming from Neil. The sensation of being filled by him slowly erases Dean and Adam.

He finally gets himself fully seated inside of me as I arch my back, grinding into him.

"Baby." He reaches around me and slips his fingers through my folds, finding that tightened nub. "Let's soak my cock up."

Fuck. The way he talks and how he works me perfectly… It's like I was made to be fucked by Neil. His thrusts are rough that my hands slip across the metal hood, my eyes rolling into the back of my head. The noises coming from my mouth sound animalistic, and my pussy is indeed soaking his fucking cock.

"I'm going to come!" I scream just as the wave crests and hauls me under, drowning me in pleasure.

"Fuck, fuck, fuck," he pants and then pulls himself out to come on the ground at our feet. Right, he still thinks he can stop the risk of a pregnancy. He's in for a shock.

"Damn," I mutter as I pull up my pants. "I came here to tell you something, not to fuck you in the middle of the road."

"What is it?" His eyes crinkle with concern as he tucks himself away.

"Look, it's my fault. I had some shit happen and the thing I was supposed to do… that thing we talked about? I forgot."

"Ivy." He shakes his head with confusion as he zips his jacket back up. "You're not making any sense. Are you still sick?"

He bends to pick up my jacket and hands it to me, the care etched into his features nearly breaking me. "I was sick, but it wasn't a bug." I shut my eyes and prepare for Armageddon. "I'm pregnant."

Quick and painless.

He stands there, unmoving, and completely silent. It's better than my reaction and the screaming I did while on my knees.

"It's mine?" This is what I was expecting.

"I don't know." I'm surprised how level my voice is as agony sweeps through him, making him wince.

His face falls as he looks at his feet. "I know we weren't exclusive, but you were fucking other people?"

"Yeah," I lie, because I can't tell him what really happened.

"Wow," he breathes out, and then his face morphs into one of anger. Anger I can deal with. "And to think I was falling for you. Why the fuck did I let myself do that? Especially knowing what type of person you are." His words hurt, but I prepared myself for the vitriol. "Who is it?" he demands.

"That's not what's important." I shake my head, trying my damnedest to keep it together just a little longer.

"Yes, it is!" he screams, and the noise startles me. "I just fucked you like you were mine! Only mine!"

"I don't belong to anyone." *I want to belong to him.*

I'm shocked to see his eyes build with tears as he sucks his bottom lip in between his teeth to stop the tremors. His pain is going to decimate me.

"You do belong to me, Ivy Greene." Finally, a tear escapes and rolls down his cheek. "You just can't face it."

"I think the sooner *you* face reality, the better." I can still feel him between my legs as his scent lingers on my clothes, and yet, his heart is in my hands, bleeding out at my feet.

"What are you going to do?" His chest rises and falls rapidly as he tries to stop his flow of tears. "With the baby?"

"I'm not keeping it." I keep my cool facade even though I'm dying on the inside.

"Of course." He laughs at the sky. "You're a murderer after all."

I knew that was coming as well. I thought I was prepared to hear those words, and I thought I could let it go, knowing why he's saying them, but my heart breaks anyway.

"I should go." I turn and head back to my car because there's no point in staying here any longer. What we had is done, and he'll go right back to hating me for the murderer I am.

"Ivy!" he calls out to me. I turn and look at him, his golden eyes simmering with rage. "You're dead to me now."

You're dead to me now. I understand why I would be, and I would feel the same way, but it still fucking hurts. Those words keep echoing in my head as I get in the car and start it up. I hope they do for the rest of my life to remind me of what I've done.

As I leave the strip and Neil behind, a sudden thought comes to me. Here in Whitsborough, you need an adult to sign a waiver for any medical procedure, and since I won't be eighteen for another few months, I need a fucking adult. I guess that leaves me with two options. One: I tell my parents, or two: I go straight to the piece of shit who raped me.

Two looks better at this point.

"Hey, Molly." I'm waiting at her locker the following week.

It's been a week of hell without being able to talk to Neil, but I keep reminding myself I've dealt with pain worse than this.

"Oh! Hi, Ivy." She looks around with apprehension before leaning in. "I'm not supposed to talk to you," she whispers like the fucking loser she is.

"Yeah, that's really unfortunate, and honestly, I would like to keep it that way. The thing is… your daddy caused a big problem and now he has to fix it."

"My dad?" Her mouth looks like a mechanical contraption you'd find in those old-ass clocks with all the metal gleaming.

"Yeah." I widen my eyes and nod my head like I'm talking to a toddler. "I need you to tell him to get in contact with me."

"Why?"

"He's been a naughty boy." I make her take down my number to pass along to her father. "Tell him time is of the importance."

Then I turn my back on her confused face and stride to my locker. Carmelo and Cam are there, horsing around as usual, and it's grating on my last nerve today. To be that carefree, not worrying about harassing men and never being raped by cops, must be fucking nice.

"Move!" I snarl at them, making them break apart.

"Why the bitchy attitude?" Carmelo asks as he raises his brow to Cam.

Idiots.

"Maybe she's hangry," Cam chirps, and I feel the rage boil.

"Can you both just leave me alone? I don't have the luxury to fuck around all the time."

"Okay, then." Carmelo kisses my cheek, the action making me soften a fraction. "Love you. See you later." He heads toward the front entrance, respecting the space I asked for.

Cam though, stays behind, staring at me. "What?" I snap.

"Are you okay?"

"Yeah." I exhale, trying desperately not to say something I'll regret. Then I blurt, "No."

"Tell me what you need." His sincere expression crashes through the wall of my anger.

"To go back in time and change my whole life," I moan and fall against my locker.

"Why would you do that?" He leans beside me, his smile sweet. "You're the strongest person I know, and it's all because of the hardships you've had to endure."

This is why I love my cousins. They can be boneheads, but when I need them, I don't have far to look. I nod and try to smile, but he sees through it because he hauls me in and smothers me in a tight hug before kissing the top of my head.

"Hang in there, Ivy. God does things for a reason. Don't change his course and just roll with it. You're only given as much as you can handle."

Don't change my course, just roll with it, and as much as I can handle. Sounds like something straight out of a self-help book, and maybe, just like he's saying, it came just when I needed it.

"Thanks, Cam," I mumble into his chest.

"Okay, gotta get back to fucking around." He tosses me a grin. "Call me if you need more Cam proverbs."

Then he disappears out of sight as I mull over his words. Do I run the course?

Chapter Twenty-Seven

I miss him.

It's been ten days and Neil hasn't strayed far from my mind. If I keep this child and it's his, what happens then? Will he change his mind? Will he want me again? The only thing these questions are proving is that I'm in love with Neil Jones and I've fucked everything up.

My phone pings and I dive across the bed, anxiously hoping it's him.

Dean: I made a compilation video. It's one I think showcases my cinematic talent and one that will destroy your family. Your mother's email is the same, correct?

Me: Don't do that.

Dean: Take a peek and let me know what you think.

I click on the link provided and nearly pass out when I see he's made a web page. There are photos of me in all different stages of undress and video links for people's 'viewing pleasure.' It feels like each of my organs is shutting down in quick succession and I may very well be dying.

None of the photos show my face, but my family will know it's me with one look. My hair, my skin tone, and my body shape. It's easy to decipher.

Dean: It's not yet viewable, but that's just a click away.

Me: What the fuck do you want?

Dean: What did we talk about regarding a young lady's language?

Me: What do you want from me?

Dean: Not sure there's anything you can do, really.

Me: I am holding up my end of the bargain and keeping my mouth shut!

He doesn't answer me, so I go back to the link. I click on each of the videos and finally come across one I wish I didn't. He has me tied up with his tie and he's beating me with a large wooden ruler. That was the time he caught me with the edge and it broke my skin. My ass cheek still has the scar.

My phone pings again and I quickly pull open the messages, seeing a number I don't recognize.

Unknown: What the fuck are you telling my daughter?

Adam Van Dyke.

I'm so fucking fed up with predators and the hold they have over me. Why am I letting this happen? I can take back my power. If I go to the police, I have the means and my family has the clout to destroy Adam's career. The same goes for Dean. He would lose his prestigious position and his fucking reputation.

Me: You should've worn a condom, you dumb fuck.

I wait for twenty minutes and then forty-five, but still

no answer. Maybe now someone else can fret just as much as I have been since my ass got back to Whitsborough. Fuck that, I've been fretting since I was shipped off to New York. I fall back on the bed with a sigh. It feels good to have someone else do it for a change.

That's right, Adam Van Dyke, you may have fathered your daughter a baby sister or brother. Now what?

"Ivy!" Dad calls out at the bottom of the stairs. "Come eat!"

My stomach growls and I laugh. Already this little thing is a fucking monster. If I'm not puking my guts up, I'm stuffing my face, and to me, that sounds like a Neil/Ivy combo. I really hope it is anyway.

My mouth fills with saliva as I walk into the kitchen, my eyes drifting shut as I inhale the scent of lasagna.

"I wish someone would react to me like Ivy does pasta."

"Nana!" I exclaim as my eyes snap open, and I run to Nana Sharla for a hug. "You're home."

"Only for a day. I fly back out to Tuscany tomorrow." She pats my back.

"Why can't you stay longer?" Mother shoots me a look and Dad's eyes widen behind her. It takes a lot of effort not to laugh at their reactions.

"I can't leave the restaurant for that long." She chuckles. "I just came to check on my grandbabies and make sure they're healthy."

Nana Sharla is still the same as she was in all the photos I've seen of her when my dad was growing up. Short, bright red hair, and enormous hazel eyes. Her skin is still smooth, even if there are deep laugh lines in some spots. She's beautiful, and even though she's a handful, we all still love her craziness.

She owns and operates a small Italian restaurant in Tuscany and is living her dream life. Dad says he thinks she has a man too, but it's hard to determine because Nana is wary of men. Again, something strange happened with our grandfather a long time ago.

"Saxon!" she exclaims when my brother comes into the room. "You're going to be taller than your father! You've shot up a few inches since I saw you at Christmas."

I give Saxon a once-over and Nana is right. He really is maturing and growing up. He's been looking after me more lately too.

"Hey, Nana." He sits at the table.

"Okay, Nana!" Dahlia runs into the kitchen with a few Barbies. "These are my favorites now. Let's braid their hair."

"Okay, angel," Nana says to her, and everyone sits at the table.

I look around at all of us and realize I really have a great family. They would still love me despite my mistakes. I admitted to killing my best friend and they're still here. Maybe one day, I can convince Neil I am worth loving despite my mistakes too.

NEIL

Her street is now ingrained in my mind. I've driven it obsessively, and I bet if blindfolded, I would navigate it perfectly.

She's pregnant.

There's a life growing inside of her and it might be mine. Maybe a child with dark hair, a bright smile, and those ocean eyes. The thought of her aborting it leaves me feeling stricken with grief.

Another mystery lost to death.

I want her to keep the baby and I want her to tell me who else the father may be. I can't decide for her, it's her body, and I would have to support her regardless, but I want to give it a chance.

It's been three days since she told me, and I've been living each one on autopilot. Then, when my thoughts become consuming, I drive along her street, hoping to catch a glimpse of her to calm the turmoil inside of me. As much as I'm being a fucking stalker, I still haven't seen her and I'm worried. Is she recovering from her procedure? Do her parents know?

Work has been the same. No one has mentioned Ivy, whether she's sick or not, and I can't just fucking ask because that will look suspicious. Emmett has been coming by more often to talk to Vin and Ember. I heard him saying something about training Carmelo in New York, which he fucking needs.

There's been no talk of Ivy though, and I would know because I've become an obsessive stalker. She could be carrying my fucking child.

I turn on her street again and notice a cop car coming in the other direction. I'm suddenly on alert because I've never seen a cop car on this street before. What the fuck happened?

I pull over about three houses before the Greenes and watch as the cop car approaches their house, slowing down to a crawl as he drives by. My skin breaks out in goose bumps with just how creepy he looks.

He drives by me and doesn't give my car a second look. I get a good look at him though. He's older, maybe late forties, with salt-and-pepper hair. He has a scar that runs through the beard on his left cheek, which stands out on his face. That was all I could get in the quick drive-by, but something is telling me he's doing exactly what I am, only not for the same reasons.

What could the Greenes have done to piss the cops off? Emmett is the fucking chief. Maybe they need me to keep a watch on shit because they don't know that's happening, right? They're obviously busy as fuck, and there may be a pregnant girl in the house. I should be here.

I throw the seat back and settle in for a bit. Might as well make sure things are okay before I go home to bed. You can never be too sure of what's in your neighborhood, even this upscale one. Isn't there a statistic that says something like, in every neighborhood, there's at least a few pedophiles? Whitsborough may be small and boring, but fuck, pedophiles probably like that.

It's midnight when I get home and I'm staring at my fucking phone, deciding if I should message her or not.

She should know that it looked like a cop was scoping out her house today.

But if I do that, she'll know I was there doing the same thing.

Only I have a reason to!

I lie back on my bed with a groan. Why did I say all those things to her at the strip? I was so angry, and I still am, but I shouldn't have been so fucking hateful. She's alone and dealing with something that will change her life forever, and I basically abandoned her.

The only thing truly holding me back is the fact that she was with someone else while she was with me. It's bothering me just as much as the pregnancy itself, and I know the way my fucking brain works. I won't be able to let it go.

Is she still fucking them?

What made her want to fuck someone else anyway?

We were amazing together.

I could pop by her school tomorrow. I mean, it's mostly for her, and to see if everything looks okay. Maybe she was fucking a classmate and now they know she's pregnant. What if they want to shove her down a flight of stairs? Or trip her as she's leaving?

I think she needs me to be close by to monitor things.

My fake cough into the phone this morning was fucking pathetic. Vin knew it too, but told me to stay home and rest regardless. But, no can do. I need to make sure his daughter is okay. So here I am, sitting in a high school parking lot, watching as students take their time getting to class. About five minutes after the bell rings, I see Ivy pull up.

She parks her car closer to the entrance and gets out. Her hair shines in different shades of brown and red, and her skin is paler than usual, but she has this rosy glow to her cheeks. She's so fucking beautiful. Her face is a mask of indifference, but her eyes are filled with the fear she's holding inside. I want to get out and pull her into my arms, tell her I'm here and I won't let anything happen to her, but then she'll probably slap me across the face and kick me in the balls.

With her backpack slung over her shoulder, she saunters to the front doors, her ass swinging in that fucking kilt, making me rock-fucking-hard. No other female has ever given me these primal responses and she's probably the only one that ever will. As fucked-up as our situation is, Ivy and I were made for each other. Does she feel that too?

When the coast is clear, I get out of my car and head around the side of the school. There's a large track and baseball diamond to the left, then what looks to be a building for the athletics department. Off to the right is another building that looks like a church, and it has a gigantic glass dome on top. The sign on the front says Precious Blood Arts Department. There are a few students walking toward both buildings, but mostly, it's quiet. I find a bench and wait out the day, and if she sees me, I'll admit everything I'm doing.

I hope she doesn't see me.

When lunch rolls around, I decide to head back to my car, not really wanting to look like an older creep scoping out high school kids. It's a waste to sit at her school and wait for her, especially when I don't know where inside the enormous building she is, but my need to see her outweighs any logic. I drive to her house instead, to wait until she gets home and make sure she looks okay.

Her street is dead, as per usual, and the gate to her house is shut tight. No one's home and therefore nobody should come around, except me.

But I have a fucking reason to!

I park in the same spot I was in the night before and relax in the seat. Maybe I should've brought something to read. I turn on my podcast and listen to a recent episode of true crime, trying to pass the time.

Around ten to three, I finally see Ivy's car pull up, her gates open, and she pulls into her driveway. Fucking tinted windows didn't show me shit. She's the first one home, which means she's home alone. I should stick around longer until one of her parents gets home just in case she needs something. I turn on another episode of the podcast and recline my seat for a bit.

It takes about two hours for another vehicle to turn on the street and my heart jumps when I see it's the cop car again. What the fuck is going on? Are the Greenes under investigation?

The car once again slows down in front of Ivy's house, this time stopping briefly to look at the closed gate, and then drives toward me. This time, when he passes my car, his head turns and we lock eyes, his narrowing slightly as his nostrils flare. He looks slightly deranged and there's so much anger in his eyes.

I guess I'm staying here longer.

CHAPTER TWENTY-EIGHT

Ivy

Dean has been quiet since I dared him to publish the website a few nights ago. I decided to take my power back and taunted him to do it. Once the initial fear was replaced by logic, I realized what that website meant. I'd love to see how the cops would react, knowing I'm severely underage in all those photos and videos. I should've grown a backbone months ago.

Officer Adam Van Dyke is another issue. He's been calling me and leaving me weird voice messages. He sounded drunk in each one while begging me to get rid of my child. As the messages went on, he got increasingly angry, and the last one I received was of him threatening to rape me again. Well, Officer Van Dyke, that's fucking stupid.

I kept all the messages because if he tries to attack me again, I will send everything to my Uncle Emmett. Beyond that, I am physically okay, save for the morning sickness, and I am still debating what to do with this pregnancy. It literally fluctuates by the hour, and I know my window of choice is closing fast. The prospect of being a single mother is scary and disappointing because I've always wanted what my parents have.

Each day, I spend about half an hour in front of the mirror, trying to see if my stomach has grown, but the only change I've noticed are my breasts. They have literally ballooned. My bras don't fit, so I've changed to sports bras. My stomach is still flat—probably because of throwing up most of what I eat—and my clothes still fit me. I don't know how much longer I have though.

Mother and Dad have been busy every day and rarely get home before six. Mother looks exhausted most of the time and has been spending almost every weekend in New York. I feel like maybe something big is happening with her business there. Whatever it is, it takes a lot of her time and energy.

Carmelo is training now with Uncle Emmett three weekends out of a month, and he's excited to learn about his birth father. Uncle Emmett knew him the best and the place where they're training belonged to him at one time. The Compound, as they call it, is a huge underground structure that houses over twenty people and has a fight ring with a massive training facility. Now, Mother and Uncle Trent own it. I've only ever been there a few times.

Saxon has become more comfortable with hanging out and we've settled into watching a few Netflix series together. I know he can sense something up with me, but he doesn't pry for any information. He doesn't really feel the need to figure it out and that's what I love about him. He says school is a pain in the ass and he wants to convince Mother and Dad to let him be homeschooled. The thing is, Saxon is extremely smart, and it's scary.

Recently, his grades have been dropping, and he's looking more and more disinterested in school. When I pressed him about it, he insisted he just hates his school and the teachers are dumbasses. I thought maybe he was being bullied because Saxon is different, but he assures me he is not. To put it in his words, "I wish someone would."

I think he's bored and the material being taught to him is too simple. Maybe he needs to be bumped up a grade.

My phone pings on the bed and I reach for it amid a flurry of emotions. Excitement, anxiety, and worry race through me. I want it to be Neil, but I dread that it may be Dean, and I'm annoyed it could be Adam.

Annoyance wins.

Officer Asshole: We should meet up. I want to help you with whatever you choose to do.

This is a complete one-eighty and absolutely unbelievable.

Officer Asshole: I know I've been harassing you, so I just want the chance to make it right. I've stopped drinking, which has led to many of the mistakes I made, like what I did to you.

He's blaming alcohol. What a fucking idiot.

Me: Fuck off, Adam.

I put my phone on silent and lie back on the bed beside Saxon, pigging out on chips and soda.

I won't let any man make choices for me. I only want one to love me through them.

It's well into the night when I hear Saxon's phone alerting us to our surveillance. It's Friday and we're the only ones home. We're not expecting anyone.

"What is it?" Saxon asks as I open his phone.

The app is blinking on the camera, showing movement,

and I expect to find a raccoon in our garbage, but I'm nearly swallowing my heart when I see a hooded figure standing outside the gate. They're not moving, just looking in, and by the body build, I don't think it's Neil. They don't move, just continue to look through the gate and wait for something to happen.

My phone lights up with a call and I curse the moment I put it on silent.

"Hello?"

"Ivy?" Mother sounds panicked. "Call Uncle Emmett."

"Okay," I whisper, keeping her on the line and using Saxon's phone to call him. "Who is that?"

"I don't know. Hurry, Emmett," she snaps as she listens to the dial tone sounding from Saxon's phone.

"Hello?" Uncle Emmett's sleepy voice fills the speakerphone.

"There's someone weird at our gate," Saxon says into the phone, his face stoic. "Get over here fast." Then he hangs up and switches back to the camera feed.

Now the guy is looking right up at it, unmoving, his face shrouded in darkness.

"Mom." The fear in my voice is clear.

"Don't worry, he can't get in," she tries to reassure us but can't hide the sound of her panic.

Suddenly, the figure looks to the right and then runs off in the opposite direction. A few seconds later, Uncle Emmett's car pulls up, and he gets out with his gun drawn, running in the same direction.

"Do not open the gate," Mother growls. "Not even for your uncle. We are on our way home."

"Okay," I mumble and hang up.

"Who the fuck was that?" Saxon jumps up from the bed to look out my window because it faces the driveway.

"I don't know." But I may have an idea. Adam? Dean? Someone hired to keep a watch on us?

Whoever it is, they're being blatant about it and know we have cameras. I'm suddenly aware that all my actions can have dire consequences. Not just for me, but my family too.

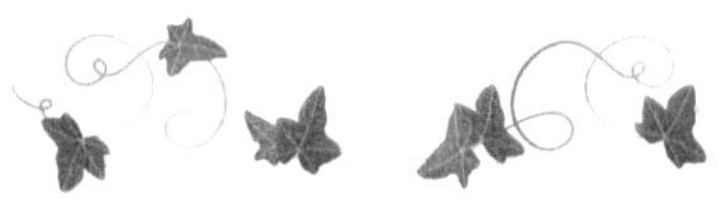

Mother and Dad get home about five hours later and the house is in a bit of an uproar. Not only is my Uncle Emmett here, but so are Uncle Travis and Aunt Adri. I can hear them in the kitchen having a hushed conversation that's freaking me out. So, I do what any normal person would do and try to eavesdrop.

The kitchen doors are shut, but there's a small gap between them, and if you stand near that, you can hear just enough. I've done it many times and listened to how much my parents moaned about their crazy kids.

First, I hear Uncle Emmett saying he saw the figure running, but he lost him farther up the street.

"It was definitely a man?" Dad asks.

"Yes," Uncle Emmett answers. "Average height and weight."

So not Neil for sure.

"Could it be Head retaliation?" Uncle Travis asks, and I hear Mother hum.

"I had a hit last weekend that uncovered one of their secret pockets in Manhattan. It could be."

Hit? Head? Secret pocket? What the fuck are they talking about? They sound like the fucking Sopranos sitting in my kitchen. This must be business lingo. There's no other explanation.

"What about Charlotte's older brother?" Aunt Adri asks, and my heart almost explodes. "I saw him on camera around the school the other day."

What?

"Nah." Dad sounds unbothered. "He has a thing for Ivy and likes to watch out for her. I think he's harmless."

"Maybe we should keep an eye on him too though," Uncle Emmett cuts in. "Just in case."

"Okay," Mother concedes. "Trent is digging up the Head I outed last weekend and will let me know what he finds. I can't go back to New York until this is all straightened out. I won't leave my kids in danger."

"If someone needs to go," Uncle Travis interjects, "Vin and I will do it."

I hear chairs scrape along the kitchen tile and rush for the stairs. I get to the top when I hear the doors open.

"All I keep thinking about is someone knew my children were here without us," Mother moans as I duck back behind the wall.

"Ivy is almost eighteen, and they did the right thing. Our children are smart," Dad assures her.

"They are smart," Uncle Emmett agrees, "and there's always someone close by.

"I can't help but think someone will start picking off

my family again," Mother whispers.

Again?

"We'll figure it out," Dad says. "We won't have history repeat itself. Our children will not be another Debra and Scott."

That's Mom's aunt and uncle, and they used to own this house before they passed away. Or were they fucking murdered?

Chapter Twenty-Nine

By Sunday, the house is bustling with activity and the nervous tension is potent in the air. Mother hired a surveillance company to come in and look over the cameras, Dad has been on the phone with Uncle Emmett constantly, and there have been cops sitting in our driveway for the last few days. Thankfully, Adam hasn't been one of them.

At the end of the night, Mother and Dad call me and Saxon into the kitchen to tell us we won't be going to school this week and to not leave the house for any reason.

"Why?" Saxon questions, his face filled with suspicion. "Who's after us?"

"No one is after us," Dad scoffs. "We're just a target for break-ins because of where we live."

"To come to that conclusion," Saxon begins, his impeccable logic about to come into play. "There must've been break-ins recently, but I haven't heard of any."

They look at him dumbfounded, and I snort. "He has a point."

"And the cops being on our property like the Men in Black is also fucking strange." Saxon leans back in his seat.

"Watch your fucking mouth," Mother says to him, and I snort again.

"Ivy, don't encourage it," Dad chastises.

"So, how long are we on lockdown?" I press as I cross my arms.

"This week," Dad answers. "Then everything will be back to normal."

Both Saxon and I nod as we get up from the table.

"Ivy." Mother reaches out to touch my arm. "Can you chill for a minute?"

I look at her as my heart thumps wildly and sweat gathers under my sweater. "Sure."

They wait for Saxon to leave the kitchen, and then she looks at me pointedly. "What's been going on with the Jones kid?"

"Neil?"

"That's the one," Dad cuts in as he leans against the wall.

"Nothing."

"He's been seen around your school, and we know he's been here," Mother states as her eyes narrow and her brow slowly rises. I know they're not mad, more curious, and this is probably something Uncle Emmett asked them to do so he could clear Neil off the suspect list.

"It wasn't him." I shrug. "I know his body type, and besides, we no longer talk."

"Is everything okay?" Dad perks up, his face becoming

serious. I know if he felt like Neil was doing something wrong, he would fire him in an instant.

"Just didn't work out," I stress as I roll my eyes. "Nothing dramatic."

"All right." Mom's eyes soften.

I get up from the table and head out of the kitchen. No matter what went down between Neil and me, he's still a great guy, but now I need to know why the fuck he was at my school. Does he want to discuss things, or is he looking to berate me some more?

NEIL

Ivy's street has been filled with cops the entire weekend, and I am *this* close to storming the fucking place and demanding to know what's going on. Friday night, I stayed in with Amelia and played Scrabble, one fucking night off. Then Saturday and Sunday were fucking crazy.

Is she okay? I've had my phone in my hand with text messages to her typed out but too fucking chicken to press send. Something was going down at the Greene residence and now it makes sense why that cop was watching it closely the week before.

Today, I will find out what happened, even if it means asking Vincent himself. I don't care if he figures out that I'm fucking stalking his house. I need to know Ivy is okay.

I get inside the building and stop short when I see the scar-faced cop standing in the hallway next to Vin's office. His brows crash together when he sees me, and I know he recognizes me from our close encounter outside of the Greene residence.

I continue walking and pass by him, both of us never breaking eye contact, and knock on Vincent's door.

"Yeah!" Vincent calls out, sounding a little irritated.

I go inside and shut the door behind me. "Mr. Greene—"

"It's Vin, Neil. You can call me Vin," he cuts me off and looks up from his laptop.

"Why do we have cops here?"

He closes his laptop and settles into his chair. "Take a seat."

My heart begins to spear up in my throat as my mind

races with different scenarios, all of them involving Ivy.

"We had an incident at the house on Friday night," he begins as he rubs his fingers into his temples, frustration written all over his face. "Someone was creeping around and caught on camera."

My mouth dries up and my stomach sinks. "Who was home?"

"Ivy and Saxon," he replies as his eyes meet mine.

"They're okay?" My voice betrays me and cracks.

"Yes." He smiles, the expression not quite meeting his eyes. "They're okay. We just haven't found the guy yet and are unsure of what he wanted. We're just playing it safe, and all the kids are home from school this week."

"Oh." I look back out to the hallway. "Is that cop out there a family friend?"

"Adam?" Vin looks around me at the cop, who is indiscreetly looking inside the office. "He's been stationed here to make sure everyone is on the up and up. Not really a family friend. His daughter and Ivy used to be close."

"Oh, okay." Still doesn't explain why he was outside of their house, and I can't shake the feeling this guy is up to something. "So, no investigation into your family then for hidden bodies on the property. Got it." I don't want to bring it up and cause trouble if it's truly nothing at all.

"What?" His eyes widen.

"Nothing, I'm just playing." I wave him off as his face pales a little. "What do you need me to do today?"

"Answer emails and take phone messages. I don't want to talk to anyone unless it's my wife, children, or brothers," he mumbles, his face already in his laptop.

"No problem."

I leave his office, and once again, stare down with the scar-faced douche. He has a look about him that screams corrupt, I don't know why. Regardless of how I feel about cops, this one stinks.

Once in my little office, I shut the door and power up my computer. The hairs on the back of my neck stand as I look over my shoulder to find scar-face walking by and looking at me.

I dare the fucker to come in here. I have so much energy from worrying and stressing out, and I would love to spend it all over his face. He doesn't come in though, and that's a fucking shame. He continues to cross in front of my window three more times in the hour though. Why does it feel like he's watching me more than the others?

It's already time for lunch when I finally finish all the emails, and I'm starving. I do my usual routine and walk around the office, asking everyone what they'd like to eat for lunch. The cop is watching me as I circle back around and head to Vin's office. This time, I don't look at him as I walk by, but I can feel him watching me closely.

"Lunch?" I ask as I poke my head in Vin's office. "Looks like everyone wants sandwiches."

"Sounds good to me. I'll take a meatball." He tosses me the company credit card.

I won't say I convinced everyone to want the sandwich place because it's conveniently near where Ivy lives and I need to talk to her.

I get to my car and finally find my balls to send her a text.

Me: Can we talk?

It takes a few minutes, but she finally texts back.

Ivy: Can't. On lockdown.

Fuck.

Me: Everything good?

Ivy: Same old.

Me: Okay.

She doesn't text me back and I'm disappointed as I drive to the deli, passing her place on the way, and when I come back, passing it once more. Everything looks good and the gates are shut. I breathe a sigh of relief as I head back to the office.

She's pissed and that's understandable. I'm simply happy she's okay. She said, 'Same old.' Does that mean the same as the last time I saw her? Like still pregnant?

I bring the food inside and look around for the cop, but I'm pleasantly surprised when he's nowhere to be found… until I question Linda, Vin's secretary, about it.

She gives me a look and says, "He left soon after you."

Is that motherfucker following me?

Chapter Thirty

This show Saxon is forcing me to watch is doing nothing to distract me from my frantic thoughts. I want to make sure Neil is safe, as well as Amelia and Shay, but I can't do anything from this house. They're sitting at home while a menacing predator lingers around their house. My warning will do nothing to help them if Adam decides to retaliate against me.

This child inside of me is my only bargaining chip, and if I agree to end it, then he says he will leave me alone. I would only have the word of a rapist to rely on though. He may never actually leave me alone. Maybe he will decide raping me is a great fucking pastime, and since he got away with it once, why not keep doing it?

My dilemma? Is the tiny life inside of me worth more than all the others here, living and breathing? Who holds priority? Are Shay and Amelia less important because they aren't my flesh and blood? What about my family? Do they deserve to live in constant fear for a life not yet born into this world?

Do I even want to bring a child into this turmoil? I can never guarantee this child a complete family unit. I may very well be a single mother like my grandmother was to my mother, and this life may be hard. Too hard for such an innocent child.

"Saxon." I turn my head and look at my brother. "What's the perfect family?"

"An imperfect one," he answers immediately. "Families with flaws and hardships end up being stronger and more resilient."

"That makes sense. Like our family."

"Nothing like our family." He laughs as his head turns from the screen in front of us to look at me. "Maybe Mom and Dad's families, but ours was a walk in the park."

I want to scream at his answer because nothing I've been through has ever been a walk through the fucking park. From the moment Nana Jenna died, my life has been a never-ending uphill battle—some of which was brought on by my own actions—but the abuse was never my decision.

At least Saxon's had an easy life and Dahlia too. Maybe if I bring this child into their lives, it will show them we are resilient, just like our parents. My hand absently strokes my flat belly as I try to imagine it growing big and round, filled with a moving little human.

"I'm tired," Saxon states and rolls off my bed. "I'm going to sleep."

"Okay."

He walks out and throws up the peace sign over his shoulder. I turn off my TV and roll over in bed. Neil is always on my mind, and right now, I hope he's okay.

Me: Is everything okay?

When I don't receive an answer, I try to cuddle into my

blankets and attempt to sleep. Then my phone pings and I am scrambling to see his answer, only it's not him.

Officer Asshole: Your boyfriend is a charmer. He told me all about fucking you.

What?

Officer Asshole: I think it's time we discuss what needs to be done.

Neil spoke to him? About me?

Me: Back off, Adam. I make my own decisions.

Thankfully, after that, my phone stays silent, and I finally fall into a fitful sleep.

Four days have gone by without a word from Neil. I need to get over to his house to check on them, just to make sure they're okay, and then I'll leave. Was Adam assigned to work on their security detail? Have they spoken about me some more?

Mother and Dad have been quiet, and no one else has been coming over to visit. Being trapped in this house is seriously an inconvenience to me right now. Dad just came home about half an hour ago, so I know Neil is home, and even though I messaged him—again—I am getting no reply. Are we back at square one?

Mother is still out, but that's been normal this week. She usually gets in after I've fallen asleep. I look out the window in my room and see a cop car sitting in the driveway. It's not impossible to get out of the house right now, but it will be difficult, and I'll have to walk my ass out in this cold weather.

I know all the blind spots of our surveillance, and I long ago created a getaway for the nights I wanted to party.

My fourteen-year-old self found out that if I go out through Saxon's bedroom window across the hall from me, it's about a four-foot drop to the first level roof over the kitchen exit to the backyard, and the camera located there points to the doorway only. I can shimmy down the column on the side of the roof and cut straight across the backyard to my hangout shed. This shed is flush with the fence that borders our property, and there's a slight gap that will bring me into my neighbor's backyard.

It's been years since I've attempted this, and I have obviously grown a few inches in that time, but I need to get the fuck out of here and see him. People have done more dangerous things for their true loves, right?

I dress myself in all black and pull my hoodie up over my head, then leave a note on my bed telling Dad I had to go see Neil and not to worry. He's going to worry regardless, but I need to do this. Thankfully, Saxon is in the shower when I enter his room and I tiptoe past the washroom door, then slowly open his window. I can't close it once I'm out, so I know my escape route will be found after this. I look out the window and giggle when the drop is much less than what I remembered. This is going to be easy as pie.

After I've hopped to the roof, I look back up at the window and let out my breath when I find it empty. It would suck to be caught at this point. I shimmy myself over the edge and wrap my legs around the column, sliding down to the ground. It's amazing how much easier it is to do this now. I run quickly across the backyard and squeeze myself between the shed and the fence, squealing when I run into thick cobwebs. I hate spiders.

Once I slip through the gap in the fence, I do a victory dance. I made it in one filthy piece. I look down at the black clothing and cringe when I see the dirt from the shed, but it doesn't matter because I'm free. This might've been the most troublesome part of the breakout, but the next part will be the most annoying, and I've always hated the cold. I pull my hoodie tighter and begin the journey I used to take almost daily a few years ago. Maybe along the way, I will feel close to Charlotte again.

Whitsborough really is filled with beautifully built homes and trees so tall they must be a couple of hundred years old. Even though they are bare of leaves because of winter, they still look majestic. Our streets are clean and lined with manicured lawns every summer. God forbid there's one yellow weed anywhere, and then the winters have perfectly plowed sidewalks, free of ice at all times. We're spoiled here.

It takes about thirty minutes to get to Neil's house from mine and the walk is slowly tiring me out, maybe because of my condition or lack of exercise lately. I'm dragging my feet and taking way longer than I should, but whatever, I'll enjoy my freedom while I have it.

I know the exact point where the scenery of Whitsborough changes. About halfway, the houses gradually become smaller, the lot sizes narrower, and the trees shorter. This doesn't mean it's no longer beautiful, simply different and still well-manicured. People in this neighborhood also take pride in their properties and maintain it well.

An intersection approaches and I remember it like yesterday. To my right brings me to Molly's house and straight ahead brings me to Charlotte's. I look down Molly's street and try to bring back that time when we were best friends, when life was so much easier. Unfortunately, it's foggy and too many horrible memories have replaced them since then.

I continue forward toward Neil's house and keep the sight of his roof in my eyesight until I am practically upon it. Then I do a quick scan of the street and grin when I don't find a cop car idling nearby.

The driveway is still the same, with a few cracks in the asphalt and the one pothole off to the left. It's almost like I'm transported back in time and I'm here to see my best friend, ready to cause some havoc. My chest squeezes and I take a deep breath to hold off the tears. They've been running easily lately.

I get to the front door and ring the doorbell, the wait making my stomach heavy with apprehension. Will he turn me away?

The door opens to reveal Shay's smiling face.

"Ivy!" she exclaims. "I thought I would never see you on our doorstep again."

Her words send a crushing blow of guilt to my chest, and I can't stop the tears this time.

"I'm so sorry," I choke out. "I'm so sorry for what I've done."

"Oh, no." She steps out to where I am and pulls me into her arms. "Ivy, we've never blamed you. We know it was an accident. It didn't change how much our family loves you."

Her words send me into incoherent sobs, and she stands there enduring the cold to comfort me. Her scent throws me back to three years ago when all I knew was the Jones' house and her cooking. Their laughter and the nights we would all play board games rushes through me. I didn't know how much I missed them until this very moment, and I feel ashamed I never came by before now.

"Come inside." She guides me inside the house. "I'll make cocoa."

My sobs slowly stop and the tears begin to dry as we head to the kitchen. Everyone looks safe here, and Adam is nowhere to be found. The stress I've been feeling these last few days disappears as I settle into a chair at the table.

"Ivy?" Neil's voice makes me freeze in my seat. He comes up beside me and leans on the table, looking down into my face. "Have you been crying?" He sounds like he cares, but then why hasn't he been answering me?

"She came by and I may have made her cry." Shay smiles at me. "Gosh, you look more and more like your mother every time I see you."

"Made her cry?" He's still looking at me. "Why?"

"Girl stuff." Shay waves him off and his eyes widen on my face.

He thinks I told her about the pregnancy. I can see the question in his eyes, so I shake my head. He visibly relaxes and plops down in the seat beside me, grabbing my hand and linking our fingers. Then he gives it a squeeze and chuckles, my head turning toward the sound.

"Aren't you on lockdown?" he murmurs so Shay doesn't hear.

"I escaped," I mumble before joining in on his laughter.

Shay turns toward us with hot mugs of cocoa.

"Young lady, I sure have missed that laugh." Her smile widens when she sees our linked hands.

Charlotte, please forgive me because I am in love with your brother, and I still love your family.

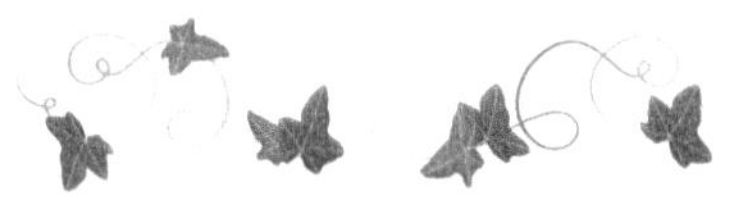

"Ivy." Neil paces the length of his bedroom. "Are you

ever going to tell me who else you were sleeping with?"

"Is it important?" I cover my face with my hands as I try to breathe through the anxiety. "It's not happening anymore. It was a onetime thing."

"Are you sure?" I lift my head from my hands to find his eyes begging me for the truth.

"I promise." I nod.

There's relief in his face, but I can also see the hurt. There's nothing I can do to take that away, and we were never exclusive. He falls onto his back on the bed beside me and runs his fingers over my back.

"We need to discuss the baby," he says, his voice lowering.

"Don't worry about anything," I assure him. "Let's just wait until it's born, and if it's yours, you can decide what you want to do."

He sits up and grabs my face between his hands. "I want to decide what to do right now. I don't care who fathered this child. I want it to still be mine, and I want *you* to be mine."

His face blurs as tears fill my eyes. "How?"

"I'll take care of you." His hand lands on my stomach. "Both of you."

I admit, I wanted to hear him say this, just like this, but for some reason, I am filled with guilt and remorse. He still doesn't know the truth about Charlotte and who the other man is.

If this relationship is going to work, it needs to be built on a foundation of trust, and we can't do that with lies unresolved. I need to come clean and beg him to somehow keep the information to himself.

I'm basically going to hand him a nuclear bomb and hope he does the right thing. I want to trust he'll see it my way, that he'll agree with me and we can move forward.

To prove it all though, I'll have to reveal the evidence I've kept hidden for three years, and then when he's done with it, I'll wait for his decision.

"I need to do a few things first," I plead for him to understand. "I need to find something to show you and then we can figure this out."

"What is it, Ivy?" His face falls. "Why can't we do this right now? Why are you always hiding something?"

I deserve that. I am always hiding something. I have my fucking reasons though, and I've been through too much for a girl my age, so I don't trust easily.

I want to snap at him and tell him to give me space, but I know he's trying to help, and I need to accept it. "I'm going to head home and sort some stuff out, and then we'll talk, okay?"

The look he gives me is filled with suspicion, and I nearly shrink from the scrutiny. "Ivy, do not leave here without sorting this out now. You don't need to go home and curl up to wallow alone. Let me help you."

His words feel like an attack, the words coated in condescension. He's trying to force me to do this right now, disregarding my feelings.

"Don't." He points into my face. "I see you retreating into yourself again. Why do you do that?"

"I need to go." I stand and reach for his door.

He slaps my hand away from the knob as I stare at him with shock. "Not until we figure this out."

"Don't touch me," I grit through my teeth, my emotions

changing in rapid succession. Anger, sadness, guilt, then back to anger.

"Ivy." He rears back from the look on my face. "Let me lov—"

"Don't!" I cut him off and wrench open his room door.

"Ivy!" he yells, but I'm already halfway down the stairs.

"Ivy?" I hear Shay, but slip on my shoes and run out of the house and down the driveway.

I just need space to figure out how to do this. Why does everything need to be sorted right now? There's so much he still doesn't know. Does he think he can just forgive it all?

He'll get my hopes up and then smash them down when he realizes he really can't forgive any of it. I can't take any more disappointment and shouldn't have to. I want him to decide our future after he learns everything. Is that wrong?

I turn onto the street, making my way back to the intersection and to the stop sign I saw a few hours ago that gave me pause—a small reminder of my childhood. The innocence I had back then was so viciously ripped away, and now I have to explain that to Neil.

My phone rings in my pocket as I stop at the corner of the street, pulling it out.

It's my dad calling, and I can imagine he's fucking pissed. I look up and down the street, swiping open the phone to answer his call.

"Dad, don't freak," I placate him as I cross the road. "I went to Neil's—"

Have you ever heard the sound rubber makes when it fights for traction on asphalt? How about when it's paired with the roar of an engine as a car is pushed to its limit? Both noises are like a symphony of disaster, and they are the very last things I hear before I'm struck.

My body is slammed into the road, then I'm catapulted into darkness.

Chapter Thirty-One

How did that get so out of hand? I was professing my love for the girl and it somehow turned into a fight. Where did I go wrong?

I storm out of my room and stomp all the way to the basement. We have a small workout area here, and I need to take my shit out on the punching bag. Once I drain all of this energy, my sleep will be deep and dreamless. I grab up my gloves and get to work, pumping my fists against the unforgiving bag, and feeling the sweat coat my skin.

I don't know how long I'm pummeling the bag for when Shay screams down the stairs.

"Neil!" I rush to the stairs and look up at her, the panic clear in her features. "It's Ivy." Her chest is heaving like she ran a marathon.

"What happened?" I ask as my feet work to get me up the stairs. I can feel myself slipping into a familiar fear. It feels like Charlotte's death all over again.

"Vin just called here and said Ivy was hit by a car on

our street." She's grabbing her jacket. "They're on the way to the hospital."

I'm locked in place and the only thing I hear is the pounding of my heart in my ears. The room spins as I try to absorb what's real and what's not. "Where is Amelia?"

"Neil!" Shay grabs my face, her eyes filling with tears. "Amelia is with Cam. It's Ivy who's in trouble. Do you hear me?"

I hear her, but not clearly because the pounding sound in my ears hasn't let up. She hands me my boots and then my jacket, helping me into them like I'm a fucking child because I can't function properly right now.

Then Shay leads me out to the car and even puts the seat belt around me once I'm in the seat. The only thing I can focus on right now is the fact that Ivy is hurt, and I just fought with her over nothing. Fucking nothing. Our last interaction was an argument about something so fucking stupid and I can never take that back.

Shay drives like she's a race car driver through the streets of Whitsborough, taking us to the hospital and swinging into the emergency entrance.

"I'll park the car. You go find your girl." Her words snap me out of my stunned state and I fly out of the car. *My fucking girl.*

I rush through the emergency doors and nearly bowl down an elderly couple, then slide to a stop in front of the desk with two nurses. "Ivy Greene," I pant. "I need to see Ivy Greene."

"Hold on, sir." The nurse looks at me with concern. "Take a breath."

"Please." I feel tears on my cheeks. "She's my girlfriend and she's been hurt."

"Okay, hun," the other nurse says as she taps on her keyboard. "Ivy Greene? She's been rushed into surgery." She looks up at me with pity in her green eyes. "Hook a left around that corner"—she points to her right—"and her family is waiting in the room there."

When I run into the room, I find everyone sitting quietly, all except Ember, who's pacing and mumbling under her breath.

"Neil!" she exclaims when she sees me. "What happened?"

"I–I w–was stupid." I'm fumbling over my words. "S–she got mad at me and s–stormed out of the house. I didn't c–chase after her." I fall to my knees and clutch my head in my hands, my world crumbling right before my eyes.

It's Travis who falls to his knees beside me, his hand landing on my shoulder. "This isn't your fault, don't let guilt eat away at you. Stay strong for her. Us Greenes are pretty resilient."

"He's right." Vin is standing to my left, his hand landing on my other shoulder. "Let's talk out everything that happened and then we can piece together the facts."

"Facts?" I look at them both. "She was hit, right? Where's the driver?"

"Hit-and-run," Ember growls and punches a hole straight through the wall.

"I'm going to call Adri and see how the kids are doing." Vin steps out into the hall.

"And I'll call Emmett and see what he's found out." Travis stands and follows Vin out.

A fucking hit-and-run?

Shay rushes into the room and heads straight for

Ember, grabbing her in an embrace. Shay's the only one crying though, and it's at this very moment I see Ivy in Ember, regardless of what Travis said.

Greenes may be resilient, but Ember is a fucking fighter, and I'm hoping that's the stuff my girl is made of.

It's been three hours.

Three hours of fucking torture waiting for news. The twisting pain in my stomach and chest just continues to worsen until the man in a white coat interrupts our silence.

"Mr. and Mrs. Greene?" Both Ember and Vin stand up, rushing to the doctor. "She's out of surgery, but there are a few things we need to discuss. We can do it in her room. She's resting there now."

What things? I stand to ask those questions, but Shay grabs my arm, pulling me back and shaking her head. "Let her parents go first."

I turn back to see their retreating backs, heads bowed together. I want to know what needs to be discussed and I want to see Ivy. *I need to see Ivy.* When Vin told me the intersection where she was hit, I nearly screamed with frustration because that's a problem area and people are running the stop signs there all the time. Amelia was almost hit the year before.

"This isn't Charlotte, Neil," Shay says quietly as she tries to once again tug me back into my seat. "Ivy will be okay."

Charlotte.

It's like God is laughing at me from up in the sky. This is another tragic accident involving a girl I love, and somehow, he connected them together.

"I love her," I confess as Shay rubs my arm.

"I know."

I hear hurried footsteps and then a flustered Carmelo barges into the room. "Where is she?" He's panting, his eyes looking frantic. "No one told me."

"Bro,"—I motion to the seat beside mine—"come sit. She's out of surgery and her parents are with her."

He nearly collapses with relief and slowly comes to the seat I pointed out.

"I thought… it was like last time…" He looks at me with sadness. "You know?"

"Yeah man, I know." I nod because I know exactly what he means. "I should've called you, but I've been pretty fucking useless for the last few hours."

He nods and we sit there in silence, waiting for answers. Right now, time is my worst fucking enemy.

IVY

"Charlotte! Pull over!" I screech, my voice panicked. "Pull the fuck over!"

"Why did you let us become this?" She sounds sad, so fucking sad. "I'm so tired of pretending."

"Charlotte." I touch my fingers to her shoulder, the trembling betraying my terror. "Stop the car."

"I'm in a lot of trouble, Ivy," she whispers as the tires screech on another sharp bend.

"What trouble? Pull over and tell me."

"Mom is kicking me out for taking her pills and my school is expelling me for selling them." Her cheeks shine with all her tears. "I needed the money."

"I will give you money. You don't need to do all of that, you know this," I beg her to see reason.

"I tried to get you out of my mind and I used him to do it."

"Used who?" I ask, my stomach dropping with dread.

"You don't know him. He goes to my school," she sobs and wipes her nose on her sleeve. The car swerves with her motion and I scream until she rights it.

"Please, Charlotte, please pull over."

"I wanted us to raise it together, like a family." She ends her words on a sob. "My family will never forgive me."

"For what?"

"I got pregnant!" she screams, and I startle at the sudden pitch.

"Oh no," I breathe out, and she turns her head to look at me.

That was the wrong thing to say because she growls in frustration and clenches her fingers on the wheel. "I love you!" she screeches. "We could've raised this baby together."

She's pregnant, and as scary as that is, she's also been heavily taking drugs. The Charlotte in front of me isn't the real version. The real one is sweet and levelheaded, and she would've never gotten herself into this trouble. No, this is something wild Ivy Greene would be expected to do, and I can't help but think maybe it's because of my influence over the years.

All of this is my fault and Charlotte is a by-product of my toxic personality.

"Okay." I exhale and dig my fingers into the passenger seat as she rounds another corner, disregarding the stop sign. "Pull over and we'll do it. We'll raise this baby and live happily fucking ever after, okay, Charlotte?"

"I don't believe you, Ivy." The sound of her resignation has me turning my head to look at her as her fingers tighten even further on the wheel. "If I can't have you, no one can."

Her face becomes still, not a trace of emotion etched into the features, as her body stiffens. I look straight ahead and see a dead end sign. Charlotte doesn't ease up on the gas. We fly down the small residential street and I know what's going to happen next. It's everything she's been promising me tonight.

I close my eyes and let myself drift out of my body, detached from my surroundings. I think of my family and how much I love them, even though I don't show it. I think of Charlotte and how much I've wronged her. And then I think of me and how little faith I put into myself. I accept all of this, and when it's over, I can only hope I end up where Nana Jenna is.

The car jolts a bit as it hits a wooden barrier, but it does little to slow us down, and then it feels like we're taking off on a runway. My eyes stay shut tight as my stomach lifts to my throat, and then we hit the ground, my body jarring with the impact.

Charlotte mutters an 'Oh God,' before the car slams into an object, and then the sound of crunching metal fills the space. It's similar to what I heard at the Demolition Derby Dad took us to one year. My seat belt locks and tightens across my chest, cutting into the skin. At the same time, the airbag deploys and my face bounces off the material like a sharp slap. It's hard to breathe as the pain slowly penetrates my insides and my body screams in protest.

The smell of burning metal and gasoline hits my nostrils, the combined scents forcing my eyes open. Charlotte groans beside me and I turn my head—the pain slicing up my neck—to look at her. The first thing I see is her face against the deployed airbag and blood dripping off her chin. Her skin is completely covered in blood.

"Charlotte." My voice breaks and my arm feels like lead as I reach for her.

She makes a weird noise every time she sucks in a breath. It's short, the effort rattling inside her chest.

"No," I moan.

I can't let her be the one to get in trouble for this. It's all my fault, and the only reason we've ended up here is because of me. Everything is because of me. I click the button of her seat belt and she slides forward, her body flush with the wheel. Then I release mine and pull the lever to open my door. It takes a few small pushes, but the door finally gives and swings open wide.

The car is on a steep slope and the drop-off at the cliff is only about five feet ahead. The large tree saved us from certain death.

"Charlotte, wait," I plead with her as I pull myself out of the car.

As soon as my feet hit the earth, my legs collapse under me and my knees sink into the mud. Standing is too difficult as I battle the gravity of the slope and the pain in my legs, so I crawl. I claw through sticks and leaves, pulling my body to the back of the car, and then let myself slide feetfirst to the driver's side door.

I reach up and grab the lever, tugging the door open and letting it fly wide like mine did. Using the door as leverage, I haul myself up to standing and lean against it as I reach inside for Charlotte.

She's so fucking heavy, her body unmoving as I pull her out and lay her in the mud.

"Charlotte." I sink to my knees beside her. "Can you hear me?"

"Ivy…" Her voice is weak, sounding like she's far away. "I'm sorry…"

"No!" I scream and gasp when I hear sirens in the distance. Someone must've heard the crash. "Help is coming, Charlotte… please."

"Ivy…" The rattling inside her chest sounds worse now. "I love…" Then her body relaxes into my hold, and I scream as the rattling noise disappears.

"Charlotte! No!" I shake her and her head lolls at the movement. "Take me instead!" I scream to the sky to whoever is taking her away. "Take me!"

The sirens are just above us now, and the lights are illuminating the surrounding area in red and blue, but I can't take my eyes off my best friend's face. She looks at peace and I hate it. I want that peace, to go with her. I want to take her fucking place.

As people come for us, I hear a few shouts and crunch of sticks and leaves, but it's useless.

Because they are too fucking late.

Chapter Thirty-Two

Voices that don't belong in my memory swim around my head. It's my mother and my dad, but they weren't with me and Charlotte that night. How can I hear them? If they were there, they would've found out my greatest secret. They would know I wasn't driving and Charlotte would be blamed.

But that's not how it went.

I remember everything about that night. About being questioned thoroughly at the hospital, about the drag marks around the car, about the severity of Charlotte's injuries, and how the officers had their doubts about my account of the night. The front driver's side of the car took the brunt of the damage, causing Charlotte's head to hit the steering wheel before the bag deployed, and then the bag broke her ribs, puncturing her lung.

But I maintained that couldn't have happened because I was in the driver's seat and she was my passenger. I had been drinking and took us on a joyride. After days of rigorous questions, there wasn't much more they could do without my story changing, and instead, suggested my penalty would be a reform school of sorts.

Charlotte's mom and dad agreed to the terms and refused to press charges, and my family shipped me off to Johnstone Academy to start my sentence. I've never told a soul about what really happened, and I always maintained it was me, but I was going to tell Neil because I wanted him to know the real me, and that meant every single secret that was festering inside of me. I wanted to lay myself bare and wait for his judgement.

As the memory fades, Charlotte's face appears in front of mine, and she looks beautiful. She's radiant and has a bright glow around her, her smile wide. I miss her smile and seeing it now makes me want to beg her to take me with her again.

"Ivy." She sounds like she's singing and speaking at the same time, a slight echo in her words. "Ivy, I love you."

"I'm sorry," I force the words out. "Charlotte, I'm so sorry."

"No." She shakes her head and her ponytail of tight curls sways behind her. "Don't be, Ivy. You were a great friend to me, and I was not in the right state of mind. I'm sorry for what I did to us."

"Take me with you," I beg her. "It's too hard to be here."

"I can't." Her smile grows wide again. "My brother will help you. Let him help you, Ivy."

"I want to be with you."

"Tell my brother the truth, okay? Tell him it was me, that I was driving, and tell him I'm sorry. I think you two were always meant to be."

Her voice fades and her face is becoming foggy. "No, wait!" I exclaim.

"Don't worry." She giggles, the sound bringing me comfort. "I'll take care of this little one. She's safe with me until we see you again."

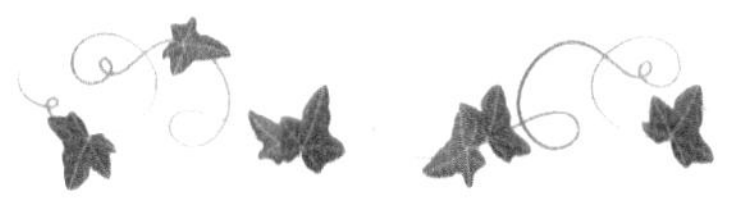

The first time I regained consciousness, Mom's face was hovering over mine, her eyes filled with worry. Then she laughed and smothered her face in my neck. Dad and Saxon were clapping in the background and my little Flower climbed up on the bed.

"Ivy!" she squealed, and even though the sound literally pierced through my skull, I was so happy to hear it. "You have been sleeping for so long!"

"Really?" My voice sounds groggy and hoarse.

"And you sound a little scary," she whispers, and everyone laughs.

"You've been out for a week," Dad says as he steps up into view. "Had us worried about you."

Every one of my family's faces gathers around me and I look into each of their eyes. I see so much love and it makes me feel stupid for how badly I've treated them over the years.

"The doctors let us all be in here because you were waking up, but it really should only be two at a time," Mother states. "Did you want to see everyone, or do you want to rest?"

"I want to see Neil." I clear my throat and wince at the pain.

"Okay." Dad smiles. "You have a few broken ribs, so taking deep breaths will be painful, and you took a heavy hit to the head. Other than that, you are fine."

Fine? My hands move and cover my stomach. Am I still fine?

"Can you guys give us a minute?" Mother asks, and everyone leaves the room. "Ivy." Her voice cracks as a tear slips down her cheek. "Why didn't you tell me?"

"It's gone, isn't it?" I wasn't far along but I could sense the life inside of me. Now it's just... empty.

"Yes, baby," she cries as she covers my hands with hers.

"It's okay, Mom." I will myself not to cry as I smile. "Charlotte has her."

"I'm sure she will love her," Mother vows through her tears. "That's the first time you've called me Mom in a long time." Her chest swells as she sucks in a breath.

"I'm sorry." I blink the tears away as I focus on her face. "This is the first time that I haven't felt like a burden. Like you're here for me, and no matter what I do or say, you'll love me regardless."

"That's right, Ivy." She smooths the hair back from my brows. "There's nothing that could stop me from loving you. Nothing."

"Charlotte was driving the car." I look my mom in the eyes, releasing the first of many truths. "I lied and said it was me because I made her angry."

"I know, baby. I always knew that, but there was no budging you to tell me the truth. I'm sorry you had to be sent away."

I nod because what else can I do? It wasn't her fault I lied, and I was a juvenile who was under the influence. Not to mention, neither of us had licenses to drive. I may have looked like I got off easy, but those two years were complete torture.

"Does Neil know?" I swallow, easing the dryness in my

throat. "About the…" I look at my stomach.

"No." She shakes her head. "Do you want to talk to him?"

"Yes," I whisper.

She kisses my forehead and then leaves the room. There's so much to tell him, and I can only hope he wants to hear it.

The creak of the door sounds in the room, and when I see his face, I begin to cry. We've come a long way and I love him so much. He rushes to my side and gathers me into his arms.

"I love you," he rasps as he kisses my temple. "I love you so much. I need that to be the first thing you hear from me."

"I love you too," I whisper against his chest. "I lost it." The grief I finally feel consumes me as I sob into his jacket. "She's gone."

"She?" His voice cracks.

"Charlotte has her," I tell him between sobs.

Then we're both sobbing together as he rocks us back and forth, his hand buried in my hair and his tears dripping onto my face.

"Charlotte will take care of her." He finally collects himself. "I promise."

"Charlotte came to see me." I hope he doesn't think I sound crazy because I don't want him to dismiss this.

"She did?" His tear-soaked face looks down into mine.

"She wants me to tell you the truth. Can I tell you the truth now, Neil?"

He crawls up into bed beside me and hauls me onto his chest, his steady heartbeat sounding in my ear.

"Please."

"When Nana Jenna died, I was so upset. She was the only one besides Charlotte who ever understood me, and I felt like my world was ending. My parents were dealing in their own way, and I was practically left alone. I drank… a lot, and then I called Charlotte to come over. She did, of course. She always came when I needed her, and when I begged her to get me out of the house, she did that too."

Neil stays quiet, the sound of his heart still beating against my ear.

"We were driving for only ten minutes when she began to ask me questions about the two of us. She confessed she loved me and thought I felt the same. To be fair, I was fooling around with her and discovering my sexuality, never taking her feelings into consideration. I wasn't in love with her and she knew it at that moment. She had been abusing oxy for a while and could be erratic with her moods, but that night was extreme. She was so angry, and I did nothing to help it. I should've been more sensitive to her feelings, but I was so messed up with mine."

"Ivy, why did you hold this inside for so long?"

"Because I wanted no one to blame her. She didn't deserve that. She wasn't herself that night when we crashed into that tree. She died in my arms…" I sob, the sound tortured. "Telling me she loved me. I loved her too. I really loved her… just not the way she wanted."

Neil's chest moves against my face as he cries, and I burrow in closer. "You let yourself be punished for juvenile manslaughter, Ivy."

"I didn't want her to be remembered as the girl who

tried to kill me and then herself. Three years ago, I kept something of hers from you and your family. I was going to go home and get it the day… When the… When I was struck," I force out as I look up into his face.

"What is it?"

"Do you remember that diary she always carried around with her? The pink one with that flimsy lock strap?" I ask him, and I see recognition in his eyes as he nods. "She brought it to my house that night, along with a change of clothes. I gave your family back her clothes, but I kept the diary. At first, I didn't want to read it, but I was afraid of what might be in there, and I was right," I whisper. "When I read it, I saw the anguish Charlotte lived through."

"What's in there?"

"Charlotte had secrets, and as much as I loved her, the last year of her life was hard on her. I'll give you the diary when I get out of here," I promise him.

I will also tell him everything else I endured, but for now, I just want him to hold me and stay here while I sleep.

"Did you see the car that hit you, baby?" he presses as his arms tighten around me.

"I don't know." I struggle to piece together that day. "I remember the sounds and the smell of burning rubber. Maybe a quick flash of green?"

I feel him tense under me and I lift my head to look at him. "Why? The cops haven't found them?"

"Not yet." His voice becomes gruffer and his face is stern.

I'm too fucking tired to decipher his mood, so I drop my head back to his chest. Maybe Charlotte will come to visit me again.

NEIL

I lift her off me and set her back down on the pillows. She saw green. The car was green. I walk quietly toward the door and look back at her, love swelling inside my chest.

She opened up about Charlotte to me and admitted the truth about the accident. I knew in my heart she was being honest. Why would she tell me lies now after doing years at a boarding school for her supposed crime? She did something that would destroy her reputation to save my sister's and now I'm going to repay the favor.

She said the fucking car was green.

I get out into the hall and Vin steps forward. "She's okay?"

"Yeah, sleeping." I scrub a hand down my face as I exhale heavily. "I'm going to head home and shower before she wakes up again."

"Did she say anything about what happened? Does she remember anything?" Ember asks me.

"Nah." The lie tastes like ash in my mouth as I shake my head. "We were talking about… other stuff."

"Right," she murmurs.

"I'll be back." I head down the hallway and out through the exit to the parking lot.

My heart is thrumming wildly and it's hard to swallow. I know who ran my girl down.

I get in my car and punch the steering wheel, the anger inside me swelling uncontrollably. My tires burn as I pull out of the parking lot and race back to my house. Maybe I'll be lucky enough to catch him on my street.

I laugh—the sound unfamiliar—when I see he switched up the green Honda Civic for a parking patrol police car. I've never felt this much anger in my life, not even when I thought Ivy killed my baby sister.

After I park my car in my driveway, I make my way back out to the street, dropping my clenched fists into my pockets. I find the hospital latex gloves and somehow find the control to saunter to his vehicle.

The sun set about an hour ago, the sky still a bit illuminated as the pitch-black night holds off a while longer. I discreetly pull the gloves on and keep my hands in my pocket. He sees me coming, and I notice him looking to his right, at the passenger seat.

I open the back passenger door and slide across the seat. In these parking enforcement cars, there's no grate between the front and back.

"Get out." His eyes flash with anger.

I do the complete opposite and push myself between the two front seats. There indeed is a gun on the passenger seat.

"Nah," I say evenly. "Ivy woke up." He has no reaction as he continues to watch me through his rearview mirror. "She can't remember the fucking car that hit her, so I came to ask you what the police know."

"I can't speak about it," he snarls. "It's an open investigation."

"I was hoping you would say that." I quickly snatch up the gun from the seat and turn off the safety. "It's not smart for a cop to have his gun just chillin' like that, right?"

I lean back in the seat and grin, the gun firmly in my hand but pointing at the floor.

"You can go to jail for a long time for taking a cop's gun." He's no longer snarling and his body is as stiff as a fucking board.

"I don't think anyone will ever find out, and if they do, I know some people." I smile wide when I see his throat working hard to swallow. "Thing is, Ivy said something about seeing a flash of green, and I thought that was fucking funny. Any idea why?"

"It's funny she got hit?" he asks quietly, mock-surprise in his eyes.

"Careful, Deputy Dipshit. I can see intelligence is not needed to enter the academy, huh?" I tap the back of his head with the barrel of the gun. "I'm saying it's funny because I know a guy with a green car." I shove his head with the gun. "Don't I?"

"Why are you doing this? Because I slept with her once? Are you jealous?" His words are like an accelerant to a flame. "Don't end up in jail for a whore."

"You're just angry you could only get it once, huh?"

He snorts like I said something funny. "I take what I want, Ivy knows that."

He takes what he wants? Like he forced her? Did Deputy Dipshit rape my girl? Was she too ashamed to tell me?

Everything in my vision flips to red and he sees the exact moment it does.

"No." He shakes his head. "Listen, I didn't hurt her."

I slam the handle of the gun into the back of his head and he falls forward with a grunt. Out fucking cold.

Then I step out of the car and walk to the front passenger side. After I press the gun to his temple, I say a quick prayer. The moment I pull the trigger, a complete sense of calm comes over me, and I'm suddenly lighter than I've been in a long while.

Grabbing his right hand, I slap it a couple times against the blood on his head, and then position the gun on the floor by his feet, letting his hand hang down over it.

Fuck, that shouldn't have felt so good. Right?

Chapter Thirty-Three

After spending two weeks in the hospital and then another month practically bedridden at home, my ribs are nearly healed. I can now laugh loudly and breathe deeply, and the whole time, I had the best company.

Carmelo spent the weekends he wasn't training in New York here with me, Cam would randomly pop in with Amelia in tow, my brother and sister barely left my side, and Neil treated me like his princess.

Mom and Dad have been attentive, and at times, really overbearing, but I love it. Uncle Travis brought over books for me to read, Aunt Adri tried to kill me again with her cooking, and Uncle Emmett solved my case. He really did.

When Officer Adam Van Dyke failed to show up to work a few days in a row, they traced his cop car outside of Neil's house. It looked like he was staking him out, but he wasn't asked to do that.

Uncle Emmett was the one who found him with a self-inflicted gunshot wound to the head, and when his location was suspiciously near where I was hit, Uncle Emmett obtained a search warrant for his house. They found the green Honda Civic with an Ivy-sized dent on the front left side and my blood on the hood. My parents also figured it was Adam standing at our gate that night. Do they know for sure? No. Do I? Fuck, yes.

Maybe he was feeling tortured about what he had done to me and felt like he was going to be caught for it. I'm not sure but I'm glad he's gone. Are all my problems fixed? Hell no. I still have Dean to worry about. He's been eerily quiet since I threatened him with child pornography and rape, but that doesn't mean shit. He may be just planning my next big problem.

On my first day home, I gave Neil Charlotte's diary and sat on the bed to cry with him as he read it. When he learned she was being bullied for being smart or when she sold pills to look cool, we cried. When he learned she began taking those pills to experiment and decided she really liked them, we cried. When she wrote about her feelings for me and still being confused because she liked a guy at school, we cried.

But when he read about her pregnancy and how she decided to somehow move to Whitsborough and raise the child with me, we lost it. It was a hard few days after that, but eventually, the heaviness of grief subsided and his healing began.

Neil has been spending as much time with me as my parents will allow, which is a lot, really. They see how he makes me feel and that he's been my rock through this entire thing.

"Babe," Neil moans and rolls into me, burying his face into my stomach. "I can't watch these true crime shows anymore."

"Fine, let's do Toy Story." I pick up my remote and point it at the TV.

"Ivy Greene, we've marathoned those movies like

three times now." He hovers over my face and gently kisses me.

Everything he does to me is gentle, and it's frustrating. I miss rough Neil, the one who couldn't control himself around me. I try to deepen the kiss, but he pulls away and gives me a stern look.

"What?" I toss my hands up in frustration. "I want my boyfriend."

"Say it again." His eyes darken and the smirk on his full lips is sinful.

"What? That I want you?"

"No, you called me your boyfriend." His lips brush over mine. "Say it again."

"You're my boyfriend, Neil Jones."

Then he crushes his lips against mine, and I moan, the opening giving him the chance to devour me. His tongue swipes against mine as I writhe beneath him, trying to press myself into him.

He pulls back abruptly and rests his forehead to mine. "Not yet, baby."

"When?" Irritation coats my words.

"I know," is his answer. "I should get home though."

"Yeah." I groan and hit him with a pillow.

"I love you." He kisses me softly.

"I love you, too," I reply.

He stands from the bed, and I watch him like he's my last fucking meal. I may be horny and all, but my man is fucking fine. I get up from the bed and only wince a little when I bend to stand. Soon, I will be back to normal.

I walk Neil to the front door and swoon when he cups

my face, kissing me softly.

"Good night," he whispers. "I'll text you in the morning."

"Good night."

After he walks to his car and drives down my driveway out of sight, I finally close the door. The house is quiet; Saxon and Dahlia are asleep, and Mom and Dad are watching TV in their room.

I decide an early night and a good sleep is just what I need as I head back to my room, so I plop on my bed and roll myself up like a burrito in my blanket.

"Get up, kid." I'm startled awake by my jacket hitting my face. "We're going for a ride." Mom is standing in the doorway of my room, and I grab my phone for the time.

"Mom," I whine. "It's four in the morning."

"You can sleep in the car. Let's go." Her voice brokers no room for argument.

I get up out of bed and follow her into the hallway.

"No, Ivy." She looks me up and down. "Go back and dress in black."

What the fuck? "Mom."

"Just do it, Ivy. For fuck's sake, listen just this once." Fucking bossy.

With a huff, I turn around and head back to my room. I find a black pair of leggings and a baggy black hoodie. When I come back out, I throw my arms up and twirl on the spot.

"Perfect." She nods and leads us down the stairs.

"Black boots," she says, and I give her a salute.

She sounds like a drill sergeant right now and I don't know where the hell we're going, but I continue to follow her out the door and into our black Mercedes. I call this our celebrity car because it's all blacked out.

"Where are we going?" I yawn and slouch down in my seat.

"Just sleep. I'll wake you up when we get there."

She's in a fucking mood, so I don't argue with her. Instead, I do what she says and fall asleep.

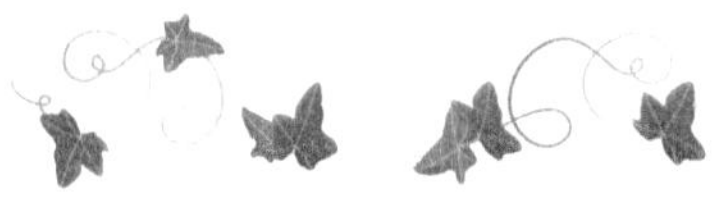

"Did you ever wonder what really happened to Mr. O'Connor?" Mom's voice wakes me up from my sleep.

The sun is bright, and I groan as I cover my sensitive eyes from the sudden light. "What?" I croak out.

"Mr. O'Connor and his partner, Mr. Pratt," she huffs like she's annoyed with having to explain herself.

"What about them?" I drop my hands as sleep completely leaves me and stare at my mom.

"Did you ever wonder why they left so suddenly?" She keeps her gaze fixed straight ahead as she drives on the highway, her jaw flexing with restrained anger. Did she find out what I was doing with Mr. O'Connor? Is she taking me back to New York?

"Yes, I asked Aunt Adri. Why?" I speak slowly.

"I'm only giving you one chance to answer me honestly."

Her voice drops as her knuckles whiten on the steering wheel. "Did they hurt you?"

"No," I answer truthfully as I swallow down my trepidation. This is my mom, she's not going to dump me back at Johnstone Academy.

"Did you do things you shouldn't do, with a teacher, with them?" My palms sweat, and I look at the car's surroundings.

"Are we in New York?"

"Answer the question." She snaps her fingers in front of my face.

"Yes," I whisper. "Only Mr. O'Connor, not Mr. Pratt."

"Mr. Pratt didn't try anything on you?"

How does she know all this?

"He didn't really, no, but I think he thought I would join him and Mr. O'Connor," I tell her, watching her face closely as she drives.

"I got rid of them."

At first, her words don't register, and I blink a few times in confusion.

"What?" I ask.

"I got rid of them." She changes lanes and shrugs. "Your Aunt Adri had her suspicions, and I never ignore those."

"Mom." I sit up straight. "Please tell me you're kidding."

"I went by Mr. O'Connor's house around eight the same evening Adri told me about seeing you run out of the school. Just to chat." She grins, her side profile looking sinister as she continues to watch the road. "Mr. O'Connor was shocked to see me and he said, and I quote, *'Whatever Ivy has told you, it's not true, Mrs. Greene.'* I told him I was there for a quick chat about my troubled teenage daughter."

"Mom, stop." I feel like my heart is about to explode.

"They agreed it must be hard raising a daughter as troubled as you, so far into drugs and partying all the time. It was evidence enough so I could do what needed to be done."

"This has to be a joke." I look around once more just as we pull into the Torres' Compound. Why the fuck are we here? "Mom!" I yell into the car's interior. "What did you do to Mr. O'Connor?"

"I wanted to kill them, Ivy." Her voice is deadly low, and the tone sounds nothing like the mom I know. "No one should touch a minor, no matter how much they ask for it." Her eyes cut to mine. "I made them leave Whitsborough, and they could only take what their pockets could fill. That's it. But I promise you, if they ever bring their pedophile asses back into my town, I will skin them alive, and you will fucking watch."

My eyes are about to pop out of my head as I feel my mouth open and shut. I make a few squeaking noises, but I can't seem to form a fucking word.

"I gave you the name Greene." Her bright blue eyes stare into mine. "But you are a fucking Torres. Maybe I needed to do this sooner because, Ivy, you became a victim of the very thing I'm eradicating."

"Mom." I'm fucking speechless. "I don't want…"

"Let's go." She opens her car door and slams it shut behind her.

I slowly get out and look around the compound. Now that I'm older, this place looks less menacing and more deserted. This area is comprised of mostly factories, and this building looks like one above land, but underneath it's a fucking village.

The large garage style door in the front opens to reveal Uncle Trent standing there with his hands on his hips.

"If it isn't my two most favorite ladies." I love the man, but I need him to give me a few minutes so I can talk to my mom.

"Hey, man." Mom pulls him in for a hug.

"Ivy!" He releases her and wraps an arm around my shoulders. "Are you here to see your mama fight? Should be a doozy one." He grins.

"She's here for the job too," Mom interjects as Uncle Trent's head snaps toward her.

"What?" His brows drop and his eyes narrow. "Did I hear that right?"

"She should be there, don't you agree?"

"I don't know, Ember." Trent eyes me. "She's not like you. At her age, you were… different."

"Ivy." She turns on me, her mouth set in a straight line. "He thinks you're weak."

"Wait!" Uncle Trent throws up his hands. "I said different."

"You're not weak." Mom walks ahead of us and toward the elevators. "And you're going to prove it."

I chase after her as Uncle Trent closes the door. "Mom!" I'm panting when I get to her side.

"What?" she asks, exasperated.

"Are you making me fight?"

Her mouth turns up into a sadistic smile and she smooths her hand down my hair. "No, baby." Then she tugs softly on the hair's ends. "Something far worse."

"Ember," Uncle Trent warns, his voice hushed.

"Tell him you're a Torres." She's staring intently at me. I want to please her, but above all else, I trust her.

"I'm a Torres, Uncle Trent." I say it with force and a bit of annoyance that he thinks I'm weak. After everything I've been through, I am far from weak.

"That's my girl." Mom pats my cheek and we step into the elevator.

"What is this going to be? Black Slaughter's apprenticeship? Her sidekick training program?" Uncle Trent drills my mom.

Black Slaughter? That's what Dean was saying.

"Black Slaughter?" I repeat my thoughts to Mom as we step off the elevator.

"Come with me." She grabs my hand and leads me down the corridor to where the dorms are.

Then she pulls me into a room and shuts the door. I look around in awe at the posters of my mom on the walls and her fight gear on the small table in the corner. It's a small room with a queen bed in the center, side tables, a desk, and a washroom/closet combo. She has a small bar fridge on her table, and when I open it, there is Gatorade and water inside.

"I think it's time I told you about our family, Ivy, and what it is we do." She sits on the bed as she rubs one of her temples to ease the tension. I don't know why I'm suddenly scared and nervous. I shouldn't be because I always knew my family's past was *strange*.

"I was raised by a single mother, this much you know, and you know I didn't find Uncle Emmett until I was about your age. But what you don't know is my father was a mob boss, the kingpin of the underground world here in New

York. He had his hand in pretty much everything. Prostitution, human trafficking, drugs, weapons, the police, and government officials."

I suck in a breath as the information seeps into my brain, the shock rendering me speechless.

"When my mother had me and Emmett, Nana Jenna helped her escape my father, but she could only take me. Emmett was stuck here to be raised as a mobster's son. My father ended up going to prison because my mother testified to the FBI. He went away for fifteen years for money laundering and racketeering. That was all they could get proof of. My father was angry, and most of all, he was angry with the woman he supposedly loved. Do you remember how my mother died?"

"You said she died in a house fire." My heart feels like it's going to fly out of my chest.

"She did." She nods, then exhales as her hands form fists in her lap. "That fire was started by my father as soon as he got out of prison."

"He killed her?" I breathe out and slowly sit down beside her.

"Yes, then I was sent to live in Whitsborough until the night he kidnapped me and brought me here. That was the same night I met your Uncle Carm."

"Here?" I look around the room as I try to imagine being in my mom's shoes at my age. She must've been terrified.

"I was kept in this very room, a prisoner, and forced to fight in the ring. Only those fights weren't regular fights, and I wasn't prepared for what he would make me do." Her throat works as she swallows, her jaw flexing with anger.

"What did he make you do?" As much as this is scaring me, I need to know everything.

"Each fight was to the death."

"You had to kill people?" My stomach turns at the thought as I stare at my mom, wondering if I'm still dreaming.

"Or be killed. So yes, I killed people. My last fight was against Uncle Tommy, and I couldn't kill him, so Carm shot him for me." Her eyes become glassy.

"But Uncle Tommy is alive." I shake my head in confusion.

"Yes, but I didn't find that out until a few years later. When I thought they had killed Tommy, something inside me flipped, and I became the very thing my father craved. He had tried to mold your Uncle Emmett into a coldhearted killer, but it didn't work, and here I was, the exact thing he wanted, only he was my target. That night, I tortured and killed my father. I was found covered in his blood with a gun in my pocket." She surprises me when she looks at me and smiles. "That's when my life became what it is today."

"What do you mean?" My words are high-pitched, filled with fear. This is my mom, but I don't truly know her at all.

"I grew to enjoy exterminating scum and began skillfully planning hits. It's my favorite pastime."

"Your favorite pastime is killing people, Mom?" I exclaim. "Do you know how crazy this sounds?" I stand to my feet. "Does Dad know?"

"Baby…" She chuckles. "I killed your dad's father for the abuse he put him and your Uncle Travis through. You bet your sweet cheeks he knows."

"Mom, who the hell are you?" I feel the tears run down my cheeks as my knees begin to shake.

"I am Black Slaughter."

"What does that mean?" I can't seem to take a full breath and my chest is hurting.

"It means I wanted to get rid of the people like your Grandfather Greene, people so sick and twisted, who spread their rot to others around them. It makes me feel good. You know what I'm talking about." She grins. "I see it in you too, Ivy. That feeling deep inside yourself"—she taps her chest—"that burns to be set free."

I know exactly what she means, and it scares me. To think that this darkness I have inside would make me want to end people's lives. I couldn't hurt anyone, no matter how vile they were.

"How many people have you killed?" I sit back down, keeping my distance as her eyes narrow on me.

"Is that what's really important right now?" She raises her brow at me and the room spins. That means a lot.

This woman sitting in front of me is nothing like the mom I know. She seems aloof and psychotic. Dean was asking me about the Black Slaughter and now I know he was talking about my mom. He couldn't know it was my mom though, and I bet he's scared shitless if she has no problem killing pedophiles.

Then a realization comes over me as my mouth dries out.

"Why did you bring me here, Mom?" My insides grow cold as I wait for her answer.

"Dean Thompson."

"Fuck." *She knows.* I fall back on the bed, my eyes strained on the ceiling. "You want to kill him?"

"No." She stands up to look down at me, her eyes blazing with rage. "I want you to." Then she walks out of the room, shutting the door softly behind her.

She wants me to kill my pedophile rapist.

Chapter Thirty-Four

It's six in the evening and we are watching as Dean's secretary gets into her car and drives out of Johnstone's parking lot.

"He'll be alone now," I whisper as fear makes my hands tremble. "How did you find out about him?" I'm trying to stall her, hoping I can still change her mind about this. We should call the cops instead and send him to jail.

"Trent and I received a tip from a co-worker about the Dean of Johnstone Academy and how much he likes to punish his girls." Her words make me feel sick. I always wondered if there were others, and the thought of him doing to other girls what he did to me breaks my heart.

"Trent does a lot of recon and he found out that much of what the tipster said was true. He found videos, photos, and even some mementos." I know those mementos. Sometimes it was a lock of my hair, and sometimes it would be a pair of my panties. "You were a part of his collection, Ivy." Her voice shakes as she takes a deep breath. "I failed you because I thought our name was enough to protect you. I'm sorry."

"Mom…" I try to make her listen. "I can't kill anyone. We should call the cops. He'll rot in jail and nobody else will get hurt."

"Jail isn't the sort of punishment these types of people deserve, Ivy. They're fed, get to go outside, and dream of the things they did while lying in their cots at night. You can change your mind, I won't force you." She turns her tear-filled eyes on me. "But understand, he will not be breathing when we leave his office."

Her reasoning begins to make sense. "Okay," I concede, knowing there's no stopping her.

"Pull your hood over your head. The makeup conceals your face, but our hair can still be distinguished on camera," she instructs as she tucks her hair into her hood.

I flip down the visor and look into the small square mirror. Mom painted my face into a decorative skull. It's gorgeously grotesque. My eyes are blackened to resemble sockets and my nose is tipped in black. She's coated my lips a bright red with black lines through it to resemble teeth, and delicate designs are on my forehead. She said it's inspired by a knife she stole from her father long ago. My face is a mirror image of her own and we look like a pair of Trick-or-Treaters.

"Let's get this over with." She rubs her hands together as we get out of the car.

The doors to Johnstone Academy are still unlocked but the hallways are empty. I can hear the faraway hum of the floor polisher, and luckily, the custodian is far from Dean's office. We hook a left at the first corridor and I see the secretary's office up ahead. Beside hers is Dean's. I'm petrified, but I'm also excited to see fear in his eyes. Maybe Mom is right. The darkness really is inside of me, waiting to be unleashed.

I'm shocked when she opens the secretary's door and softly closes it behind us. Dean's office is always locked from the corridor. To get to him, you have to use the adjoining door from the secretary's office.

I open my mouth to ask her how she knows, but she turns on me abruptly and presses her finger to her mouth. I nod and gulp back my words. I can't believe I'm doing this.

Mom opens the door and I hear a bit of rustling. "Carol, did you forget something?"

His voice has me freezing on the spot and I can't seem to collect my thoughts. Mom steps into the room and I hear Dean jump from his chair with a shout.

"Hello, Jerry Thompson," Mom literally coos. "I heard you've been asking around about me."

I can't move from this spot in the secretary's office, and even though he is not in my line of sight, hearing him is having the same effect.

"Black Slaughter." He sounds… terrified. My body relaxes and I take a few steps forward, liking the way he sounds.

"Ding, ding!" Mom claps her hands, and I can't help but grin at her antics. "You deserve a prize."

"No." His voice shakes, and it stirs something in the pit of my stomach. "No, I don't need a prize."

I take a few more steps inside his office, but the door blocks me from his view.

"Too bad." Mom takes a step toward him. "Sit in your seat, *Dean*." That's what he makes everyone call him because he's so proud of his position.

I hear his seat creak as he sits back down, and my chest is brimming with adrenaline. Mom walks toward his desk and out of my line of sight.

"Wait, don't take that out." I hear his voice squeak with

fear. "We can talk about this."

I want to see what she does to him, and most of all, I want him to see me.

I step out from behind the door and walk up to the front of his desk, the very spot he continuously raped me on. Mom twirls a large hunting knife in her hand, and I note that it has the same skulls carved into the handle. The knife she stole from her dad.

"Wait." His hand trembles as he points to me. "There are two of you? What's that one's name?"

"Name?" Mom turns to look at me. I don't have a fucking name. Should I have a name? "Neither of us have names, Dean. We are Black Slaughter."

He stands abruptly and Mom tenses, her stance changing slightly. His eyes look wildly between us before he darts for the side of the desk I'm on, clearly making a run for it. Mom pushes me to the desk as she intercepts Dean with a quick punch to his ear and then a hard kick to his kneecap. He drops to the floor with a shout, and I watch in astonishment as Mom punches him hard on the cheek. His skin splits and the blood swells around the wound.

"That wasn't smart, Dean." She undoes his tie. "Black Slaughter, get the chair."

I bring one chair by his desk to her side, and once again, I'm shocked as she tosses him into it. Dean is not a small man. He's not as big as my dad, but he's not small either. Mom is fucking Hercules.

He struggles, and she punches him another two times in the mouth, his lip splitting open.

"Keep testing me," she snarls. "I fucking love this shit."

Nope, definitely not my mom.

Then she takes his tie and wraps it around his neck as his head lolls from the blows. He's on the brink of passing out, and I can't believe I'm feeling disappointed. I want him to struggle more so Mom will continue to punish him.

Mom is now standing behind him and the chair, tightening the tie, forcing his head up. His eyes widen and his fingers dig at the silk material, bloodred in color. Didn't he want to see if it would match my blood?

I walk forward slowly, and Mom's black-painted eyebrow raises in question, but she doesn't stop me. I swipe my fingers over his cheek, gathering the blood, and then hold it against the tie.

"It really matches the color of blood."

The color drains from his face, and he struggles again until Mom's fist hits the side of his head, which snaps to the left before he slowly lifts it up again.

"Ivy?" he questions.

I don't answer him because there's no point. I know he knows who I am. Instead, I watch Mom knot the tie to the back of the chair, and then she's back in front of him. If he struggles too much, the fabric of the tie will dig deeper into his throat and he'll choke. Then Mom undoes his belt, pulling it from the loops, and once again stands behind him, putting me back in his view.

"I can't believe you set this up," he says to me. "Did you kill Serrano too?"

"No," Mom replies. "I made sure he received a warning." She laughs. "I guess the coward ran."

The more I hear his words and smarmy voice, the angrier I get. That feeling builds more in the pit of my stomach and works its way upward. Mom wraps the belt around his left arm and tightens it to the back of the chair.

"Your belt." She points to the one around my waist.

I undo it and hand it over, my gaze never leaving Dean's face. His eyes are pleading with me, but I can't muster up a bit of remorse. I remember begging him to stop and pleading with him not to hurt me. He never listened.

Mom straps his other arm to the chair and then she's methodically cutting away his dress shirt with her knife, revealing his chest, which is dusted with black and gray hairs. Dean is handsome in a sinister-looking way. His hair is jet-black, graying at his temples, his eyes are a dark brown, and his skin is pale like wax paper. He takes care of his physique because he's not fat, but he's not built either.

She bares his chest and then presses the tip of the blade to his skin, the indent cushioning around the edge.

"Look," he pleads again, "I will leave the country and never come back again."

"But you'll still be a child raping piece of shit," Mom states matter-of-factly. "You won't be able to control yourself."

"Give me the knife." My voice is sure, but my arm shakes when I extend it.

I have so much energy coursing through me that I can't seem to keep it contained. I want to make Dean bleed and really saturate that tie. I want him to cry and beg me to stop, and then I want to do it all again.

Mom hands it over without a second thought and strokes the hair on top of Dean's head.

"She didn't want to hurt you coming in here," she mutters to him. "I think the sight of you and how weak you look is pushing her to do it."

"Don't do it, Ivy." Tears roll down his cheeks, mixing with his blood. "You're not a murderer."

"Don't say my name!" I scream as I grip the knife in my hand.

Then I walk forward and he kicks out his foot, trying to hit my legs. The movement shocks me, and I stab the blade down into his thigh. The scream he makes is exhilarating and the blood soaking into his pants is mesmerizing.

I pull the blade out and cringe when blood squirts out quickly.

"Looks like you hit an artery." Mom chuckles, sounding strangely proud. "He'll bleed out soon. What else do you want to do?"

"This isn't you," Dean pants. "You're not strong enough to live with this."

"Shut up." I shove the knife forward and it slices through the skin of his stomach like butter, sinking to the hilt. His blood is warm as it coats my fist as he grunts, but I can see he's quickly dying.

With each stab, I imagine all the things he did to me and release them. This is my revenge, and Dean can no longer haunt me.

"He's almost dead." Mom's voice slips through my murderous haze as his head falls forward, the tie choking him. I pass the knife to her when she holds out her hand.

Then she pulls his head back up by his hair and his eyes are nearly shut, unfocused. She watches my face as she brings the sharpened edge of the blade to his throat and presses in, dragging it just above the tie. Blood flows out from his throat and down over his chest, blending beautifully with the tie.

"I hope you rot in Hell," I snarl.

Mom undoes my belt from around his arm and hands it back to me, which is glistening with his blood.

"There you go, baby." She smiles. "Now you have your own memento."

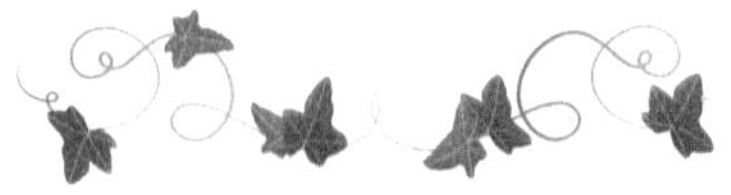

Mom is training with Carmelo and she's kicking his ass, even though he's all fiery and angry. She just keeps whipping his back to the mat and dancing circles around him. It's been two hours since we killed Dean and I am petrified about the police.

Mom assured me nothing would happen, but I'm still scared and it's hard to concentrate on what's going on.

"You okay?" Uncle Trent asks as he sits beside me.

Am I okay? Yes. I'm better than I was before, but I'm now scared for different reasons.

"Will we get arrested?" I whisper.

"No." He chuckles and shoulder bumps me. "We own the cops here."

Oh.

"I'm proud of you for sticking up to him, and I want you to know I removed all the photos and videos he had of you." He lets out a large breath. "I wish you would've told me when I went to see you."

"I couldn't at the time," I mumble. "I thought I deserved it."

He pulls me in for a hug and kisses the top of my head. "You won't hide that shit again though because now you are Black Slaughter."

"That's Mom." I look up at him, his eyes swelling with

pride.

"No, that's the both of you."

I don't know why my heart warms at the prospect, and maybe I am twisted in the sense I enjoy killing, but only if it's justified.

"I used to kick your father's ass on these very mats too," Mom taunts as she hugs Carmelo. "You remind me a lot of him."

"Thank you, Aunt Ember." He grins.

Then he turns, and I don't miss the look he gives Uncle Trent's daughter, Catalina. She's a few years younger than us, but she's well-trained. I remember her a bit from when we were younger, but I don't know her well.

"If your cousin keeps eyeing Catalina, I am going to murder him," Uncle Trent growls, and I laugh.

I don't watch Mom's match later that night, because I'm fucking exhausted and I don't want to see any more violence. I think I've seen enough. I've been given a room across from Mom's to rest, and even though I need sleep, my mind is still racing. I flop on the bed and finally open my phone, noticing the battery is running low. I didn't bring a charger and I know I will need to text Neil before it dies. I open up my messages to find a few from him.

Neil: Good morning.

Neil: Hello?

Neil: Is everything okay?

Neil: I'm calling your house.

Neil: Spoke to your dad… Call me when you can.

Me: Sorry! Mom dragged me on an impromptu trip to New York.

Neil: It's okay. I was worried. How's the trip?

Me: I want to come home now.

We text for a bit longer and then my phone dies. I roll over with a huff and shut my eyes, finally feeling something like contentment settling inside my chest. I no longer feel guilty about Charlotte and I'm free from my abusers.

Maybe now, life can just be normal.

Epilogue

Neil

Our second-year anniversary is tomorrow, and my plan is suddenly making me anxious. I know Ivy loves me and wants to spend forever with me, but I'm still nervous. I pull the ring box out of my pocket and stare at it. This cost me a near fortune, and I thank the fact that I am now Vice President of Legendary Wheels.

Ivy comes home from school today for reading week, and I can't wait to sink myself so deep inside of her, then I'm going to ask her to be my wife. My family is so excited and even Dad has decorated the backyard.

Rodney Jones came out of rehab a changed man and has never looked at another drink. He's forgiven himself for Charlotte's death and is now focusing on his other children. Amelia is doing well in high school and I'm so proud of her.

Everything fell into place perfectly after Ivy's accident and I just want to make the rest of her life something she is deserving of.

I guzzle down my bottle of water. I wish I could have something stronger, but we don't have alcohol in this house, and I respect my father's wishes. I hear a car pull up in the driveway and I know it's the Greenes because Vin texted me when they were leaving.

My stomach tries to force itself up my throat as I breathe to pull myself together. She won't say no to me. She wouldn't, right? Ivy is independent, and we've never discussed marriage. It took everything to sit her down and talk about our relationship, making it clear we were exclusive.

"Hey!" Vin's voice bellows from the front door. "We're here!"

I rush out and I'm nearly plowed down when Ivy jumps up on me, wrapping her arms around my neck.

"Hi, baby!" she screams, and I chuckle.

"Hey." I kiss her softly.

"Hi, Neil." Ember kisses my cheek and Vin shoots me a wink.

"'Sup, bro?" Saxon nods, his voice cracking with puberty.

"I want, like, four hotdogs!" Dahlia squeals and runs for the backyard.

"Oh, I want a hot dog too," Ivy breathes in my ear, and I'm instantly hard. "Let them go outside. I think I can have you coming down my throat in two minutes, tops."

"Ivy," I say her name with warning.

She drops her feet to the floor and yanks on my arm, pulling me into Shay's pantry. It's fucking small and we need to press together for the door to even shut. Then my girl drops to her knees, and I freak out she'll find the box, so I rush my slacks open for her.

"Impatient, hmm?" She laughs as she pulls me from

my boxers, giving me a few quick tugs.

I am impatient but also nervous. I haven't seen Ivy in two weeks because she's been studying for midterms and stays in a dorm in Toronto. So yes, my dick is ready to come down her fucking throat.

She flattens her tongue and runs it over the head of my cock, making me jerk against her lips. She hums and drops her jaw, then takes me down to the base of her throat. I groan and toss my head back, causing a bag of pasta to drop to the floor.

Ivy gags and pulls back, laughing when she sees the pasta on the floor.

"Don't make a lot of noise," she whispers. "Our families are here."

You don't fucking say?

Then she's sucking me back into her mouth, her saliva dripping down my shaft, and her throat constricting as she forces me deeper. I don't think I'll last the two fucking minutes because I already feel my balls tighten and the sensations spreading up my cock.

"Fuck, I'm…"

I drop my head back as I feel myself explode inside of her mouth. She slurps me dry and then tucks me gently back into my boxers. I watch as she stands, a small drop of my cum sitting on her full bottom lip.

I wipe it with my thumb and press it inside her mouth. "Don't waste it, Jones," I whisper.

"You mean Greene." She rolls her eyes as she sucks my thumb.

Not for much longer.

We make our way out of the pantry and follow our

family outside into the backyard. Ivy rushes over to her uncles and aunt while I fret some more.

"You look like you're going to puke." Vin gives me a disgusted look.

"I feel like I'm going to puke."

"You think she'll say yes?" he questions, and I look at him with shock.

"Do *you* think she will?" I whisper harshly.

"It's a toss-up. My girl doesn't need a man, you know?"

I fucking hate him right now.

Then he fucking throws his head back and laughs, his locs swinging back and forth. "I love fucking with you, man."

"Fucking stop it," I mumble as he continues to chuckle.

I step out to the middle of the backyard and a hush settles over everyone but Ivy. She's still bragging to Carmelo and Cam about something.

"Ivy," I call out to her, and she turns, looking around curiously. Then I hook my finger and beckon her to me.

"What's going on?" she asks when I take her hands.

"Don't kick me in the balls or anything like that. Deal?"

"Why is everyone so quiet?" I get down on my knee and pull the tiny box out of my pocket. "Oh, shit," she rasps, and I don't know how to take that, but I continue onward.

"Ivy Greene." I look up into her bright ocean eyes and the fear in them. "I think I have loved you since the night I saw you hop up on the hood of your car at the strip."

"Neil!" she hisses and looks around.

Carmelo laughs heartily.

"She won that night, by the way," I tell everyone and hear chuckles.

"Shut up," she growls and kicks my knee lightly.

"I will love you for the rest of my life if you'll let me. I will take care of you and do anything necessary to keep you safe. I want you to have my children and I want to grow so old together we can't even remember each other's names." I hear a few more chuckles, but it's the tears on my girl's cheeks I'm paying attention to. "There will never be another for me, Ivy Greene. Will you marry me?"

She gnaws on her bottom lip and my stomach crashes to the ground. Then her mouth widens as she tosses her head back.

"Fuck, yes!" she screams to the sky.

EMBER

It's a little chilly out tonight and the wind bites at the tip of my nose. I pull my jacket around me and turn onto his street. After everything I worked for, putting my actual blood, sweat, and tears into this town, somehow my daughter still fell through Whitsborough's cracks. I'd find it almost laughable if it wasn't *my* daughter.

My firstborn, the one who tested me at every turn and laughed at the most sadistic things. How did she fall through the cracks?

I blame myself.

It was my responsibility to teach her about these things, that monsters exist, living right under our noses. Even the vilest wear pretty faces and smell like heaven, waiting for their prey to be at their most vulnerable. Ivy has been through enough and it breaks my heart, knowing it all happened under *my* nose.

I see his house and grin when I feel that familiar feeling swirl in my belly. I really want to kill them, bleed them dry, and watch the life slowly leave their eyes. Vin seems to think they should just get the fuck out of Whitsborough though, and I can't bring myself to stress him out even more. He's telling me our daughter wanted it and she even has a taste for men in authority positions. It wasn't necessarily rape.

In my eyes, his dick shouldn't have been anywhere near her, but again... less stress for my family.

I walk up his driveway and see both of their cars are here. Perfect. I crack my neck and wince at the pain that skips down my spine. I'm getting older. Killing and fighting are going to have to slow down, and I may have to consider retirement, but I will need a replacement first.

The doorbell rings and I swear it's to the tune of "It's

Raining Men." It should sing something about schoolgirls in kilts instead. My jaw clenches as the door swings open, showing a slightly perturbed O'Connor. His face quickly transforms into one of horror, and I can't help the snort that falls from my mouth.

"M–Mrs. G–Greene," he sputters. "Are you here about Ivy? Whatever it is she said, I assure you it's not what it seems. I just…"

"I was hoping we could chat regarding my daughter, whom I can't seem to control for the life of me." I put on a super sugary tone.

"Oh." His shoulders relax and he brushes back his hair. "Sure, of course. Come in. I am worried about her too."

He leads me into his house and straight to the family room where his partner, Mr. Pratt, is sitting. His eyebrows shoot up to his hairline as he gives O'Connor a look.

"Mrs. Greene is here to talk about Ivy and how troubling she's becoming," O'Connor explains as I take a seat across from Pratt.

"Oh, the drugs." Pratt nods. "Some kids experiment, but Ivy has taken it to extremes…"

"Shut the fuck up, both of you." The room instantly falls silent. "Did you actually fucking think I came here to talk to you about my daughter?" They don't answer and I chuckle. "I guess I am. Which one of you stuck your dick in her?"

I know which one did, I just love making pedophiles squirm.

"Mrs. Greene…" O'Connor clears his throat. "I'm going to have to ask you to leave…"

I jump to my feet and grab his wrist, twisting it behind his back. He leans forward when I apply pressure and screams.

"Hey!" Pratt jumps to his feet.

I press the arm up a little more and O'Connor screams again, halting Pratt.

"I wouldn't try anything," I warn him. "Or I will break his arm and then I'll kill you both."

I really want to kill them both.

"Here's how it's going to go down." I speak slow and calm, because even though they're teachers, they must be dumb as fuck. "You're going to walk your asses straight out that door, get in your car, and drive the fuck out of Whitsborough."

"What about our stuff?" Pratt asks. See? Fucking dumb.

"Maybe you should've thought of that before thinking it was a good idea to stick your dick in my daughter," I snarl.

"I didn't…" Pratt starts.

"I know." I grin at him and break O'Connor's arm.

The sound of the bone breaking is delicious, but then coupled with his screams? Nearly orgasmic.

I kick him to the ground as Pratt takes a step toward me, his jaw ticking. He's bigger than O'Connor and I really want to see if he can use his size.

"You want some too?" I grin.

"Don't." O'Connor pants as he slowly stands on his feet. "We'll leave."

"We will?" Pratt stares at him dumbfounded.

"Yes, we'll go to my mother's place in Manitoba. Is that far enough?" He looks at me.

"Not really, but I'll allow it." I shrug. "I wanted you in Hell."

O'Connor grabs his keys in his one good hand and tosses them to Pratt.

"You need a hospital," Pratt growls.

"Let's get out of Whitsborough and then we'll go to the nearest one." O'Connor's eyes keep flicking back to my face.

"Our clothes?" Pratt whines.

"Get new clothes, bitch." I clap. "Hurry, I don't have all night and neither do you."

"My car…" Pratt whines a bit more, and I bitch-slap him hard across the face.

"Get the fuck out of this town. Sell your fucking car with the house." I hold my hand out. "Give me the keys."

He drops his keys into my palm while rubbing his cheeks, his eyes alight with anger, but he's at least smart enough to shut his fucking mouth. Finally.

They walk slowly out the door, one cradling his arm and the other rubbing his face.

Bunch of fucking pussies.

For all book updates and social platforms, check out my website

C.A. Rene lives in Toronto, Canada with her family, where most of the year varies from chilly to frigid. Most days you'll find her wrapped in her many blankets in bed while reading or writing her next dark, twisted story.
Her stories boast of inclusivity and refusal to be conformed in any small box. Writing across genres is a hobby and drinking wine is a must... Or coffee ... with a splash of Baileys.

ALSO BY C.A. RENE

The Whitsborough Chronicles
Through the Pain

Into Darkness

Finding the Light

To Redemption

The Whitsborough Progenies
Ivy's Venom

Carmelo's Malice

Saxon's Distortion

Gabriel's Deception

Desecrated Duet
Desecrated Flesh

Desecrated Essence

The Reaped Series
The Reaper Incarnate

Hunting the Reaper

Claiming the Reaper

Hail Mary Duet

Blue 42

Red Zone

Steel Dragons MC

Dragon Slayer

Dragon Strife

Dragon Scorch

Hell's March MC Duet

Hell's Viper

TBA

Fusion Core Duet

Tension

Release

Second Chance Standalones

Fighting the Tide